I0592491

CELESTIAL SHIFTERS BOOK 1

# SHARDS OF VENUS

## TJALARA DRAPER

*To Kevy Wevy Woo Woo*
*My rock, my joy and my best friend.*
*Thank you so much for believing in me and for reading this book*
*even though you don't like fantasy and think I spend too much time*
*with "my silly dragons and fairies."*
*Love you forever.*
*x x x*

## CREATING COLD CASES

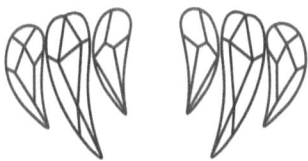

NATHAN DELANO WANDERED THROUGH THE DIM CABIN'S living room, careful to watch his step. Police lights flashed garishly off countless crimson puddles and smears as he greeted each uniformed Erathi in turn.

*Humans*, he reminded himself, shaking his head. Even after all these years, the word *Erathi* still leaped to mind first.

Detective Judith Walker was inspecting a bedroom door's heavy bolt mechanism with a gloved hand. When she noticed him nearby, she waved him over.

"Hey, Jude," he said, sweeping his gaze once more over the room. "What's the situation?"

"Hey, Delano." She yanked off her glove with a *snap* and gestured to a black body bag being zipped up by a paramedic. "One deceased teenage girl."

"Do we know who?"

"Yeah. It's the missing Branstone girl." Jude handed him her phone. "Here, have a look. I took these when I arrived."

Nathan swiped through Jude's photos, immediately recognizing the blonde victim, Lyla-Rose Branstone. In grisly contrast with the wide smile from the yearbook photo in her case file, her eyes were open and glazed. Four horrific grooves were carved into the side of her head, running from behind her ear to her chin. The ear itself had been sliced clean through in several places.

"Check this out." Jude reached across him to zoom into the area between the victim's neck and shoulder. "If I didn't know any better, I would have thought that was some weird bite mark."

Six bloodied puncture wounds formed an incomplete arc with a gap at the peak, which fell just below Lyla's left collarbone. The inner two marks were the smallest, while the middle ones were about the width of a ballpoint pen.

Nathan's chest tightened. *No. Not here. Not in Brookhaven.* Only one species made that distinct bite mark: his own race, the Veniri.

And he'd spent the last fifteen years hiding from them.

"Any weapons found?" Nathan asked, hoping Jude wouldn't notice the deflection.

She shook her head. "Nothing. At least, not yet. An abandoned vehicle was located down the road. I've sent an officer to go over it. I've yet to check out the surroundings myself."

Nathan nodded and handed back her phone. "What about witnesses?"

"The owner of this cabin lives farther down the hill. He and his wife were about to go to bed when they heard screaming coming from this direction. He came to investigate and dialed nine-one-one straight away when he found the victim."

A muscle twitched in Nathan's jaw. "Did he see anything else? Maybe catch a glimpse of who did this?"

She shook her head. "Whoever else was here cleared out by the time he—" A melodic tune from Jude's phone cut her off. "It's one of my kids," she said, glancing at the screen. She gave Nathan an apologetic look.

He gestured for her to answer. "I've got this."

"Thanks, Nathan." She patted his shoulder before quickly accepting the call and making a beeline for the exit. "Hi, sweetie . . . ?"

As the two paramedics with the body bag followed her out, Nathan turned back to the room. Time to set to work.

The quaint shack was likely several generations old, possibly built by one of the owner's ancestors. Knitted and patchwork throw rugs added a cozy touch, or at least, they would have if they hadn't been lying crumpled among splintered furniture. A decorative gun rack was mounted on one of the exposed timber walls, along with a collection of animal heads on plaques: deer, foxes, a bear, a zebra, and a tiger. Nathan had never understood the human desire for trophies, the need to display bits and pieces of their targets with pride.

With deliberate precision, he picked his way through the chaos, taking in the details of each gouge, splatter, and smear of blood and periodically snapping a few photos of his own. His boots thunked with each step on the timber floorboards. When he reached the open back door, a gust of icy wind bit into his face and neck, and he raised his collar and tightened his jacket. Peering into the darkness, he sucked in a deep breath of the cold night air.

A familiar tingle crept under his tongue.

He glanced back, ensuring none of the remaining officers were paying attention. The tingle grew into a fierce prickle as he allowed the simple transformation to take its course.

Within seconds, a forked tongue shot out from between his lips like a whip, then flicked back into his mouth. He assessed the night's aromas and flavors, a lingering bouquet of potent scents from the evening's activities.

The Veniri ability to scent someone's essence, or their soul-scent, was something Nathan heavily relied on for his

Erathi work as a detective. Deducing the inner workings of a crime scene was so much easier when he could scent the residual intentions and emotions of the moment. But with all the extra cops, paramedics, and civilians traipsing through this area over the last hour, this time he would need more than his tongue to isolate the information he needed.

He scanned the stars. They were almost startlingly luminous, but none were brighter than Venus, sparkling straight ahead through the silhouetted tree branches. Nathan closed his eyes and took a deep breath, basking in the Venusian beams.

Beneath his closed lids, thin membranes glided over both his eyes. When he blinked them open again, the scenery before him was still drenched in darkness—until he flicked out his forked tongue. This time, the soul-trails illuminated like phosphorescent tendrils of smoke, gleaming wisps against the black of night. Each one glowed a different hue of the rainbow, leading into the forest beyond.

The leaf litter crackled and crunched beneath his feet as he stepped out of the shack. The trails started to fade but pulsed back to life with another flick of his tongue. With each taste of the air, he processed the flavors infused in each soul-trail, gathering valuable data.

After a few moments of walking, his boot kicked against something. He slid back the inner membranes of his eyes and pulled out his flashlight. The incandescent beam revealed a man in a hoodie and jeans, lying in a heap. Next to him, about a foot away, another person lay sprawled on the ground—a teenage girl. Patches of deep red speckled her clothing.

When his flashlight beam caught her face, he swore under his breath. Another kid from one of his case files. *Violet Chambers, 16 years of age. Legal guardians: Norman and Connie*

4

*Hopkins. Address: 42 Daisy Crescent. Missing. Last seen approx 11:15 p.m. on Thursday, July 18.*

Her dark brown hair was matted with blood, dirt, and leaves. Compared to the photo, her features were hollow. Muddied cuts and bruises covered most of her face, and her right eye was almost indiscernible from the surrounding swelling.

Nathan hung his head, covering his face with his hand and wearily rubbing his temples. After a few breaths, he reached down to her neck to look for a pulse.

A faint beat tapped against his fingers.

\* \* \*

Nathan hurriedly retraced his steps back to the shack, careful to avoid jostling the young girl in his arms. Violet gave a low groan.

"Hold tight," he said. "We're nearly there."

He barged through the back door and straight out the front. "I need a paramedic!"

Jude's attention snapped to him. She let out a gasp, eyes wide, then barked out some orders. Within seconds, two paramedics wheeled over a stretcher. Nathan laid down his bundle and stepped back, giving the paramedics space to perform their flurry of choreographed procedures.

The next few moments were a blur as he recounted to Jude what he'd found, leaving out his discovery of the second body. He'd hastily cleared it out of view, but he would have to clean that mess up soon—before anyone found it and started asking questions. Especially Jude.

His jaw tensed as he studied her. Her chin was resting on one hand in her signature thoughtful pose. He could almost see her mental processes breaking down and analyzing the new pieces of evidence he'd provided. Her intelligence and intuition always impressed him; it was what made her such a great cop. It was also what made him work overtime to keep her in the dark. She could never know who was responsible for this hellish mayhem. Her life would be in danger, not to mention his own.

He scoffed. Who was he kidding? His life had been in danger for years now.

His derisive snort broke Jude's trance. She shook her head and focused back on him. "Sorry for zoning out. Just thinking."

He gave her a knowing smile but didn't reply.

"Here." She reached into the car Nathan was leaning on and pulled out a red vacuum flask. "Have some coffee. It might still be hot."

He took a sip, cringed, and forced himself to gulp down the bitter, lukewarm liquid. "Ugh, maybe a little sugar next time." He wiped his mouth with his sleeve.

"No time for sugar," said Jude, drawing a long mouthful from the flask.

Over her shoulder, Nathan noticed one of the paramedics waving to him. "Coffee break's over. We're being summoned."

They headed over to the ambulance, and Nathan nodded a greeting to the paramedic by the stretcher. "How's the vic?"

"She's awake and stable for now. We've given her a dose of morphine to help with the pain until we can get her to the hospital."

Nathan nodded. "Mind if I ask her a few questions?"

The paramedic shrugged. "You can try. You might be able to get something out of her, but maybe not much tonight."

Nathan stepped closer to the girl. "How ya doing, kid? You warm enough?"

She looked up at him with wide, glassy eyes.

"Your name's Violet, isn't it?"

After some hesitation and a quick glance at Jude, she nodded.

"Violet, can you tell me what happened?"

No answer.

"Can you tell us who did this to you?" Jude asked.

Nathan's stomach churned at her question. Violet's expression grew distant. Finally, she shook her head and looked away.

Nathan relaxed. "It's okay, Violet. You're safe."

One of her hands clenched the top of her silver foil blanket. Dry blood was caked under her fingernails, and half the nail of her index finger had been completely torn off. Her knuckles were shredded and bloodied. Whatever had happened to this kid, she'd certainly fought hard to defend herself.

Nathan's mind raced, imagining the horrors she must have faced as she screamed and begged her attacker to stop. A fiery rage boiled in the pit of his stomach. His elbows started to burn as the screams in his mind grew louder and louder. A slicing sensation replaced the burning in his elbows, and he felt the sleeves of his jacket beginning to tear. He needed to regain control of himself, *fast*.

But the female face screaming in his mind was no longer Violet's. It morphed into—

*Stop it!* Nathan slammed his eyes shut and turned his face away from Violet. He took a few deep breaths, forcing himself to relax until the blades in his elbows melted back into his flesh.

He turned back to the girl. "Violet—"

"He had a tattoo," she said in a raspy voice.

Shock gripped him. Her gray-blue eyes captured his with sudden, sharp intensity.

"A tattoo? What kind of tattoo?" Jude asked, taking out her phone.

Violet's next words were slow and deliberate. "He had a tattoo of a crystal scorpion, right here." She pointed to the side of her neck.

Nathan furrowed his brow and scratched his head.

"Are you sure?" Jude asked, tapping more notes into her phone.

Violet nodded.

"Was he a friend of yours?" asked Jude.

"I . . ." She screwed her face up, clamping her eyes closed. After a few heartbeats, she let out a quiet sob. "I . . . don't . . . I can't remember."

"That's okay," Jude said gently.

Violet turned toward Nathan, a tear rolling down her swollen cheek. "I don't know who he is," she whispered.

"It's okay, Violet." He gave her a soft pat on the shoulder.

Silver foil crinkled as she gripped the thermal blanket with both hands, her whole body shaking with silent sobs. Tears carved clean trails through the blood and grime on her face.

"That's enough for now," said the paramedic. "We've kept her here too long already. We should get her to the hospital."

Nathan and Jude stepped to the side as Violet was wheeled into the back of the ambulance. The lights flashed on, and the engine roared to life.

Jude let out a heavy sigh. "I suppose we should go process the area where you found—" Once again, her ringtone cut her off. She checked her watch and clicked her tongue. "It's my kid again. She's been really sick, and with the long hours I've been doing lately . . ."

"It's okay, Jude. If you need to head home, just go."

Jude pursed her lips. "I really shouldn't."

"Yeah, go on. Your kids need you." He patted her on the shoulder. "You've been here longer than me anyway. I'll deal with this mess."

She hesitated. "You sure you don't mind?"

"Not at all." He steered her toward her car. "Get home and kiss those kids goodnight."

Jude gave him a weary smile and stood up a little straighter, as if a heavy burden had been lifted off her shoulders. "Thanks, Nathan. I can always count on you."


Two hours later, Nathan stood at the side of his car, watching the last police vehicle pull away from the scene. As soon as its taillights drowned in the night, he ducked under the police tape and walked back toward the cabin.

Time to shut this investigation down.

As much as he hated tampering with the evidence, cases involving shifters were better left to go cold. What Jude didn't know couldn't keep her and her kids awake at night.

He needed to get rid of the second body, but first, there was something else he needed to do. Violet had remembered a tattoo, and if she saw it again, all hell would break loose.

The wind whipped around him as he squinted into the inky blackness of the cabin. Nothing. Blinking, he raised his face to the heavens and, like before, sought out Venus. The radiant evening star sang to him in a faint melody only he could hear, and his body responded, his inner eyelids once again hazing into existence.

He flicked out his tongue, and the darkness flooded with colored phosphorescent mists, each hue of the glowing rainbow alive with its own collection of flavors. The ethereal light began to fade but, with another flick, pulsed back to vivid clarity.

Like a bloodhound, he followed the trails, veering left or right according to the prompting of his forked tongue. But unlike a bloodhound, instead of odors, he followed emotions and intentions, desires and interests, the distinct medley that makes up a being's very soul.

He gradually filtered out the familiar scents of Jude and the other officers and paramedics, reducing the rainbow to fewer colors. Soon he'd isolated Violet's and the deceased girl's scents as well and also filtered them out. Only a handful of trails remained.

He called on his internal Venusian energy and, like blowing out a foggy breath in winter, expelled some of it into the remaining trails, brightening and sharpening them against the dark. Clouds of the subtle light had gathered in various areas. These were echoes of moments past—snapshots of the subject's strongest emotion. With another gust of Venusian energy, he channeled his attention on these places until misty faces came into focus within. He inspected each one until he found what he was looking for.

Nathan released a burdened sigh. Right there, in the vaporous echo of the man's neck, was a tattoo of a crystal scorpion.

Ignoring his rising emotions, Nathan continued to follow the trail back out into the night.

## ASSAULTED TASTE BUDS

Violet jerked awake; someone had taken hold of her arm. Strobing memories of her abduction flickered through her mind, and she yanked away.

"It's okay, Violet," said a female voice. "I'm just checking your vitals."

Violet's panic subsided when she recognized the nurse by her bed. She relaxed back into the pillows and rubbed her eyes.

"I'm going to check your blood pressure, okay?"

Before Violet could reply, the nurse slipped on the blood pressure cuff and switched on the electric pump. The squeeze on Violet's arm had just passed uncomfortable when the nurse released the pressure and noted down the reading. Then she briskly moved on to checking Violet's temperature and heart rate.

Violet silently berated herself. She should be used to this routine by now, considering a nurse checked her vitals roughly every six hours. She'd been well looked after by the nurses and doctors at Brookhaven Hospital, but that didn't do a thing to change how much she hated being there. As far as she was concerned, all hospitals were odious, with their stark white walls, the promotional "Ask your doctor" medical posters, and the nose-pinching aromas of infected bodily fluids mixed with the sharp tang of antiseptic.

But even the smells and ambience were infinitely more bearable than the lifelong ache of what hospitals meant to her—the stinging reminder that her mother had abandoned her in one of these cold, lonely buildings shortly after she was delivered. Violet had long ago given up on the idea that her mother would one day return to claim her, but that didn't stop her grief from resurfacing every time she was forced to step into one of these godforsaken places.

"Hmm," said the nurse, jotting down some notes on the clipboard at the end of Violet's bed. "Your injuries are healing beautifully, but you're still showing a low-grade fever. I'll make sure you get another dose of Tylenol."

Violet nodded, blinking away the sting of tears, and swallowed the growing lump in her throat.

Despite the heavy weight of emotions, staying at the hospital was still preferable to the alternative. A slight shudder raced through Violet's body at the thought of being sent back to her foster parents.

The nurse frowned. "Are you cold?"

Violet responded with a small nod. It was better than giving the real explanation. How could she stand to face her "home" now that Lyla-Rose was gone? Lyla had been her lifeline, the spark in the darkness, the breeze under her broken wings. Lyla had kept Violet going, her only friend in the world. And now she, too, was gone.

"I'll get you a warm blanket." The nurse gave her a reassuring smile and left the room.

Violet stared up at the bland pattern of ceiling tiles, trying to breathe through the growing tightness in her chest.

*Dead. Lyla's dead.*

This time, she didn't even try to blink the tears away. They cascaded down her cheeks, and she turned her face into her pillow. The aches and pains that hadn't fully healed roared back to life as her body shook with sobs.

The last few days had been a blur, clouded by pain and tangled up in a constant string of nurses, doctors, social workers, and police officers. The police had questioned her for every detail. *What happened? Who?* But no matter how hard Violet tried, she still couldn't remember anything—except for one blazing image. A neck tattoo of a crystal scorpion.

Violet squeezed her eyes shut and dug her fingertips into her skull. *Come on. Think! Try to remember.* It didn't change a thing. Her memories remained locked away. For the space of a few heartbeats, fear shoved aside her frustration. What was wrong with her? Why couldn't she remember?

Faint chatter cut through Violet's thoughts. As it grew louder, Violet recognized the baritone voice of her doctor and the lighter voice of her social worker, Miranda. Judging by the tone of their conversation, they were discussing something serious.

Violet quickly nestled into her pillows and feigned sleep as the two paused outside her door.

"We can't keep her here forever, Miranda."

"I know, I know . . . I was hoping to have another home ready for her by now, but at her age it's becoming next to impossible."

A slight panic began to churn in Violet's chest.

"I understand, but she's been here for almost two weeks, and that's only because we aren't overrun with patients at the moment. She's more than ready to be discharged. I'm not running a halfway house here."

"You're right. I get it. And I can't thank you enough for

keeping her in longer than necessary. I just can't stand the idea of taking her back to those god-awful people."

"I wish there was more I could do to help. Really, I do. But for now, all I can give you is the rest of the afternoon. You need to take her today."

"Thanks, I really appreciate it. That should be enough time for me to make some more calls."

"Great. For now, we'll leave her to sleep. I'll make sure one of the nurses gives you the discharge forms."

Footsteps tapped away on the hospital linoleum.

Violet's eyes flew open.

Today. Miranda was taking her home *today*. Her eyebrows pinched together as she analyzed her options. Sure, she didn't have anywhere else to go, but she was sixteen. She wasn't a child anymore. She could fend for herself—hitch-hike to the city, find a job, lie low until child services forgot about her. The plan wasn't foolproof, but there was no way she was going back to a foster home. Of that, she was sure. She was done.

She threw her blanket off and winced. Another thing she was sure of was that she needed some painkillers for the road.

A few moments later, Violet was dressed, and her small denim bag, packed with the few belongings Miranda had retrieved for her, was slung over her shoulder. She poked her head into the hallway and checked both ways before leaving the room.

Over the years, she'd become a pro at sneaking around. She stayed clear of the nurses' station and ducked out of the hallway whenever someone passed by who might recognize her. With a bit of luck, she made it to the hospital pharmacy without any problems.

The patient roller window was shut, as was the access

door around the side. The pharmacist was either doing ward rounds or out to lunch. With a casual glance around to make sure no one was watching, Violet dug into her bag and pulled out some hairpins. Wedging one in her teeth, she bent the metal out of shape, then stuck her makeshift lockpicks into the pharmacy door handle with a finesse gained from hours of practice.

*Click*.

*Perfect*. She eased the door open.

"You know," said a deep voice behind her, "it's one thing to run away from the hospital, but stealing meds is a shortcut to juvie."

Violet froze. She barely had the door open an inch. In her periphery, a guy leaned against the wall next to the pharmacy door—one of the cops who had frequently visited and questioned her about Lyla's murder. He wasn't looking at her. Instead, he casually inspected his nails.

She glanced toward the hospital exit at the opposite end of the hallway.

"I wouldn't if I were you," he warned. "I'll have you crash tackled and handcuffed before the sliding door sensor even registers your existence."

Violet frowned. With her ribs, thigh, and ankle still not one-hundred-percent healed, he was probably right.

"But what I *would* do," he continued, "is contemplate very carefully which decisions to make next." He looked at her from the corner of his eye. "If you make some wise decisions, then it's likely I'll forget to say anything to my partner and the hospital's superintendent. Not to mention Miranda. She'd be crushed if she knew what you were up to. She's been singing your praises the whole time."

Violet hesitated, but the steel in his tawny eyes warned her to act soon, or he would. With a juvenile huff, she

15

removed her hairpins from the lock and let go of the door, which slowly closed with a pneumatic wheeze. All her adrenaline had dried up, leaving only shame. The cop was likely to snitch anyway, and Miranda was going to kill her.

"This way, kid," said the cop. He headed down the hallway, in the opposite direction of the hospital exit. Violet shot a mournful look at the door to freedom. She could still make a run for it; the cop hadn't even bothered to check if she was following him.

She winced. *Who am I kidding?*

With a defeated sigh, Violet trailed after the cop, but after a few paces, she frowned. He wasn't leading her back to her room. Instead, he pushed through a glass door and held it open for her.

"This isn't my room."

"I know" was all he said as he gestured for her to enter.

The world she stepped into was a complete contrast to the sterile hospital: the facility's botanical gardens. Trees towered high above. Instead of stark white walls, every hue of green imaginable tumbled and climbed in all directions, broken up only by a vast spectrum of bright flowers. Water trickled musically down a rocky feature wall by the door, and a gentle breeze, heavy with the scents of rich earth and flowers, chased away the smell of antiseptic.

Other patients were wandering along the weaving path or sitting on the benches provided. A nurse pushed an elderly lady in a wheelchair, but she stopped to allow her patient to stroke a low-hanging flower with her wrinkled hand.

"What are we doing here?" Violet asked.

"Remembering for a few minutes that life isn't always crap."

He walked up the path a few paces and settled on a bench overlooking the pond, which was fed by an artificial waterfall.

Violet frowned. What was this guy's deal? He'd just busted her for trying to steal drugs, and instead of gloating, he wanted to zen out in nature?

After a few moments, Violet sauntered over and plonked down on the opposite end of the bench. She peeked at him from the corner of her eye. He had his eyes closed, and his face was tilted up, catching patches of sunlight that speckled through the leaves. She figured he was maybe early forties, judging by some silver streaks in his dark hair and the salt-and-pepper stubble along his square jaw. The creases around his forehead, eyes, and mouth gave him resting I'm-about-to-kick-your-ass face, and his towering height and muscular build only added to his edge of intimidation.

Still, Violet didn't feel scared around him the way she had with previous cops—the ones who liked to use their badge and brawn to bully culprits into so-called justice. Something about him felt soothing.

"So, kid, you wanna tell me why you were trying to run away?"

Violet picked at the ends of her sweater sleeves, glaring at the orange koi fish gliding leisurely through the water. "I wasn't trying to run away."

"Oh, really? Then what would you call it?"

She folded her legs up onto the seat and hugged her knees. "I was . . ."

A few silent moments passed. She couldn't bring herself to finish the sentence. There was no point. The cop was probably mentally rehearsing his lecture, including threats to use his taser to make her go back to her awful foster parents. Because it was the right thing to do. Because she wasn't old enough to take care of herself. Blah, blah, blah . . .

Instead he unzipped his jacket halfway, reached in, and pulled out a white paper bag. He opened it and held it out to her, revealing some kind of candy in the shape of black discs.

She took one. He took one too and popped it in his mouth before putting the bag back in his jacket.

Violet inspected both sides of the disc. One side was smooth, while the other had an embossed impression of some kind of European coin. With a small shrug, Violet put the disc in her mouth. Immediately, her tongue wanted to commit suicide. Her whole face screwed up as the intense flavor of salt and licorice coated her mouth.

"What the—?" she exclaimed right before involuntarily spitting the rubbery gunk into the garden behind her. Warbled sounds of disgust followed as she tried to hack out the lingering flavor. When that didn't work, she rubbed her tongue with her sleeve.

"What a waste," said the cop. His expression held a hint of amusement.

"What *is* that stuff?"

"In this part of the world, it's called Dutch licorice."

Violet's whole face twisted in revulsion. "Ick! Remind me never to put one of those in my mouth again."

His amusement spilled into a smile. "Aw, c'mon. It's not that bad."

"Are you kidding? I'd rather lick the road! *Ew!*"

He chuckled at that, a bass resonance from deep in his chest.

"Violet, there you are!"

Violet turned to see Miranda barging through the door a few feet away. Her face was calm, but her eyes were blazing. *Uh-oh, she's pissed.*

"What is the meaning of this?" demanded Miranda. "Please tell me you weren't trying to run away *again*? Do you seriously think living on the streets is a better option for you? It's bad enough that one girl has died already, and now you—"

"It's okay," a new voice cut in. Another cop Violet recognized, a middle-aged woman, came up behind Miranda and touched her shoulder. "We found her."

Violet curled into a ball and hugged her legs again. Her eyes stung with fresh tears.

"Come on, Miranda," said the lady cop, steering her away from Violet. "How about we have a chat? Nathan, do you mind?"

"I'll be back, kid." He patted her on the shoulder and went to join the ladies.

They huddled a few feet away, close enough that they could keep an eye on Violet—and close enough that she could still hear their conversation despite their hushed tones.

"I'm sorry, Jude," said Miranda.

"There's no need to apologize to me."

"I know. I'm just . . . I don't know what to do. I understand why she's running away. I get it. I would be doing the same thing in her situation. I've been making calls for days to try and get her into a new home, but even all my emergency housing is over capacity. I just . . ." She dropped her head into her hands and gave a restrained groan of frustration.

"I hear you, Miranda," said Jude. "I don't like the idea of her going back to those people either. Hell, if I wasn't already raising two kids of my own, I'd offer her a bed in a heartbeat."

"Thanks, I appreciate it. And you too, Nathan. Thanks for making sure she didn't take off. I don't know what I would've done if she'd disappeared again."

"Can she stay here for another night?" Nathan asked.

Miranda shook her head. "I've already tried that. Violet has stayed past her welcome. I have to take her today, and the best I can do for the moment is a group home back in the city—at least, until I can find a home willing to take on a sixteen-year-old. If only she were ten years younger."

Violet dropped her head against her knees.

"Well, I do happen to have a guest bedroom that isn't being used," said Nathan.

"Oh my gosh! Would you?" exclaimed Miranda.

"Look, I don't know whether it's appropriate or not for a cop to take her in, but—"

"Don't worry," cut in Miranda. "Leave it to me. It would only be temporary. I promise."

"Nathan, are you sure?" said Jude. "It's not like taking in a puppy, you know."

"Yeah, I know. But the kid's had a rough ride. I can at least give her a bed for a few days. Besides, you can give me some pointers, can't you, Jude?"

Jude scoffed. "I've yet to experience the teenage mood swings. It might be a case of the blind leading the blind."

"So what else is new?"

"Great, it's settled." Miranda rattled off a list of forms she needed to prepare before bringing Violet around to Nathan's place.

"Hey, Violet," said Jude.

Violet raised her head to see Jude looking down at her, Nathan at her side. Miranda was already making a phone call behind them.

"Some temporary arrangements are being made for you to stay in Nathan's spare room until better accommodations can be found." Jude inclined her head to Nathan. "Do you think you can handle putting up with this guy for a few days?"

Violet gnawed on the inside of her cheek. The idea of staying with a cop was a foreign concept. But what other option did she have? As far as cops went, he wasn't too bad. He certainly hadn't needed to give her a chance after busting her for breaking into the pharmacy, and he hadn't snitched on her. Yet. In fact, so far the worst thing he'd done was assault her taste buds with that tar-flavored disc.

"Yeah," she said, giving them a slow nod, "I think I can handle it."

## STUPID ROSE

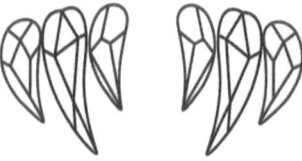

Nathan sighed with relief when he spotted a vacant parking spot near the college entrance. "Must be my lucky day," he said in a low voice.

The jeep rolled to a stop, and Violet's sleeping form jolted in the passenger seat. Her arms flailed, smacking against the dashboard, and she cried out, eyes still clenched shut.

Nathan leaned over and took hold of one of her arms. "Wake up! It's just a dream."

She released a strangled growl, fighting his grip.

"Violet!"

Her eyes flew open and harried pants replaced the screams. She looked around, brow furrowed in confusion. When she spotted Nathan, she slumped back in her chair and groaned. "Sorry, I must have fallen asleep. Was I screaming again?"

Nathan nodded, his lips in a tight smile. "Same dream?"

Violet rubbed at her eyes with the heels of her hands. "Yeah, the faceless man with the neck tattoo."

The familiar wave of guilt surged through Nathan's chest.

*That damn neck tattoo.* Violet's trauma had latched so fiercely on to that image that it was impossible to erase. He sucked in a breath and held back his sigh. "No need to worry, Vi. It was just a dream."

"Yeah, I know." Her tone was edged with a chronic frustration. She turned her attention to the buildings outside. "Wow. We're here."

They hopped out of the car and gathered up Violet's things from the back.

A guy with greasy blue hair and a black metal-spiked vinyl jacket bumped into Nathan, causing him to drop the cardboard box he carried. The kid didn't stop or even apologize. Nathan growled a string of choice words as he bent to gather the box's scattered contents. He stopped mid-curse when Violet came to stand next to him.

"Damn, kids these days," he gruffed, rummaging through the hastily repacked items with one hand. "If he's broken your camera, I swear I'll—"

"Don't stress. I have it here." Violet held up the camera, which was suspended from a strap around her neck.

Nathan secured his grip on the box, still scowling. "If anything's broken, you can blame the blue-haired punk over there." He jutted his chin toward a cluster of college kids with freakish colored hair. Along with the shiny black vinyl, several wore studded dog collars, and he winced when he spotted one guy sporting black lipstick.

Violet looked over, adjusting her hold on her pillow and suitcase. "I'd say they're goths, not punks."

Nathan snorted. "What's the difference?"

Violet bit her lip. He knew it was her way of holding back a smirk. "Well, if you put on some spectacles, old man, you'll notice the lack of safety pins and mohawks."

"Mohawks or not, they're lucky I'm not going over there," Nathan deadpanned.

This time Violet did smirk. "Why? Afraid they'll figure out you smell like mothballs?"

"For the record, it's not mothballs. It's Old Spice."

She threw her head back and laughed. "Seriously? You're wearing something that literally has the word *old* in its name."

Nathan smiled. She had such a great laugh—a recent development for the girl who continued to bloom and shed the husks of her old life. The image of her from the night he'd first found her would always be seared into his brain, but the girl standing before him was a complete contrast. Her gray-blue eyes—stark against the frame of her dark brown, shoulder-length hair—held more sparkle and amusement. When she smiled, her defined, angular cheekbones became plump and rounded—proof of how a healthy diet and exercise had filled out her previously gaunt frame.

She'd had her nineteenth birthday a few weeks ago, and as per her request, it was a low-key barbecue with just Jude and the kids. As much as Nathan held concerns about her moving out into the world, he knew she was more than ready. He'd done the best he could to prepare her to look after herself. Her instincts were killer—as long as she didn't panic first.

He nudged her with his elbow. "Yeah, yeah. Come on, this stuff's getting heavy."

They took several steps, then Nathan stopped short. "Almost forgot." He balanced the box with one hand and fished a set of car keys out of his jacket pocket. "The last thing I want is some greaser stealing my new ride." He pressed the lock button on the remote.

Violet smirked again.

"What?" He put on a defensive tone. "I've only had it a week."

She laughed and shook her head. "Come on. Your jeep will be fine."

A wide stone staircase led from the parking lot to the college entrance, which consisted of two red brick pillars with white cornerstones, standing a couple stories high. At the top rested a decorative black arch bordered with gold. The college emblem, an open book backed by a shield, was situated at the top, and beneath it was MONARCH GROVE COLLEGE spelled out in silver. The tall black gates hinged open, inviting newcomers into the college grounds.

Violet paused at the entrance, her forehead creased. Her expression reminded Nathan of the first day she'd arrived at his place three years ago, not long after she was discharged from the hospital. Back then her skittishness was clear even during the tour of her new room.

He leaned in and gave her a gentle nudge. "You know that blank canvas life you keep talking about? It's through those gates."

She sighed. "I know." She still didn't move.

"It's not here on the steps, Vi."

He didn't receive the sarcastic reply he expected. Instead, her eyes became more agonized. "I don't know if I can do this, Nathan."

Nathan blinked a few times and scratched the top of his head. "Um . . . well . . ." It was times like these he wished he was more of a "pep talk" kind of guy. "Look, the way I see it, you can give up now and spend the rest of your life wondering 'what if,' or you can walk through those gates with your head held high, knowing you damn well deserve to be here. You'll make friends, you'll go to parties, you'll study hard, then you'll leave with your hard-earned diploma. Either way, it's up to you."

She nodded a few times, chewing on her lower lip. "But I've never done anything big like this before."

Nathan shrugged. "Yeah, well, you'll never know whether you're capable if you don't try."

She snorted, and to his relief, the corners of her mouth twitched up into a smile.

"So, Violet. What's it going to be?"

"Okay." She nodded. "I'll give it a go."

"Great! I'd hate to think we drove two hours for nothing."

She laughed and gave him a playful punch before stepping through the gates.

Sunlight glittered through the leafy canopy arching over the path, and the manicured greenery beneath thrived with hundreds of bold flowers. Benches were scattered around the gardens, most of them already occupied. The campus buildings, which generally followed the red brick and white cornerstone design, could be seen beyond the trees. Dormitories were easy to spot by the bay windows that waved in and out of the buildings' facades, contrasting with the linear lecture halls and community establishments.

Violet's room was on the second floor of one of the dormitories. They navigated through the countless students, parents, and college welcomers, making sure not to trip on any of the boxes and bedding that hadn't made it into rooms yet.

Finally, they stood outside room number 2052 of the west wing. The door was ajar, and Violet hesitated.

Nathan laid a hand on her shoulder. "Blank canvas, remember?"

When she turned to him, he was relieved to see her expression wasn't fearful. Instead, her eyes held a glint of excitement. With a smile and a nod, she shoved the door open.

"Ouch!" yelped a male voice from inside.

"What the—?" Violet stumbled back into Nathan, and the

box he carried toppled and spilled for the second time that day.

The door slowly swung back open, revealing a guy clutching his face. A few agonized groans escaped from between his fingers.

"What happened?" asked a female voice from farther in the room.

The guy just moaned.

A petite girl with chestnut dreadlocks that hung down to about mid-waist came into view. She wore an oversized heavy-metal band shirt with blue denim shorts edged with white lace. Her skin was golden, either sun-kissed or spray-tanned; she looked as if she'd just stepped off a beach.

"Show me." She yanked the guy's hands away from his face.

"Ouch! Careful, Autumn."

"Quit being a baby and show me." After a moment of inspection, she released him and whacked him on the shoulder. "There's no blood. You're fine."

His reply was a groan of derision. Then he pointed to Violet. "I think your roommate is here."

Dreadlocks fanned out as the girl spun around.

Violet's eyes bugged. Her hands covered her mouth and her cheeks turned red. "I'm so sorry. I had no idea that—oh my gosh. Are you okay?"

The girl smiled. "Don't worry, he's fine." She put her hands on her hips. Her slender nose crinkled as she looked Violet up and down with dark brown eyes. "So . . . you're my new roomie."

Even though the girl was a few inches shorter than Violet's five feet and eight inches, she radiated an intensity that made Violet shrink back against Nathan.

"Yep," said the girl after a few heartbeats. "I think you'll do."

The guy behind her groaned and rolled his eyes. "Don't mind Autumn. You'll eventually get used to her overbearing ways." He stepped in front of her and held out a hand. "Hi, I'm August."

He was taller than Violet, but he still had a few inches to go before he would reach Nathan's eye level. His dark brown hair was styled in a messy quiff. Faded, ripped jeans were matched with a low-cut white V-neck and about a half-dozen necklaces made from black thread, gemstone beads, copper, and silver.

After a slight hesitation, Violet shook his hand, which sported a faded turquoise wrist cuff adorned with a few bracelets that matched the guy's necklaces. "Hi, I'm Violet."

"Awesome." He grinned.

"I'm sorry again for hitting you with the door."

August waved his free hand; the other hand still held Violet's. "Don't mention it. No permanent damage done. It'll take a lot more effort to ruin this pretty face."

The handshake continued for what Nathan figured to be the longest handshake in history. Finally, he cleared his throat, and the boy dropped both his grin and Violet's hand.

Violet inclined her head. "This is Nathan."

"Cool." August nodded in a manner that reminded Nathan of a bobblehead doll. He held out his hand. "Nice to meet you."

"You too," Nathan replied, making sure his tone held a note of warning. He restrained the temptation to crush the boy's hand but still went for a firmer than normal grip. The boy hid his wince of pain pretty well, but his relief was obvious when Nathan released the handshake.

"So," Nathan said after a pause, "Autumn and August?"

"Yeah, you can blame our hippie mothers," said August. He put his hands in his pockets, rocked back on his heels, and donned a tight grin.

Autumn gestured between herself and August. "We're cousins, born a week apart. Our mothers are sisters and thought it would be so cute for their babies to have semi-matching names."

August forced a laugh and attempted an indifferent look. "It obviously didn't occur to them exactly how cute it would still be once we reached adulthood. And in case you were wondering, I was born in May, not August." He paused a moment. "And yes, to be honest, I am actually glad that my mother didn't call me May. But if you ask me—"

"You can just call him Gus," Autumn cut in.

"Right. Yes. Gus is fine." His head bounced in a nod again, and he crossed his arms. "So, Violet, what do you think of your new room?"

"She hasn't seen it yet," said Nathan.

Autumn snorted a laugh, and Gus's cheeks turned a little red.

They all picked up Violet's things from the spilled box, and the cousins ushered Violet into her new home. Two beds, two bedside tables, two desks, two desk chairs, and two wardrobes mirrored each other on either side of a bay window seat. To the right of the entryway, a door led into a small bathroom, and to the left was a kitchenette with a mini fridge and microwave.

Autumn had obviously already claimed the right side. Clothes, shoes, power cables, power boards, and a number of other items were strewn all over that half of the furniture. Violet dropped her bedding on the free bed, and Nathan set his box on the desk.

Autumn planted herself on the bay window seat, her legs folded beneath her, and patted the space next to her. "Come on over and make yourself at home, roomie."

Violet flicked her gaze to Nathan. He mouthed, *Give it a*

*go.* She gave him a slight smile and crossed the space between the two beds to sit next to Autumn.

"So, Violet, what brings you to Monarch Grove University?" Autumn asked.

"Uh, nothing special." Violet picked up a cushion and placed it on her lap. "I'm just doing photography."

Nathan folded his arms. He hated it when Violet downplayed her talents. Since the day she picked up his dusty old camera, he knew she had a keen eye for photography. He would never forget the smile on her face when he bought her a new camera, one with enough buttons and functions to rival a spaceship. His walls back home were lined with her framed handiwork.

"What about you?" Violet asked.

"I'm studying cybersecurity and program engineering," said Autumn, lying back and snuggling deeper into the cushions. She selected a dreadlock and twirled it in her fingers. The sun streamed in through the window and enhanced the girl's golden skin.

"Oh." Violet stroked one of the cushion's tassels. "What's that?"

"It's just a fancy way of saying 'hacking.'" Gus had slumped into Autumn's desk chair and was swiveling from side to side. "She just wants to learn what the regular people of internet land are doing these days to secure themselves against the likes of her." He jabbed an accusatory finger at his cousin.

She rolled her eyes. "Shut up, Gus. You know full well you wouldn't be here if it wasn't for my 'hacking,' so drop your high and mighty attitude and show a little gratitude."

He shook his head. "Nope. I still maintain I worked hard for those pitiful grades. You just ruined my bad boy rep. Seriously, not *everything* needs to be manipulated to get your way." He gestured to her laptop. "You treat that thing like it's a genie that grants wishes."

Autumn rolled her eyes. "Whatever. Just admit how glad you are to be rubbing shoulders with college girls right now instead of flipping burgers."

"Pfft. Don't pat yourself on the back yet. I haven't rubbed shoulders, or any other body parts for that matter, with any college girls."

Autumn sniggered.

"Wait, hold up," said Violet. "Are you serious? Did you really hack into your school's network to change his grades?"

"*Hack* is such a crude word," said Autumn. "I like to think I was doing the world a favor. Not only was I helping a cousin out, but I also discovered our biology teacher was using his school computer to stash his disgusting collection of taboo porn. Let's just say, after an anonymous tip to the cops from me, he's no longer teaching biology." Autumn shuddered in disgust. "Ugh!"

"Damn, girl," said Violet. "Where were you when I needed help with my grades?"

Nathan cleared his throat and gave her a pointed look.

"What? Totally joking," she said, stifling a smirk. "And what about you, Gus? What are you studying?"

"Nothing major. I've taken up a few random classes until I figure out what I want to do."

"Such a waste," Autumn scoffed. "I keep telling you that if you just applied yourself, you could be a doctor like your mom. I've already fixed your high school grades, so no one will know you were trying to make out you were a slacker."

"Just leave it, Autumn." The tone in his voice suggested this was an old argument.

"Come on," whined Autumn, "it's not too late for me to change your status to 'med student.' Seriously, you're wasting your time with Greek poetry and textile classes."

"You never know. The textile class might come in handy with helping Aunty Skye with her hemp-weaving business."

"Quit joking around," growled Autumn. "I'm not going to let you give up on medicine. I just don't know why you—"

"You *do* know why," Gus said through gritted teeth. "Now drop it." His cold glare could have turned water into ice.

Autumn's mouth clamped shut, but her own glare matched Gus's level of severity.

Nathan and Violet exchanged an awkward glance.

Gus groaned and rocked his head back to look at the ceiling. "Can we please discuss this later when we're not trying to make a good impression on our new friend here?"

"Fine," Autumn relented. "But this isn't finished."

Gus rolled his eyes. "Of course. Why would I ever think you'd let this go?"

Autumn *hmph*ed and crossed her arms.

Gus gave Violet and Nathan an apologetic smile. "Sorry for the drama."

"It's fine," said Violet.

Nathan just gave a tight-lipped smile and waved his hand indifferently.

"So . . ." Gus floundered through some small talk with Violet until the tension started to ease up. Autumn eventually dropped her attitude, and the three of them commenced a lengthy discussion about their anticipation for their college careers, the towns they moved from, and other trivial things like movies and fashion.

Nathan watched as Violet smiled and responded to whatever Autumn and Gus were saying. He hadn't seen her look this content and confident in a long while. In fact, come to think of it, the whole time he'd known Violet, he'd never seen her act like . . . well . . . like a teenage girl.

"Oh my gosh!" Autumn exclaimed. "I can't believe you don't know who The Wanderers are."

"Uh, sorry." Violet's lips compressed into a half wince, half smile.

Gus groaned. "Brace yourself. You're about to be baptized into one of Autumn's obsessions whether you like it or not."

"It's not my fault you haven't developed a taste for great music, cuz," retorted Autumn.

"It's not your *taste* in music I'm opposing, *cuz*. It's the time, place, and consistency. Violet, I suggest you invest in a decent pair of earmuffs if you want to get any sleep."

Autumn tossed a cushion, which smacked him square in the face.

Gus yelped. "Autumn! Door! Hurt! Remember!" He wiped at his nose with his shirt collar. "Sheesh! What's it take for a guy to get a bloody nose around here?"

Autumn leaned back into her cushions, her hands behind her head and a victory smile on her face.

Violet hid a laugh behind her hand.

Nathan shook his head. He didn't envy Violet putting up with these two. His phone buzzed, and he pulled it out of his pocket to read the message, then noticed the time.

"Damn! Dinosaur alert!" Gus pointed at Nathan's flip phone, a ghost of a smirk playing on his lips. "I had no idea people still carried those antiques around."

Nathan gave him a stare he reserved for the perps he interrogated. After a moment, Gus awkwardly folded his arms and dropped his gaze to the floor. *Ha, that was too easy.* He wished the people he grilled cracked as easily as this kid.

He closed his phone and put it back in his pocket. "Violet, sorry to interrupt, but I gotta go."

"No problem. I'll walk you out."

A few paces down the hallway, a young man holding a stack of flyers approached them, flashing a big toothy grin at Violet. "Hi, am I right to presume you're new here?"

Violet nodded. "Uh, yeah. Just arrived."

"Awesome!" The guy very enthusiastically held up his thumb. "Welcome to Monarch Grove College, or MGC, if you're into acronyms. I can guarantee you're gonna love it here. And in honor of your first day, we're having a party." He handed her a flyer.

"A party?" said Violet. "Already?"

"Of course! What better time than the present to show off our amazing school spirit?"

"Because all we have is the present right?" Violet gave him her own toothy grin.

"Right! A girl after my own heart."

Nathan inwardly cringed. Peppy guys like this grated on him, but he couldn't overlook his appreciation that this kid was giving Violet a warm welcome.

Violet scanned the flyer and pointed to the name of the venue. "Um, sorry, but where is this?"

"Oh, it's super easy to get to." The guy turned and pointed, explaining the directions. In doing so, he exposed a tattoo of a rose on his neck.

Nathan felt Violet stiffen beside him. Her breaths grew shallow and uneven. The flyer crinkled as her hands clenched into fists, her knuckles going white.

When the guy turned back, neither Nathan nor Violet responded, and his toothpaste-commercial grin faltered.

"Ah, like you said, super easy to get to," Nathan blurted. "Thanks for your help."

Violet nodded and smiled, although not as bright as before. Instead it was the tight smile Nathan knew so well— the one that held no joy behind it, only masking the turmoil rising inside her. He took hold of her shoulders and gently guided her away.

"Breathe, Violet," he said in a soothing voice only she could hear. "It was a rose. It's not him. Just breathe, okay?"

Her anxiety, triggered by something as unassuming as

an unfortunately placed tattoo, was plain to anyone who cared to look closely enough. It was evident in the tightness of her shoulders, in the way her eyes darted around, in her uneven breathing, in the way she fidgeted with the flyer.

Nathan directed her outside, hoping some fresh air would help. They found an empty bench under one of the ancient trees in the garden.

"I'm sorry, Nathan. I know you have to get going," said Violet, taking a seat. "Don't worry about me. I'll be fine."

"It's all good, Vi." He sat next to her and patted her back. "I can spare ten minutes."

He remembered when Violet first started showing her post-traumatic stress symptoms, not long after she'd been found. The numerous episodes at school had ranged from catatonic to frantic screaming. Nathan promptly had her referred to a psychiatrist and the school counselor.

It took some trial and error, but as soon as she began working with someone specialized in trauma, Violet's mental health improved in leaps and bounds. Over time, she'd learned to recognize her triggers and developed methods to cope.

He was proud to see how well she was handling this one. Some triggers were worse than others, and even a year ago, the sight of a neck tattoo would have resulted in a full-blown panic that would have had Violet reaching for the switchblade tucked securely in her back pocket. Now she managed the situation like the trooper she was.

She took several more deep breaths, regulating her breathing and lowering her heart rate. Slowly, the tension in her shoulders released, and she sat back against the bench with a little less rigidity.

He knew she had this under control, but he added some words of encouragement just for good measure. "Violet, you're safe. No one is here to hurt you. You're not in any danger. And you're doing great at managing this anxiety."

That made her chuckle. She nodded and took a few more measured breaths as Nathan released a quiet, grateful sigh. The worst of it was already over.

It had been a few months since she'd had a full-blown panic attack—the last, Nathan hoped, she would have to experience. But he couldn't help worrying about how she would cope on her own, at a new and unfamiliar place, by herself.

He stopped reviewing his mental list of worries when Violet stood up.

"Okay, I'm all good now." She forced a grin, but it didn't quite reach her eyes. Even though her expression was calmer, the flyer still shook with the slight tremor in her hands from the residual adrenaline rush.

Nathan had half a mind to grab her wrist and take her back to the car. And if he was reading her expressions correctly, she was afraid he was going to do just that.

He forced his own smile. "So, you got everything you need?"

"I think so." Her voice shook a little, but she raised her chin and said in a bolder tone, "Yes. I have everything I need. I'll be fine."

He had to give her credit, she was determined to prove she wasn't going to let one little near attack break her on her first day of college. With a genuine smile, he gave her a nod of approval.

"Good. Oh, and before I forget"—he pulled out the keyset for the jeep and placed it in her hand—"these are now yours."

Her eyes bulged and her jaw dropped. "What? No way. That's your new car. I can't take your car." She attempted to give the keys back.

He shook his head and closed her hands around them.

"You've already used all your savings on school fees. Think of this as a late birthday present."

She shook her head.

"Fine. If you can't take it for you, then at least take it for me. This old man wants to sleep at night knowing you have a safe way to get home from off-campus parties and shopping sprees in the city and whatever else you college kids get up to these days. I'll be honest, I don't fancy the idea of you catching trains or buses and especially walking home in the dark."

She gave him an *are-you-kidding-me* look. "Really? And what about from the parking lot to my dorm? It's still a good ten-minute walk, and there are lots of dark places attackers could be lurking, you know."

"I know, but that's what this is for." He pointed to the place where her switchblade was hidden. "Don't tell me you've already forgotten all your self-defense training from the past few years. In case you have, a swift kick to the balls should do the trick."

Violet put her hands on her hips. "And what if it's a girl who's attacking me?"

"I . . . um . . ." Nathan frowned and rubbed the back of his neck. "I don't know, kick her in the teeth and yank on her hair, or something."

She laughed. "Or something?"

He smiled. "Anyway, I'll let you get back to your new friends." He patted her on the shoulder. "And don't forget, you can call me whenever. Day or night, no matter the time."

She nodded.

"I mean it, Vi."

"I know." Her teasing smile dropped into seriousness. "Thanks, Nathan."

"Don't mention it."

"No, really. Thank you. For everything. I wouldn't have made it here without you."

He waved a hand. "Ah, someone had to drive you. It beats catching the train with all the stuff you had to carry."

She hit him on the arm. "You know what I mean."

He nodded, and before he could react, she hugged him. He hesitated for a second, then hugged her back. "You know, I think you're going to do great here." He didn't have to see her face to know she was smiling. "I'll catch you later, Vi." He turned and walked down the path.

"Wait," she called after him. "How are you getting home without a car?"

Without stopping, he called over his shoulder, "I bought a train ticket. The station is only a few minutes' walk from here."

"But the train station back in town is still a twenty-minute drive to your house."

"Jude's picking me up."

"What? Are you telling me you finally—"

"Bye, Vi. Enjoy your first day."

## ANGRY PIXIES

Violet sat alone on the bench for a few minutes once Nathan was out of sight. After her near attack, all she wanted was to curl up on her bed and go to sleep.

Living in Nathan's spare room for the past three years had been a godsend. It was only meant to be a temporary arrangement, but even after three months, her social worker hadn't been able to find her a suitable housing situation. A few discussions later, Nathan had offered to have her stay on a permanent basis, and without a lot of hesitation, Violet had agreed. After all, Nathan was about as chill as a guardian could be, and having her own space—a place to hide away whenever she felt the need, no questions asked—had given her a safe haven, somewhere she could heal and recharge after losing Lyla.

Living with someone else in the same space wouldn't be an easy adjustment. She wasn't one to trust people easily, if at all. Still, Autumn and Gus *were* the kind of people she would like to get to know. Given a little time, maybe she would even come to call them friends.

She fidgeted. Something in her jeans pocket was digging

into her. She pulled out her switchblade, another gift from Nathan. He had given it to her not long after he started training her in self-defense. At first he'd just taught her the basics—things like how to break free from headlocks and choke holds—but after a few weeks, he'd moved on to how to defend against someone with a weapon, starting with a knife. Not only had he trained her to defend against a blade; he'd also taught how to use one effectively.

When he'd presented her with the switchblade, claiming it had been in his family for several generations, of course she'd refused to take it. She'd never owned anything so valuable. But he had insisted.

She twirled it in her palm. There was no denying how beautiful it was. When she pressed the button, a double-edged blade glided out from the center of the handle with a *shnik*.

She held it up, the handle fitting snuggly within the contours of her hand. The sun reflected subtle changes of color along the pearlescent hilt, and a crest of some sort was ornately carved on the topside of the pearl finish. Along the back were ten embedded black gemstones.

On either end of the pearly white handle, both the bolster and guard were mostly teal, but when she rotated the knife from side to side, veins of emerald green and magenta glistened in the sunlight. They matched the blade itself, where the emerald and magenta glimmered through the teal in an organic whirled pattern right up to its deadly tip.

She pressed the button again. *Shnik*. The blade disappeared back into the handle.

Violet switched her attention to the keys in her other hand, shaking her head. Nathan's generosity was staggering. A part of her had wished over and over again that he'd shown up much earlier in her life, but another part knew he'd arrived at the perfect time.

She'd spent most of her life watching her world be destroyed piece by piece, and Lyla's death had been the final Armageddon. But Nathan had shown her how to rebuild, helped her claw her way out of her wretched abyss and learn how to fight her demons. He'd become her beacon, a reason to trust not only in him but also in herself. He was there when she'd needed someone the most.

She took in a deep breath and slowly exhaled. Now she was at college, by herself. He was no longer just down the hallway. The thought of doing this next chapter in her life without him almost brought on a new wave of panic.

She squeezed her eyes shut. *Stop it!* She couldn't do this anymore. She couldn't keep falling to pieces and waiting for Nathan to mend her. *Come on, Violet, get yourself under control. It's going to take a little adjustment, that's all.*

She needed to grow up, embrace her new reality, remember that this college life was what she wanted. She just needed to take it one day at a time.

For now, maybe caffeine would help. Earlier she'd seen a quaint little coffee shop near the parking lot outside the college grounds. The walk there and back might give her enough time to clear her head and prepare herself to face the dynamics of her new home life.

About twenty minutes later, she pushed through the glass doors of the café and placed an order for a chai latte with extra foam. She then leaned against the wall, out of the way of the other customers, and twirled a tassel on her scarf while she waited.

Glossy wallpaper and various artworks decorated the café's walls. A television mounted in one corner played a black-and-white Marilyn Monroe movie with the volume on low. People came and left with Styrofoam cups, steaming croissants, and other snacks-to-go. A barista called out an order, and a woman with blonde wavy locks and a tan jacket moved past Violet to collect her latte.

Violet's heart skipped a beat. *That woman . . . Was she . . . ?*

The woman turned and happened to catch Violet's eye for a second on her way out. Violet's shoulders sagged. What was wrong with her? Of course that woman wasn't Lyla.

A lump formed in her throat.

She'd lost count of how many times she'd wished she could remember what happened the night Lyla died. She only knew what Nathan and Jude had told her, but none of it explained *why*. Why were she and Lyla kidnapped? Why did Lyla have to die? Why was she still alive? Lyla was more deserving of life than she was. Lyla had a family: a mother, father, and brother who missed her.

Self-loathing clung to Violet like gelatinous goo. No matter how hard she tried to scrub it away, a sticky residue always remained—just like how the tattooed man from her dreams remained. The faceless one with that stupid tattoo she saw every time she closed her eyes.

Violet inwardly cringed, replaying how she'd reacted to the guy handing out the flyers. *It was a stupid rose tattoo, for crying out loud!* Rubbing her eyes, she let out a sigh.

"Miss? Excuse me, miss."

She blinked a few times. The young female barista behind the counter was waving at her. "Your chai latte is ready."

"Oh, sorry." Violet walked over and handed the barista a few bills from her wallet. "Here you go."

"No worries, love," said the barista, taking the cash.

*Love?* Violet hated it when younger girls called her "love." She offered a tight smile, picked up her latte, and turned.

And crashed right into someone.

For a second, brown liquid and white foam blocked Violet's vision. The aroma of cinnamon and other spices overtook her senses.

She froze in horror.

A man about her age looked down at his scarf, jacket, pants, and shoes, now covered in a murky tinge. She regretted asking for extra foam. Both he and she watched as a white glob smeared a trail down his scarf, then splattered into the milky puddle at his feet.

He looked up at her.

Her heart pounded, her cheeks grew warm, and her eyes couldn't open any wider. Her whole body tensed, preparing for what was about to come next. The rage. The shouting and screaming about third-degree burns and ruined clothes. Memories flashed through her mind's eye, each one more violent than the last. She braced herself.

Then he grinned.

She blinked.

He was actually grinning at her.

Her panic hitched.

His smile was lopsided but genuine. A hint of amusement twinkled in his golden-brown eyes.

"You know," he said, wiping a few specks of white foam from his blond goatee, "when I figured some coffee would warm me up, this isn't exactly what I had in mind."

"I'm sorry?" Was she missing something? Was this usually how people reacted after being baptized in hot chai?

He shrugged, still smiling at her. "Apology accepted."

*Apology?* Violet gasped. *Oh, right!* She threw her hand over her mouth. "I'm so, *so* sorry."

She turned and grabbed a nearby stack of napkins. She should probably help him wipe down his clothes, but the idea of touching a stranger made her slightly uneasy. Instead, she stooped and attempted to sop up the pool at his feet.

He chuckled and bent down to her level. "Here." He reached a hand toward her, and his fingers grazed her wrist. "Let me hel–"

On instinct, Violet flinched away and stood up. A look of horror instantly replaced his grin, and he stood up with deliberate slowness, both palms held out.

"I'm sorry . . . I didn't mean . . . I just . . ." His eyes darted over and around her. He took half a step back as if preparing to flee.

"Oh!" *He was just reaching for the napkins in my hand.* "No, I'm sorry." *Sheesh, soon this guy is going to think that the only word I know how to say is* sorry. She offered an apologetic smile just as she realized her other hand was resting on the switchblade hidden in the back of her jeans. She forced herself to relax and let her hand drop to her side. *It's fine, Vi. He wasn't actually going to—*

She blinked. Going to what? Attack her in the middle of the coffee shop? Latch on to her wrist and drag her out to his white van and stuff her inside?

She gritted her teeth and gave a slight shake of her head. *Seriously, get a hold of yourself. Not everybody is a kidnapper.*

"Um, you just . . . startled me. That's all." She held up the napkins. "Here."

His eyes narrowed at the napkins. He still had his hands raised, palms out.

*Gosh, this guy is acting like I'm pointing a gun at him instead of holding a stack of napkins.* His focus on her was intense. Violet's cheeks grew warm. Could she blame him? Her recoil had been a little over-the-top for an accidental graze of the wrist. From his reaction, she may as well have yelled, "Stick 'em up, homie, and give me all your money!"

He took a step back and started to turn.

She cursed herself. It was the second time she'd overreacted that day. Did she have to act like a psychotic jerk every time a cute guy tried to be nice to her?

"Let me pay for your coffee," she blurted out before he

could completely turn away. He paused, but when he didn't say anything, she added, " . . . for the whole week."

He still didn't respond, but his intense expression relaxed a little.

She glanced at his scarf. "I can also replace your scarf, if you like. I'll get you one with, um . . ." She winced. " . . . less milk stains."

"Hmm . . ." He tilted his head to one side, then to the other, making a show of considering her offer. To her relief, he dropped his hands; the act made her feel less gangster.

At last he nodded, a half smile appearing on his face. "I think I'll take you up on that free coffee. But don't worry about the scarf. I've never liked it anyway." He held up a soppy tassel with his finger and thumb. "In fact, I think you've improved it."

Two new lattes and an extra stack of napkins later, Violet and the guy stood at the door of the café. She put her hand on the door handle, then hesitated. The wind had picked up, tugging with greedy tendrils at the coats, jackets, and scarves of the people who passed by. Clouds covered the sun, blocking any of its efforts to shed some warmth.

She sighed and hugged her chai latte close.

"If you're not in a hurry to leave," said the guy, "why don't we sit for a few minutes and see if the sun is willing to show its face again today?" He gestured to an empty table with two chairs by the floor-to-ceiling windows. Before she could respond, he held up a warning hand. "Just promise that you won't throw another latte at me." A corner of his mouth twitched, amusement twinkling in his eyes.

Violet couldn't help smiling, despite the remaining butterflies of embarrassment in her stomach. She took one last look at the dreary view outside. It was going be a good twenty-minute walk back to her dorm, and all she planned to do when she got back was take a nap.

"I promise I won't bite," he said.

The butterflies in her stomach fluttered harder. Not butterflies—more like angry pixies buzzing and banging to get out.

He smiled at her.

Her nap could wait.

She nodded and followed him over to the table.

Once settled, he shed his still damp jacket. Violet's embarrassment flared again at the blotchy latte stains that had bled onto his long-sleeved shirt. He adjusted his scarf, then took a sip of his drink.

Violet dipped her head, hoping her red cheeks weren't obvious. She took a sip of her latte, relishing the scald and the decadent flavors dancing over her tongue.

"So, I didn't catch your name." The guy turned his cup in a slow spin on the table.

"My name?"

Again, a corner of his mouth twitched. "Yeah, you know. The word that people use to get your attention. I figured if a lovely lady such as yourself has offered to buy me coffee for the rest of the week, I should at least know her name."

She raised an eyebrow. "'Lovely lady'? That makes me think of an elderly woman with poodles."

He chuckled. "All right, how about I change that to 'beautiful lady'?"

Violet's cheeks and neck grew warm. She dropped her gaze to the lid of her drink, at the four raised domes labelled *White*, *Capp*, *Latte*, and *Choc*. The dome for *Latte* was pressed in, and she circled her thumb in its dip. "It's Violet."

"Violet." His voice was velvet.

She bit her lip.

"So, are you a student?" Violet asked.

He shook his head. "No, thankfully I'm all done with my degree. I now work from home."

"Oh, really? What do you do?"

"I'm a marketing consultant."

"That sounds fancy."

He let out an amused sigh. "Not really. Basically, I assess a business's marketing strategy and develop a plan that outlines proposals for improvements."

"Nice."

"Yeah, it's not a bad gig. I'm my own boss and I get to choose my hours. At the start I didn't have the luxury of picking and choosing my clients, but I've developed a bit of a rep, and I can now take on the ones that interest me."

"Wow, that sounds awesome." Earlier, she'd guessed he was about her age, but if he'd finished a degree and was already running his own business, then he had to be at least twenty-three. It made sense; his masculine features easily outpaced the pubescent boys from her high school, who were still growing out of their delicate childhood phase.

"So, Violet, if you don't mind my asking, why chai?"

Her brow crinkled and she tilted her head. "What do you mean?"

"I mean, forgive me if I'm wrong, but you don't strike me as someone who would like . . . chai."

"Oh." Violet shrugged. "I don't know, what's not to like? It's like drinking a cup of Christmas. All of those festive flavors—ginger, cloves, vanilla, star anise, and cinnamon. Now, who doesn't like cinnamon?"

He crinkled up his nose.

Violet's jaw dropped. "Don't tell me you don't like cinnamon?"

He pursed his lips and shook his head. "Sorry. Not a fan."

"Come on, man, what about cinnamon doughnuts? Freshly cooked."

He crinkled his nose again. "I prefer glazed."

"What? You're kidding? There's no way that glazed doughnuts are better than cinnamon ones."

He laughed and held his hands up. "Okay, okay. How about we agree to disagree? I'll leave you to your chai preference, and you leave me with my glazed doughnut preference."

Violet laughed and nodded. "Okay, deal."

He smiled. "Great."

The distance between them was short over the tiny table. From this proximity, she could see his eyes were actually deep chocolate with dazzling flecks of gold, which together emitted the golden-brown hue from a distance. His trimmed goatee, now free from foam, matched the sandy blond of his hair, which was streaked with vintage gold and sun-kissed white. His scarf hid his neck and most of his chest, but his gray sleeves were tight enough to showcase the muscles in his shoulders and arms.

She realized he was studying her as she was him. Once again, her cheeks flushed, and she dropped her gaze to her coffee lid.

"So, I don't suppose I get to know your name?" she asked. "Because, you know, I figured my friends would want to know who the poor unfortunate soul was that got assaulted by my chai."

He laughed. "Ah, in that case, we can't let your friends down."

"No, we can't," she said, biting her lip.

"Well, you better tell them my name is Thane."

\* \* \*

Violet walked back into her room, the remainder of her chai latte in hand.

"So, your dad's pretty cool." Autumn was sitting in her

desk chair, twirling a dreadlock around a finger. Colored thread and beads decorated a few of her locks, and silver bell earrings reflected sparkles of sunlight onto her face. They tinkled when she moved her head.

Gus sat in Violet's chair, casually swinging from side to side. "Yeah, he's also kinda . . ." He half squinted an eye, searching for the word. ". . . intense."

Violet dropped onto the bay window seat, smiling. She shook her head as she wrapped her arms around a cushion. "Nathan's not my dad."

"Oh," said Gus. "So, what, he's your uncle? Much older brother?" He gave Violet a conspiratorial grin and waggled his eyebrows. "Is he your sugar daddy?"

Violet scoffed and threw the cushion at him. "He's just a friend."

Gus *ooph*ed when it hit him in the face. "For the love of doughnuts, would you girls please stop attacking my beautiful face? I'm starting to think you're jealous of my good looks."

"If that were true, I would have thrown my chai at you instead."

Gus laughed. "From now on, I'll keep an eye out for flying hot beverages."

Violet laughed and drained the rest of her chai, then set the empty cup down on the windowsill. Chai always triggered her small cluster of happy memories—most of which involved Lyla.

"So," said Autumn, "other than carry boxes, what does your friend do?"

"He's a cop."

"Oh," said Autumn at the same time Gus exclaimed, "A cop!"

Gus smacked himself in the forehead and groaned. "Why,

49

oh, why did I have to mention Aunt Skye's hemp business in front of a cop?"

Autumn rolled her eyes. "It's not illegal, doofus."

"Maybe *he* doesn't think that. And what about you? That was a great time to bring up your illegal online activities. He's probably already on his radio requesting backup."

"Stop making it sound so shady," Autumn ground out.

"I knew you'd be caught one day!"

"Nathan's cool," said Violet. "Trust me, he doesn't care about stuff like that."

"Says you." Gus stabbed an accusatory finger at her. "How do we know you aren't a plant sent here to report on Autumn's hacking activities?"

"A what?"

"You know, a *plant*. It's cop language for 'spy.'"

"Umm, actually, I don't think it is."

Autumn groaned. "She's not a spy, Gus."

"How do you know?"

"Because I just know."

"How? You think you can just do a little *clack-clack*"—he motioned typing on a keyboard—"and you know everything?"

Autumn kicked his chair. "Shut up, Gus."

"I'm serious. You're going to cross a line one day and find yourself seriously screwed."

"You're freaking out over nothing."

"You're not freaking out enough!"

Autumn gritted her teeth and let out an exasperated grunt. Gus just glared at her. For a few moments, the two stared each other down.

Violet was starting to think she'd come back too soon.

Then, as if snapping out of a trance, Autumn said, "*Anyway*, moving on to more important matters"—she held up a flyer like the one Violet had been given earlier—"some guy came by to give us one of these. We're totally going, right?" When Violet didn't answer straightaway, she turned to Gus. "Right?"

Gus sighed and threw his hands up. "Sure, let's go party."

Autumn squealed. "How 'bout it, Vi?"

"Um . . ." Violet hesitated. When she'd received the flyer earlier, she'd been keen to go try it out. But parties meant people, lots of people, and after her near panic attack, the idea of pasting on a cheerful demeanor for the rest of the night was too overwhelming to think about.

Plus, she'd had her fill of meeting new people for the day. There were sure to be more parties later. This was college, after all.

"You two should go. I think I'm in need of an early night. I want to be fresh and ready for tomorrow."

Autumn put on a pout.

"You're kidding, right?" said Gus. "This is college! Now's the time we get to let our hair down and party till we puke. And seriously, we don't need to worry about classes until at least the week before exams anyway."

"Yeah, I know," said Violet, trying not to cringe. "But I've had a long day. I'll postpone the puking until later."

Autumn and Gus gave up trying to convince her after a few more attempts. They stuck around for a little longer, then to Violet's relief, they left to set up Gus's room, which was in the south wing of the building.

Violet curled up on the window seat and hugged a cushion tight, overcome with exhaustion.

Outside, the final rays of the setting sun tinged the world a warm yellow. Below, she could see the network of paths cutting through the garden from each dormitory. Every path was filling up with students, the majority of them headed in the same direction.

They were all going to the location of the impending

party, based on the directions the guy with the flyers had given Violet earlier. That guy probably thought she was a moron. He was probably telling all of his friends right now how much of a freak she was.

She groaned and buried her face in the cushion.

*It was a rose tattoo. A stupid, stupid rose!*

With a huff she leaned on the windowsill, propping her head up on one hand. Hopefully, tomorrow would be a little better. Although the day hadn't been *all* bad.

Cinnamon and spices still lingered on her taste buds, and her thoughts drifted to Lyla. A fierce, familiar ache stabbed through her chest and clutched at her throat, and before she could stop it, a tear rolled down her cheek.

"I've done it, Ly. I've made it to college."

## 5

# THERE YOU ARE

THE THUMPING MUSIC, LAUGHTER, AND CONVERSATIONAL chatter drifted out to where he stood in the night's inky blackness, the dark shadows of various trees and bushy shrubs providing him perfect camouflage.

The first party of the new school year was being held in one of the dorm's social rooms on the ground level. He angled his head to peer through gaps in the foliage, searching each floor-to-ceiling window. The partygoers had divided themselves into their typical roles: dancers near the DJ stage, seasoned partiers observing a game of beer pong, those who needed alcohol to boost their confidence around the punch bowls and kegs, and the socially awkward scattered throughout the outskirts.

His nose crinkled at the raucous behavior. He'd never understood the appeal of making a fool of oneself under the influence of spirits and narcotics.

He turned his attention to the dorm buildings, scanning the windows until he spotted the one he was looking for. A light inside silhouetted a female student sitting at the bay window, watching the partygoers spilling out onto the lawn below.

He smiled. "Ah, there you are, Violet."

A mosquito hummed by his ear and landed on the side of his neck. He slapped it, then rubbed the irritated skin, momentarily wrinkling the sharp outline of a crystal scorpion tattoo. He folded his arms and leaned against the brick wall, never once dropping his gaze from the girl in the window.

## 6

## THAT CHANDELIER

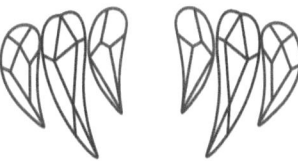

Nathan wound down the car window, letting the wind caress his face as he scanned the houses and stores that flew by.

"How was Violet's first week of college?" Jude asked from the driver's seat of the unmarked police car. He preferred it when she drove; he'd never really gotten the hang of maneuvering these Erathi vehicles.

"Well, she—"

He was interrupted by someone from the precinct reporting a break and enter. Nathan reached for the handheld radio and replied that he and Jude would check it out.

"Great," said the voice on the other end. "Here's the address."

The address was familiar to Nathan, though he couldn't pin down why. Then again, which address in this town wasn't familiar?

"No rest for the wicked," said Nathan as Jude veered the car toward their new destination.

"If they did, we'd be out of a job."

"Would that be so bad?"

"It would for me. Your kid might be in college, but I've still got to get my two kids there. Lord knows my ex-husband isn't paying enough child support to even cover piano lessons. But back to my original question. How is Violet doing?"

"Not too bad," he said after a slight pause.

"Uh-oh, what happened?"

He looked at her and shook his head. "How do you do that, Jude?"

She waved a casual hand. "Years on the job. I can always tell when someone is trying to downplay an event."

Nathan looked out the car window. Since he'd started working with Jude three and a half years ago, he'd gone to extreme lengths to hide his true identity not just from her but from the rest of the town. Suppressing his nature had meant learning to rely on his human abilities to read and predict the emotions and motives of those around him— something that had turned out to be infinitely trickier when it came to raising a teenager.

When Violet had moved in, he'd turned to Jude for advice on how to deal with not only the female but also the adolescent variety of tenants. Jude's experience in raising two preteens had been invaluable. Without her, he never would have known the power a bar of chocolate had when consoling moody girls.

He didn't get too deep into his thoughts before a fist thumped his arm.

"Hello? Spill. What's up with Violet?"

"Ah, you know. Violet's tough. She's been through more than we can imagine."

Jude hissed out a breath. "That's an understatement. It still kills me that we couldn't find Violet and Lyla's kidnappers. I can't believe every lead we had was a dead end." She thumped the steering wheel. "I *hate* cold cases."

Nathan shifted in his seat. It was a sure bet he wouldn't stand a chance against Jude's wrath if she ever found out how many of their cold cases were a result of his influence.

"Anyway"—Jude glanced in his direction—"you didn't really answer my question. What's up with Violet?"

He opened his mouth to reply.

"Nevermind," she said. "We're here."

He'd been too caught up in the conversation with Jude to notice the affluent area of town they'd driven into: the manicured lawns, sculpted hedges and gardens, terraced entrances, and sandstone pillars. Each house competed with the next in grandeur and complexity of design. Locals called this street "millionaire lane." Politicians and a few minor celebrities owned houses here. With a sinking feeling, Nathan recognized the house next door to where they'd parked as belonging to Mayor Clearwater.

Dread agitated his gut as he realized where they'd stopped.

The Branstone house. Lyla-Rose's house.

The Branstones had neither political nor celebrity status. Instead, they came from a wealthy family business that spanned several generations. The talk around town was the family owned a few well-known franchises across the country, ranging from jewelry stores to home decor.

Nathan did his best to suppress his apprehension as he and Jude stood at the front double doors. He'd never been inside the Branstone's home. During the investigation of Lyla's death, he and Jude had used the "divide and conquer" approach. He'd focused on studying the crime scene and the forensic side of things, taking part in the interviews when they were held at the precinct, but it was Jude who'd done the necessary home visits with Lyla's family.

Jude pressed the doorbell. A few seconds later, a woman wearing a hot-pink sports top and leopard-print leggings answered the door. A towel was over her shoulders, and her bleached blonde hair cascaded down in soft waves.

"Yes?"

"Hi, Mrs. Branstone," said Jude, "you might remember me. I'm—"

"Of course I remember you, detective," said the woman, cutting her off. "I remember him too." She gestured to Nathan.

He tried recalling the last time he'd seen Lyla's mother. Previously she was brunette, and he also noticed some changes in her lips and nose. Cosmetic surgery, maybe?

"Great," continued Jude. "We got a call about a break and enter."

The woman's face changed from wary to relieved. "Oh, right!" She gave them a broad smile. "Great timing. I've just finished my workout."

Nathan doubted that, based on her flawless full-faced makeup.

"Come on in."

He waited for Jude to go first.

"Oh, wait!" Mrs. Branstone held her hand up to prevent Jude going any farther.

"Stars above," Jude muttered under her breath before taking a step back.

"I've just had the floors waxed," continued Mrs. Branstone, "so take your shoes and socks off before entering."

Nathan looked down and noticed the wooden floorboards under the woman's red-nailed feet. Jude breathed out an "Okay" before stepping back to remove her shoes and socks, and Nathan suppressed a sigh and an adolescent eye roll before taking off his own. Mrs. Branstone tapped her red fingernails on the door while she waited.

Once they were both barefoot, the woman gave them a winning smile and beckoned them inside.

The entry expanded into a grand foyer with high ceilings, lit by an enormous crystal chandelier dangling down the center of the room. A staircase to the right swooped up and to the left, the railings made of intricately carved wood. Family photos adorned the stark white walls along the stairs. A few closed doors led off the landing, and Nathan couldn't help wondering which one might have been Lyla's room.

"Give me a second to change. I'll also bring out some refreshments," said Mrs. Branstone, leading them through a doorway at the foot of the stairs and into a sizable lounge. "Please take a seat." She gestured to one of the sofas before leaving through another doorway.

Nathan and Jude sat down across from a stone fireplace. When he guessed Mrs. Branstone was out of earshot, Nathan leaned closer to Jude. "I don't remember Lyla's mom being so blonde."

"Yeah," said Jude, matching his low voice, "or so full in the lips."

He snorted a low laugh and inspected the room, scanning the extravagant furnishings. He was trying to recall the name of the family's decor homewares franchise when he spotted something that made his gut churn. Crystal vases and lampstands on a mantel over the fireplace glistened in sunlight streaming through the windows. He checked the rest of the room, noting more glass and crystal-like trinkets.

He hadn't heard Mrs. Branstone return, so the appearance of a glass of water in front of his face made him startle.

"Here you go," she said in a sing-song voice.

Light glimmered off the necklace around her neck. Three large colorless gems were draped center stage across her collarbones, with smaller stones framing the larger ones. To the untrained eye, they looked like diamonds or possibly cubic zirconium, but Nathan could detect a difference in the way the sun's rays reflected off the facets. A distinct whirled pattern. And the scent—

Nathan fixed his eyes on the glass of water still in Mrs. Branstone's hand. The churning in his gut turned to nausea, and he forced himself to concentrate on the glass—not to turn his gaze anywhere else. He focused on his breathing in an attempt to stave off his oncoming gag reflex.

Jude elbowed him, her own glass of water in her hand. She frowned, a question evident in her expression. He forced what he hoped was a smile, then took the glass of water.

When Mrs. Branstone sat down on an adjacent sofa, Jude said, "Sorry, it's like he's never seen a cup before."

"Do you like them? My husband got them for me last week. Antique crystalware from Japan."

Nathan closed his eyes, trying to drown out the woman's rattling on about all the other "crystalware" her husband had acquired. Jude even commented on her necklace.

He tried to force his mind to other things, anything to get himself under control. But his thoughts slipped back to the crystal chandelier in the foyer.

A cold sweat erupted all over his body, and saliva flooded his mouth as his nausea intensified twofold.

*Diamantium. But how many?*

That necklace alone would be at least one.

*But that chandelier—*

He was about to vomit all over the floor.

He bolted up. Jude and Mrs. Branstone stared at him, obviously startled.

"So sorry," he blurted out, "must have been the Chinese food last night. Where's your bathroom?"

## 7

# WHAT DO YOU WANT, BLONDIE?

VIOLET INHALED THE FAMILIAR SCENTS. THE BITTER ROASTING coffee was, of course, the most pungent, but something else added an edge of caramel-syrupy sweetness. A waft of melted butter and cheese mingled with the other aromas: a grilled croissant sandwich for someone's breakfast-to-go.

It had been only a week since her first day, and so far her adjustment to college life hadn't been *too* bad. Once she'd received her schedule, the routine of classes and studying—with occasional meals and sleep slotted in—had swept her up and never put her down. She hadn't felt so exhausted in her life.

The busyness was a welcome change from the mundanity she'd left in Brookhaven. Still, with each new class came a new list of assignments, each one more overwhelming than the last. In one particularly dark moment, she'd considered quitting college altogether. She'd had to remind herself that this was what she wanted, this was what she'd worked for.

And this was what Lyla would have wanted.

Violet clung to all her memories of Lyla. The day they first met six years ago was still as clear as crystal.

*  *  *

*The door shut, leaving Violet alone in the bedroom while the muffled voices on the other side gradually moved back downstairs. Miranda was likely filling in the new foster parents about Violet's history.*

*She winced. She'd already seen through the sugar-sweet facade these foster breeds put on whenever someone from the department visited. She'd inwardly shuddered and tasted bile when the new foster dad had given her a sleazy grin and a wink when Miranda wasn't looking. Violet had glanced at the guy's wife and quickly gathered she was the turn-a-blind-eye type.*

*Violet had heard stories of other foster kids finding loving and caring foster families, even eventually being adopted. But in her thirteen years in the system, she had yet to be lucky enough to find that mythical home.*

*She threw the trash bag containing her few belongings onto the floor and collapsed onto the bed, not bothering to acquaint herself with the new room. Instead, she stared at the ceiling and planned her exit strategy. She'd probably be able to get out of here in a few weeks, two being the best-case scenario, three months being the worst.*

*A noise outside the window interrupted her train of thought.*

*Violet bolted up off the bed when the window slid open. A socked foot and then a leg poked inside, soon followed by the whole body of a young girl about Violet's age. The intruder dusted off her tan trench coat and black leggings, brushed a few leaves out of her long blonde locks, turned to Violet, and smiled. A tartan scarf of pale cream, black, and red was draped loosely around her neck, and . . . was she seriously wearing a beret? And where were her shoes? Was she another foster child? If she was, she'd clearly been out knocking over a high-end fashion store.*

*"Hello." The girl extended her hand. "I'm Lyla-Rose. Pleased to make your acquaintance."*

*Violet didn't move. She scanned the girl's stance and expression, trying to guess her intentions.* Hmm, she's probably not in the system. *She was too smiley and . . . polite. Violet had never met any other teenagers who used the phrase "pleased to make your acquaintance."*

*When Violet didn't respond, the girl dropped her hand and shrugged a shoulder.* "All right, how about I start with the basics?" *She reached into her coat pocket and pulled out a notepad and pen before taking a seat on the edge of the bed. She flipped the pad open, hovered the pen over the page, and looked up at Violet.* "What's your full name and date of birth?"

*Violet stared at her.* What on earth was going on? *She'd seen a lot of things over the years, from crazy to nightmarish, but nothing like this had ever happened before. She clenched her fist, refusing to drop her guard, just in case.*

*Lyla-Rose frowned at her.* "Um, do you speak English?"

*Violet frowned.* "What? Yes, of course I do."

*The girl beamed in relief.* "Oh, good. For a minute there I thought you were either a foreigner or possibly mute."

*Violet's eyebrows shot up. She half wondered if this girl had escaped from a nearby mental asylum, then mugged a model before climbing the tree to Violet's second-story window.*

"So, name and date of birth?" *repeated the girl.*

*Violet crossed her arms, not entirely sure how to handle this odd encounter.* "Um, why are you here? Are you another foster kid?"

*The girl's eyes bugged.* "What?" *She laid a hand on her chest.* "Me? No way! No, no, no." *She waved her arms as if Violet had suggested she sprout wings.*

"Then what do you want, blondie?"

*Lyla-Rose tilted her head.* "Isn't it obvious?"

*Violet frowned.*

*Lyla-Rose sighed and dropped the notepad and pen on the bed beside her.* "Okay, look." *She took a deep breath.* "The thing is, Miss Graham told me I need a very compelling human-interest piece to*

63

compete for the editor position for the school magazine. However, Cynthia Clearwater"—she wrinkled her nose as she said the name—"has already completed her interview on the mayor, which is totally cliché and totally unfair, because her father is the mayor." Lyla-Rose stood up and started pacing from the window to the bed. "So of course she was going to get an 'unfiltered' and 'emotional' angle compared to every other person who has ever interviewed him." She threw her arms up to gesture the air quotes. "But when I explained to Miss Graham that nothing ever happened in Brookhaven and anything worth doing a human-interest piece on has been done a million times before, all she said was"—she put her hands on her hips and put on a high-pitched British accent—"'You're a clever girl, Lyla. If the editor position is truly important to you, then surely you of all people can find a compelling topic to write about.'"

She paused mid-pace and beamed. "So, here I am."

Violet squinted at her. "Umm, sorry, I still don't understand what's going on."

Lyla rolled her eyes. She ran over to the bed to retrieve her notepad and pen and held them up for emphasis. "I'm here to interview you. Duh."

"What? You've got to be joking." Yep, Violet was now totally convinced this girl had escaped from a mental asylum.

Lyla giggled. Her green eyes sparkled, and her face glowed with triumph. "Of course not. Don't you see? This is perfect." She threw her arms wide. "Not only are you the newest person in town, but you're also in the system. Here is an opportunity for me to write a fascinating human-interest piece that the school magazine has yet to see. You could give me all the gory details of an insider's perspective on what it's really like to be one of our country's 'forgotten orphans' who is 'overlooked by the Man.' I'll list the pros versus the cons, the myth versus the truth."

Violet's jaw dropped. This girl must also be on crack. Never in

her life had anyone summed up her foster career as "fascinating."
And exactly what "pros" was this bimbo expecting?

Violet started to shake her head. "I don't think—"

"Please let me interview you. I just know this will be my best
article yet. And it will be exactly what I need to win the editor position for the school magazine. Please say yes." Lyla rushed over with
a desperate look on her face and grabbed hold of Violet's arms.

Violet instantly screeched in pain, jerking out of Lyla's hold.

Lyla stumbled backward, eyes wide with shock, her gaze glued
to Violet's arms.

At some point, Violet realized, she must have pushed her sleeves
up, revealing the ugly blue-and-purple bruises on her forearms.
Her cheeks grew warm. She hastily tugged her sleeves to her wrists
and re-crossed her arms before daring a glance back at Lyla.
Curiosity gleamed in the girl's eyes, but another emotion flickered
behind it—something Violet couldn't really decipher. Whatever it
was, it was too much for Violet to handle.

"Get out," she said in a low voice.

Lyla's mouth dropped open. "What? But—"

Violet pointed to the window and growled, "I said get out."

A moment passed, and Violet considered grabbing the girl by
her expensive scarf and hammer-throwing her out of the window.

Lyla pursed her lips and raised her chin. "Fine." With that, she
climbed out the window and back down the tree. When she reached
the ground, she put on a pair of rollerblades that had been left
beside the tree trunk. She glanced back up at Violet and, with a
defiant huff, stomped her rollerblades through the grass, then glided
away when she reached the concrete sidewalk.

A few days later when Violet started at her new school, she wasn't
impressed to find that Lyla was in her grade. The school was small
compared to a few of her previous ones in the city, and with the smaller
student population, it would be next to impossible to avoid Lyla
completely. But to her relief, Lyla seemed to be ignoring her as well.

*Violet also didn't take long to discover who the Cynthia girl was whom Lyla had spoken about with such vehemence. It did, however, take a little longer to discover the reason why. From what Violet could decipher, the girls were neighbors and had been best friends since kindergarten. But apparently a few months before Violet had arrived, they'd had a falling out. Depending on who was telling the story, the reason ranged from boyfriend stealing to family rivalry. Whatever the reason, the result was Cynthia came out on top as the school's social queen, and Lyla became the target for gossip.*

*However, Lyla had two things going for her: her family's reputation and her brother, Sagan. He was two years older, and the story was he was being groomed to take over the family business, which included frequent absences from school to join his father's business trips. Other than that, Violet didn't know a lot about Sagan, except he was highly respected and the majority of the female body had a crush on him. Cynthia especially.*

*Even so, Sagan couldn't shield Lyla from all the vicious text messages, social media humiliations, or sniggers and sneers in the school hallways and girls' bathroom. And things were worse whenever he was away.*

*One day, a few insidious creeps sat behind Lyla during a documentary video in history class and took turns snipping off locks of her hair until Lyla finally noticed. Later, Violet found her in the girls' bathroom, sobbing while she looked at herself in the mirror and clawing at the ends of her freshly cut hair, as if to force it to grow.*

*The raw emotion and desperation were painfully familiar to Violet, along with the relentless wishing that someone, anyone, would stop and pay attention.*

*But this time someone was paying attention.*

*It was Violet who had noticed, and it was Violet who was there when Lyla needed someone the most.*

*She should . . . what? Comfort her? But . . . what does one do to comfort another? This seemed out of her league, better suited to a teacher, a counselor, or a . . . a friend.*

*Violet's mind raced and her heart thumped. She stepped forward until Lyla could see her in the mirror's reflection.*

*"Okay, I'll do it," declared Violet.*

*Lyla's sobbing paused. A few emotions flickered over her face before her expression landed on confusion. "What?"*

*Violet ducked into a stall, then emerged with a handful of tissue, holding it out. "I'll do your interview."*

*Lyla turned to face her but made no move to take the tissue. Instead, she fixed Violet with an intense stare.*

*Violet fought the urge to squirm, recognizing the same look she herself had given Lyla when the girl had broken into her room. Even though Violet hadn't been involved in any of the cruel treatment toward Lyla, she also hadn't made any attempt to intervene, which was just as bad as those creeps cutting her hair. She knew Lyla was searching for falsehood—questioning Violet's true intentions.*

*After a slight hesitation, Violet took another step forward, bringing herself toe-to-toe with Lyla. "Look, name the time and place, and I'll answer any questions you got." She placed the tissue in Lyla's hand. "I swear there's no hidden agenda and no strings attached."*

*Lyla's gaze never wavered. Instead, it seemed to intensify. After a few moments, Violet was starting to think the girl was never going to respond.*

*"My place, after school," Lyla finally said, all hints of recent sobbing gone from her voice.*

*"Great. See you then."*

*Lyla patted down her cheeks with the tissue, and Violet turned to leave.*

*"Before you go . . ." said Lyla.*

*Violet looked back to see Lyla holding up a pair of scissors.*

*"You don't happen to have any hairdressing experience, do you?"*

*Violet gave a small smile. She took the scissors and began trimming away the jagged pieces of Lyla's golden hair.*

\* \* \*

If Lyla were still here, they would have gone to college together, maybe even been roommates. She could have been with Violet right now, waiting for her own coffee while chattering about her latest assignment and disagreements with the class tutor.

Violet sucked in a breath. The pang in her chest was a familiar companion to the bittersweet what-ifs. She couldn't completely say that life was worse without Lyla. It was just that life would be better if Lyla were still in it.

Since losing Lyla, Autumn and Gus had become the closest thing to friends she had, apart from Nathan and Jude.

Living and sleeping so close to Autumn was a little claustrophobic at times, but it wasn't all that different from bunking with half a dozen other foster children. And as far as roommates went, Autumn wasn't too bad. She spent the majority of her time lost in her computer, laptop, or smartphone. The constant *clack-clack* of the keyboard had begun to disappear as white noise.

Violet was also getting to know a few other classmates who frequently visited their dorm room between classes. The main one was an Irish girl named Bessie, a bubbly go-getter with an unhealthy addiction to Hello Kitty, Japanese confectionary, and Quentin Tarantino movies. Autumn and Gus had met her at the party on their first day. They said they'd approached Bessie thinking she was Violet, but when Bessie started talking, the Irish accent immediately gave away the mistake. Other than the same hair color, Violet didn't see the similarities, but several other classmates had since made doppelgänger comments.

One week into college and both Gus and Bessie were practically part of the furniture in Violet and Autumn's room. The four of them got along really well, but Violet still made sure to set aside small amounts of free time for herself outside the dorm—usually in the mornings.

She'd woken early and sneaked out, even though it would be another hour or two before Autumn would be awake and vertical. This was the time she and Thane had agreed to meet, just as they had every day since the chai baptism.

The café was crowded with its usual morning rush. One of the baristas was whistling a light melody, barely audible beneath the grind and hiss of the coffee machines. Patrons huddled in for their morning buzz of caffeine, bringing biting gusts of wind each time one of them opened the door.

Violet scanned the café for a spare table and nestled into a seat. She still had a few minutes to kill before Thane arrived, so she snuggled into her jade-green woolen scarf and pulled out her camera. She'd been inspired on her walk over to snap a few candid shots of students taking advantage of the rare sunshine. She scrolled to a photo of a couple sitting on one of the garden benches. The guy had his arm draped casually around the shoulders of a girl in mid-laugh, her head thrown back, white teeth glistening. He was smiling at her as if he were entranced.

Violet had never had a boyfriend. *What would it be like to be that girl?* Their companionship seemed so close and comfortable. If either he or she were taken away, the photo would be incomplete.

She smiled, thinking about her recent conversations with Thane. Talking and laughing with him was surprisingly easy. It was hard to believe they'd already reached the last day of her promise to buy him coffee for the week.

"Friends of yours?"

Violet glanced up as Thane took the seat across from her. He shed his jacket and hung it on the back of his chair, then unwound the scarf from around his neck and bundled it on the table.

Violet blinked. "Sorry?"

Thane smiled and gestured to the camera in her hands. "The couple in the photo. Are they friends of yours?"

"Oh." Violet looked down at the digital screen. "No, I was just taking some shots of some randoms on the way here."

Thane's eyes widened. "Oh. So you're a stalker."

Violet's eyes bugged. "What? No! I'm not . . . What I mean is—"

Thane grinned and held his hands up. "Relax. I was just kidding." He laughed. "You should see your face."

Violet pressed her palms to her burning cheeks. How could this guy have this effect on her?

He chuckled once more. "I'm sorry, I shouldn't tease. What I should have said was 'That's a great photo. You have a real gift.'"

Something fluttered in her chest, and she couldn't help smiling. "Thanks. You're a real jerk."

His eyes crinkled as he laughed. "You're right. I deserved that."

Their laughter died down. After a few heartbeats, Violet realized they were both staring at each other.

She cleared her throat. "I'll, um, go order." She swiveled in her chair and was about to stand when a young girl in the café uniform placed two takeaway coffee cups on their table.

"One cappuccino and one chai latte, am I right?" asked the barista.

Violet and Thane exchanged a look.

"Yeah," said Thane.

"Great! You can pay when you're ready, love." The barista smiled and winked.

After she left, Thane gave Violet a conspiratorial grin. "Only seven short days and we've become regulars."

Violet laughed. "Actually, I think it's taken *you* seven short days. If you ask me, the barista's crushing on you. Once my week of paying for your coffee is over, I'm pretty sure you could milk some more free ones out of her, especially if she figures I'm no longer in the picture."

Thane's brow furrowed. "No longer in the picture?" He looked down at his cappuccino and spun the cup a few times with his fingers. "Is that what you'd prefer?"

Violet tilted her head. "No, I was . . . I was just trying to make a joke."

This time when he looked up at her, his eyes sparkled. "Great, because I was, um . . . I'd like to keep seeing you. That is . . . if that's all right with you."

Violet's pulse raced. "Ah, yeah. I mean yes," she said, nodding her head with a little too much vigor. "Yes. I'd like that too."

Thane's grin stretched from ear to ear. "Great! So, how about next week, and this time the coffees are my treat."

"Perfect," said Violet.

## 8

## SHARK GRIN

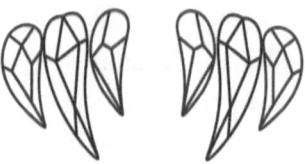

Nathan splashed water onto his face, then took a mouthful to rinse out the acidic burn of the bile he'd just retched into the adjacent toilet. This human life must be making him soft. He'd seen so many detestable things—even done some himself—but none had had the same effect on him as the decor of this house.

When he turned the tap off, he was plunged into silence. His mind raced as he looked up into the vanity mirror, trying to process the previous few minutes.

*How many?* That necklace alone was at least one, but that *chandelier*!

Emotions broiling in his torso overflowed, manifesting a piercing agony that stabbed into his elbows. He hurriedly took off his jacket before the sleeves could get shredded.

The slicing sensation intensified. Over the years, he'd learned to suppress it, but this time he allowed it to break free. He held up an arm and watched in the mirror as a glistening edge pierced through the skin of his elbow. It grew parallel to his forearm, gliding out until it almost reached his wrist. He lifted his other arm, where a crystalline multifaceted blade also protruded, a twin version of the first.

He inspected the blades, noting the distinct whirled pattern within the facets—a pattern similar to Mrs. Branstone's necklace, as well as, most likely, to each crystal shard of the chandelier. Except the pattern on his Diamantium blades were his own, unique, like a fingerprint.

The image of Mrs. Branstone's so-called diamond necklace flashed again in his mind, and he covered his face with his hands, remembering the scent of it. A knot tightened in his throat. He tried to clear his mind of the violent images, of the horror of his shifter race being butchered, their crystal bones broken into tiny shards and then reassembled into a graphic display of human wealth.

He shook his head in disbelief. Why was this making him so nauseated? He'd seen and handled the dead of his own kind before and never had this reaction. But then, except for one particular Veniri, he hadn't been around any others since he'd absconded from his hive fifteen years ago, let alone any of the deceased. Maybe he was developing some kind of sensory sensitivity.

How had he not known about these hunters sooner? More importantly, did they know about him? For the past ten years he'd been so focused on keeping his Veniri identity a secret even Jude and Violet didn't know. But he wasn't privy to the hunters' inner workings or how they discovered and tracked their prey. He doubted he would have lasted this long in their house if they did know. Maybe Jude was his saving grace, an unwanted witness.

. . . Or maybe she was in on it, helping to lure him into some elaborate trap?

He shook his head. That was crazy. There was no way. He was with her almost every day; he'd know if she was the duplicitous type.

He froze. *Jude.*

She was still out there. He doubted she was in any danger. If there was one thing he did know about Erathi hunters, it was that they didn't hunt humans. Still, he didn't like the idea of her being out there without him. He turned his attention back to his reflection and raised his arms. The slicing pain was less severe this time as the Diamantium blades melted back into his flesh.

His jacket securely back in place, he left the bathroom and headed back down the hallway. The lounge was empty. His heart skipped a beat, and blood rushed instantly to his head. His staccato pulse thumped in his ears as pressure built behind his temples.

Before panic could completely set in, he heard voices in the next room. He followed the sounds through a doorway on the other side of the lounge, unclicking the safety strap on his gun holster as he walked. He was just about to draw the weapon when Jude came into view. He recognized her business posture: back straight, shoulders squared, head down and nodding as she entered notes into her phone. She was muttering "mm-hmm" as she listened to whoever was speaking.

He let out a breath and re-strapped the gun, but just as he was about to enter the room, a baritone voice made him pause in the doorway. His relief evaporated.

Two males had joined Jude and Mrs. Branstone.

One was maybe in his late teens or early twenties, with white-blond hair. Nathan recognized him as Lyla's older brother, Sagan. He was slouching against a wall, his arms crossed and his expression sour. When he spotted Nathan, his eyes grew wide, then venomous. He pushed himself off the wall and stood to attention.

The man who'd spoken was older and stood at Nathan's

six-foot-two eye level. He had dark brown hair with graying sideburns, a trimmed moustache, and a goatee. The tight black sweatshirt he wore outlined his broad shoulders and muscular physique, and an intense severity radiated from his every expression, movement, and even stillness.

Matthias, Lyla-Rose's father.

Nathan's elbows flared when he locked eyes with him, and he suppressed a scowl. He needed to pull himself together—maintain his "*human* detective" facade. Even so, he couldn't help making some mental preparations in case the worst-case scenario arose.

He played out a few hypothetical escape plans to get Jude and himself out of this house, cataloguing the weapons he had on his person along with the ones he knew Jude carried. With their collective stash, there was a chance they could fight their way out against these two—three if he counted Mrs. Branstone. And in the end, if it turned out he needed to rely on his Diamantium blades, he would practice his truth speech to Jude later. Or at least a watered-down version of the truth. Assuming they both got out alive.

Matthias paused his response when Nathan walked into the room.

Jude looked up, following Matthias's gaze over to Nathan. "Mr. Branstone, you remember Detective Delano?"

Matthias's mouth curved into a grin, an expression that reminded Nathan of a shark right before it bit into its prey. "Of course, Detective Delano." Matthias held out his hand. "It's been a while since we've been acquainted."

Nathan hesitated, then rebuked himself when Mr. Branstone's shark grin deepened. He forced a smile and shook the man's hand. "Yes, Mr. Branstone. It has been a while."

"Please, call me Matthias."

Nathan replied with a compliant nod.

Matthias's grip tightened. His eye contact never faltered, nor did his smile.

Nathan's elbows blazed with pain, the savage sensation increasing by the second. His jacket was in danger of being punctured. He fought against the urge to step in front of Jude and shield her from this man. Matthias would surely notice, not to mention Jude would probably shove him aside and question his weird behavior.

Nathan opened his mouth to speak, to tell Jude he'd received a phone call from the station and they were expected back, but Matthias spoke first.

"My wife tells me you've been sick, detective."

"Oh, yes," piped up Mrs. Branstone. "How are you feeling?" She crinkled her nose. "You don't think you've caught a nasty bug, do you?"

"Of course not, ma'am." Nathan smiled, relieved when Matthias took a step back to put an arm around his wife.

"Oh, good," said Mrs. Branstone. "I'd hate to think you'd caught something to pass on to the rest of us."

"No need to worry, dear," said Matthias, patting her on the shoulder. "I'm sure whatever has the detective's insides squirming is probably a very recent development."

Her lips pursed. "Regardless, it still might be a good idea to disinfect the guest bathroom, just in case you are contagious."

Matthias gave a close-mouthed chuckle. The intensity in his eyes gave Nathan a chest-tightening suspicion that Matthias knew exactly what he was. He recognized the undeniable look of greed hunters possessed when appraising their target. Matthias would know exactly how much he was worth dead and exactly who'd be willing to buy his Diamantium skeleton.

Nathan's eyes roamed over Matthias in what he hoped was a casual manner. A gun holster was cinched at his waist, securing two handguns, one on each hip. He doubted they were the only arms on his person, hence the sweatshirt. Long sleeves were convenient for concealing many other weapons, ones specialized in slaying beings like himself.

Nathan kept a close eye on the man's hands, his teeth gritted. Deciphering this man's intentions would be so much easier if he could partially shift and use his forked tongue.

Matthias's grin grew even wider, as if he knew what Nathan was thinking. Nathan restrained his desire to wipe that smug grin from the man's face by any brutal means necessary.

Jude cleared her throat. "So, Nathan, just before you walked in, I was going through the details on their son's stolen laptop."

"Indeed," said Matthias, "the matter that has brought us all together." He gestured to the young blond man. "Come on over, boy. Detective, you recall my son, Sagan?"

Nathan had almost forgotten Sagan was still in the room. "Yes, of course," he said, holding out his hand.

Sagan made no move to shake it.

Now that Sagan was standing beside his father, the similarities between the two were conspicuous. His eyes, nose, and cheekbones were a younger carbon copy of his father's, and he too wore a black sweatshirt over a broad, muscular physique. The main difference was the eyes. Where Matthias's were brown, Sagan's were a striking pastel blue, and where Matthias's held a glint of savage amusement, Sagan's held pure poison.

Matthias put his hand around the back of Sagan's neck. His fingertips turned white, and steel edged his next words. "Go on, son. Shake the good detective's hand."

Sagan's jaw tensed as he dutifully shook Nathan's hand once, then dropped it immediately.

Matthias gave a crooked smile and patted Sagan twice on

the head. Nathan half expected the phrase "good boy" to follow.

With the unpleasant introductions over, Jude proceeded with her investigation.

Nathan folded his arms and tried to recall his interviews with the Branstone family, sifting through memories for anything that would have alluded to their true identity, but his recollections had grown fuzzy over the last few years. As hard as he tried, he could only remember them as a grieving, broken family desperate to find out who'd killed their loved one, and why.

He caught Sagan's scrutinizing glare. After a heartbeat, he passively assessed him as he had his father. A black chain was peeking above the neckline of Sagan's sweatshirt, and the subtle outline of an amulet was visible beneath the fabric at his chest. Nathan flicked his attention to Matthias. He too had the same black chain and subtle impression of an amulet under his shirt.

Amulets were clan crests hunters received during their initiation. Each contained ten tiny vials embedded in the metal crest, one for each known species of shape-shifter. Hunter initiates used the vials to store a sample of luminescent blood from their first kill of each shifter species. The more colors in an amulet, the more revered the hunter.

Nathan had never encountered a hunter with all ten colors. The most he'd seen was five. A friend of his claimed to have seen an amulet with six.

He wondered how many colors were on Sagan's amulet. And for that matter, what about Matthias's? How many colors would a hunter need to be as arrogant as him?

"Oh, by the way . . ." Matthias turned his attention back to Nathan. "I've been wondering about that girl. What was her name?" He squinted and snapped his fingers a few times. "You know, the girl that was there when Lyla died."

Nathan clenched his fists, and Sagan snapped his attention to his father.

"Oh, you mean Violet," said Jude.

"Yes, Violet." His grin broadened with triumph. "How is she these days?"

"Actually, she's doing great, all things considered."

"Marvelous." Matthias's eyes glittered, and Sagan's glare faltered. "Thank you, detective, for all your help here today," Matthias said to Jude.

She pocketed her phone. "We'll give you a call as soon as we know anything."

"In that case, call my wife. I'm heading out of town for a few days."

Jude nodded. "Will do."

Once back in the car, Jude started her rant. "What the hell was that all about? Did you see how that kid was looking at you? What a creep." She went on about ungrateful rich kids and "It's his laptop that was stolen, after all."

Nathan hardly registered what she was saying; his mind buzzed. When Jude stopped the car, he realized she'd asked him a question. "Sorry, what did you say?"

"I said I'm hungry and going to grab something to eat. Do you want anything?"

Nathan winced. His stomach was currently empty, but he still had a trace of nausea left from having to walk past the Diamantium chandelier a second time on the way out of the Branstone's. "No thanks. I'm fine."

"Okay, I'll just be a sec."

Once she was gone, Nathan pulled out his phone and dialed a number. After a few rings, a male voice answered.

"Yeah?"

"Where are you?" Nathan asked. "Are you in town?"

"No, not at the moment. Why?"

"Good. Don't come to my place. I've attracted the attention of some Erathi hunters."

There was a pause. "Oh, you sure you don't want me to—"

"No," said Nathan. "It's best you stay away. I'll call you when . . . if it's safe to come back."

## 9

## PSYCHO DEATH GRIP

VIOLET STEPPED OUT OF THE SHOWER AND DRIED OFF, catching a glimpse of her body in the mirror on the bathroom door. Pale lines raked over one side of her ribs, mottled scars covered her elbows and knees, and ghosts of small cuts and grazes were still evident on her face, her palms, and most of her fingers. Yet she held no memory of receiving any of them.

The most perplexing scars were the ones on her back. She swiveled around and craned her neck to inspect her lower back in the mirror. On either side of her spine were her Venus dimples, but instead of two little divots, they were raised mounds of marbled tissue, as if burned from either acid or fire. These scars were set apart from her other signs of abuse; they were too symmetrical, too *planned*. No doctor or nurse could explain the scars when Violet had asked about them in the hospital.

Shaking her head, she once again dropped the unsolved mystery and wiggled into her dress. Should she put on makeup or not? Leaning close to the mirror, she inspected her face and frowned. She'd never liked the color of her eyes.

They were more gray than blue, as if the blue pigment had run out when her eyes were being made. And, ugh! Was she getting eye bags? The dark shadows under her eyes stood out against her pale skin. The assignments were coming in thick and fast, and the late study nights were already catching up with her. How did everyone else seem to maintain both their study and social lives?

A wave of exhaustion enveloped her, and she considered changing into her pajamas and falling asleep to a movie on her laptop. But there was no way Autumn, Gus, and Bessie would let her stay home, especially not after skipping out on the last party. Besides, she may as well make the most of her college experience.

She rummaged around in Autumn's makeup bag. "Hey, Autumn, do you have any concealer I can borrow?" she called out.

Makeup was one thing about the female prerogative Violet had never gotten on board with, although she'd stolen a watermelon-flavored lip gloss from a store once when she was fourteen. She'd lost track of it after about three foster homes; another foster child had likely snatched it.

Autumn poked her head into the bathroom and leaned on the door frame. "I've got a few concealers, but I'm not sure I can help you. None are the color 'corpse.'"

Violet pouted, admiring Autumn's golden skin tones. She could definitely pass as a beach babe. All she needed was a bikini and surfboard.

Autumn folded her arms. "Why the interest in makeup all of a sudden? You've never put any on since I met you. Not that you need any, by the way." She screwed up her nose. "You're one of those annoying girls who always looks like she's 'hashtag-woke-up-like-this.'"

Violet laughed. "More like 'hashtag-what-does-the-sun-look-like?'"

Autumn laughed. "A little sun wouldn't hurt, right?"

"Yeah, well, not all of us were raised to embrace a hippie alternative lifestyle."

"Hey, don't let the dreadlocks fool you. The city life is what I crave, regardless of how much I complain about store-bought milk."

Violet chuckled.

"You better go change, Vi." Autumn checked her watch. "We only have a few minutes before the others get here."

"I'm ready to go," said Violet, trying to make sense of Autumn's numerous makeup products.

"What do you mean?" Autumn frowned at Violet's outfit. "You can't wear that."

"Why? What's wrong with it?"

Autumn put a hand on her hip. "It's black."

Violet tilted her head and furrowed her eyebrows. Autumn's dress had a galaxy print on a navy background, and she'd dyed a few of her dreadlocks various fluorescent colors to match.

"You can't wear black to a black light party," said Autumn.

"What?" Violet stroked her hands on the soft fabric of her dress. "Why not?"

"Because an all-black outfit will make you invisible, and not to mention, every bit of lint and white fluff will be super obvious."

"Oh." Violet tugged at the hem of her dress and inspected it a little closer.

"Hey, guys, we're here," called Gus.

"We're in the bathroom," said Autumn.

"If the bathroom door's open, then I'm expecting you to be fully dressed. It's too early in the evening for nudity," said Gus.

Bessie appeared in the bathroom doorway. "Hey, girls, what do you think?"

Violet's eyes bugged as Bessie twirled to show off her outfit. She wore a bob-length neon-green wig and matching green lipstick. Glow sticks and neon armbands complemented her hot-pink tank top and fluorescent tutu skirt.

Bessie held out her hands. "Check this out. I've just had them done." Her nails were a neon blend of hot pink at the bases and green at the tips. "You like?"

Autumn smiled and nodded. "Awesome! They look so cool."

"Is it safe to look?" said Gus, still out of view.

Violet grinned and Autumn rolled her eyes. "Yes, Gus. I know you're dying to show us your outfit. The stage is all yours."

Gus jumped next to Bessie and let out a "Ta-daaa."

"Woah," said Violet.

Gus turned to give the girls full view of his all-neon attire. He was wearing lemon-yellow dress pants with a pink button-up shirt under an orange jacket.

"I couldn't find any neon shoes, but I did find a can of neon-blue hairspray." He held up a foot, showing off the new color of his once white sneakers.

"Wow!" said Autumn. "Amazing!"

Gus hooked his thumbs under the collar of the jacket, a salesman smirk on his face. His smirk turned into a frown when he looked at Violet. "You're not wearing that to a black light party, are you?"

Violet rolled her eyes. "There's nothing wrong with what I'm wearing. Let's just go."

"Nuh-uh. Nope." Autumn grabbed her by the shoulders and shoved her out of the bathroom until they stood in front of Autumn's wardrobe. "Bessie, you do hair, and I'll do the outfit."

* * *

Their shoes tapped rhythmically on the city street pavement, falling into sync with the aid of the thudding rave music a few blocks ahead. A mixture of hot food fragrances from various surrounding restaurants and food trucks floated past. Violet's stomach grumbled as she caught a whiff of butter chicken, spiced rice, and other delicacies from the Indian restaurant across the street. She doubted this party was going to have food anywhere near as aromatic or appetizing. She should have eaten before they left.

Violet wrapped the collar of her jacket tighter around her neck. She'd lost count of the number of things she was already regretting on this freezing cold night, but Autumn's choice of outfit for her definitely topped the list. She tugged on the hem of her all-white dress. The stretchy fabric hugged tight to every curve, leaving very little to the imagination. It also persistently glided up as she walked; a pair of hot-pink leggings—Bessie's suggestion—was the only thing saving her from complete shame. She couldn't keep her switchblade on her person in this getup, so she'd hidden it in a flamingo clutch, another item Autumn had let her borrow for the night.

Violet yanked a little harder on the thigh-high hem, and Autumn slapped her hand. "Stop it. You'll ruin my dress."

"There's not enough fabric in this thing to even be considered a dress," Violet gritted out. "I can't believe I let you convince me to wear this out in public."

Autumn rolled her eyes. "You look fine, Vi. *Amazing*, actually. Now, stop whining."

When they reached the end of the street, Autumn flung her arms out, stopping the group before they turned into the alley. "Wait! Before I forget, you're gonna need one of these." She opened her shiny gold clutch and handed each of them a card. "You can thank Prophecy03 for the fake IDs."

"Who?" said Violet.

Gus groaned. "It's one of Autumn's hacker buddies."

Bessie squealed in delight as she took her card.

"You've got to be kidding me." Violet eyed the photo of herself next to the name Vanessa Smith. "Seriously, Autumn, if Nathan finds out, he's going to kill me."

Autumn smirked. "So don't let him find out." She linked arms with Violet and Bessie and dragged them around the corner.

Two bouncers stood in front of the doorway of a seedy establishment scrawled with graffiti tags. The fluorescent attire of the patrons flowing in and out contrasted starkly with the dark, derelict alley.

"Wait," said Violet, "this is a club. I thought you said we were going to a college party."

Autumn tilted her head and shrugged one shoulder. "Well, technically, I said a lot of people from college might be going to this party."

Violet scanned the faces of the neon people, not recognizing any of them.

"Come on, Vi." Autumn nudged her. "Lighten up. A night off campus isn't going to hurt. Seriously, a change of scenery will be good for us." She latched on to Violet's arm and dragged her forward.

The others glided through the bouncer's inspection with ease. Violet's heart pounded when the bouncer glanced a few times between her and the fake ID, and when he finally waved her through, she barely avoided a visible sigh of relief.

Once inside, Violet sucked in a breath, the full-force electronic beats vibrating through her chest. "Wow."

Deep indigo bathed the club, cut through by pops of illuminated yellows, greens, blues, pinks, and magentas. The patrons' clothing ranged from glowing neons to strobing LED lights. One guy even had on a shirt that illuminated to each pounding beat of the music, while another was wearing UV orange contact lenses. Another girl's black vinyl corset had pink LED lighting in a geometric pattern, accentuating her curvaceous body. A tight crowd writhed on the dance floor, watched by onlookers from a U-shaped balcony on the second level.

Violet turned to her friends and gasped at the illuminated transformation of Bessie's and Gus's outfits and Autumn's galaxy print. She looked down at her own white dress, now glowing an icy blue.

Autumn giggled and shouted over the music. "See, I told you. You look great. You should see your hair!"

Violet reached for a handful of her loose hair and grinned. The fluorescent hair chalk Bessie had put in was lit up in a vibrant rainbow.

Bessie grabbed Autumn's arm and shouted. "Come on, let's get some drinks."

A few minutes later, the two returned with a tray of about twenty glowing shot glasses, with Bessie grinning as if she'd just won the lottery.

Violet's jaw dropped. "Whoa! How drunk are you guys planning on getting?"

Bessie shrugged. "I didn't know what to get, so the bartender suggested I try an assortment."

"Tell them the truth." Autumn smirked. "You just got hustled by the hot bartender."

Violet laughed, once again eyeballing the crowded tray. "Just how hot was this guy?"

"I dunno, I couldn't tell under the black light. But he had an epic mohawk."

Violet and Gus shared a look of disbelief and joined the girls in a few group shots. It took a few rounds, but Violet got used to the tangy burn the alcohol carved down her throat, and before long she started to enjoy the warm buzz.

To her surprise, the four of them managed to empty the tray in no time.

Bessie squealed and pointed to a corner of the club. "Yes! They have body painters here!"

Before anyone could respond, she'd already dragged them halfway to the body-painting station.

Later, at a table Autumn had miraculously managed to snag—the girl certainly had a flair about her—Violet admired a UV floral design painted up the length of her arm.

"What do you think?" Bessie shoved her own face into Violet's view, pointing to the neon butterfly on her cheek. Violet grinned and held up both thumbs.

"I can't avoid it any longer. I need to dance!" Gus took hold of Bessie's arm and dragged her to the dance floor, yelling a warning to Violet on the way. "Keep an eye on Autumn, will ya? She can be sneaky."

He and Bessie joined the edge of the crowd. Gus's orange jacket and Bessie's neon-green wig stood out like beacons, even among the fluorescent horde. Violet couldn't help giggling at their outrageous dance moves. If only she could be that carefree. Lyla would have been up there with them. Not only would she have matched their crazy dancing; she would've stolen the show.

She checked her watch and her eyes widened. "Whoa! Do you have any idea what time it is, Autumn? We should probably think about heading home soon."

Autumn shook her head and took another sip of her drink. "Nope. Can't leave. I haven't seen him yet."

Violet's brows drew together. "Him? Him who?"

"Actually, speaking of guys . . ." Autumn waved her hand dismissively, her words a little slurred. "When are you going to tell me about this guy you keep talking about? I hear he likes scorpions."

An icy chill crushed Violet's warm alcoholic buzz. "What?"

Autumn slid across the booth seat closer to Violet and propped a hand under her chin expectantly. "I said, 'I hear he likes—'"

"I heard what you said. I've never spoken about a guy. Or . . . or any guys." She hadn't even told anyone about Thane.

Autumn nodded, her head bouncing up and down with more vigor than necessary. "Yes, yes, you have. I heard. I heard when you were sleeping." She leaned her head on Violet's shoulder and looked up with glassy eyes. "Did you know you talk in your sleep?"

The muscles in Violet's face tensed, and the alcohol in her stomach turned sour. "I need a glass of water." She stood up, and Autumn toppled into her vacant spot.

"Violet, wait! You haven't told me what he looks like. You haven't—" The thumping music drowned out the rest as Violet shoved through the dancers, making a beeline for the exit.

Bodies and limbs jostled her in all directions, hindering her quick escape. Violet's chest heaved as her world spun in a frenzied tangle of illuminated colors. She needed to run. To get away from this demon that ruled her past and her nightmares.

Her knees buckled.

The features of the dancers around her became unfocused, blurred. Faceless, like the man in her dreams.

She clamped her eyes shut, but it did nothing to erase the image of her deepest fears. The crystal scorpion on his neck burned into her eyes, more vibrant than ever. In her mind, the faceless man reached toward her.

"Violet!" A heavy hand clapped against her shoulder.

She screamed and spun around, panic battering at her chest.

It was only Gus.

"You almost gave me a heart attack," Violet panted, clutching and bunching the fabric over her rapidly beating heart. She moaned and pressed a hand to her forehead. "I think I've had too much to drink."

"Where's Autumn?" Gus shouted.

"What?"

Gus's eyes were huge, intense.

"Gus? Are you okay?"

"Where's Autumn?" he shouted again.

"She's . . . um . . ." Violet cast a look around, getting her bearings.

Gus shook her shoulders. "Violet, where is she?"

She pointed in the direction of the table she'd left just moments ago, but a new group of clubbers now occupied it, none of which were Autumn. "Um . . . She was—"

Gus spat out a few choice words. The decibel of his exclamation competed with the volume of the music. "I knew this would happen! You guys don't know her like I do. We have to find her." He linked his arm through hers and barged through the crowd.

"Wait, where's Bessie?" Violet yelled.

"She's at the bar."

Violet spotted a green wig in the long lineup for drinks.

"Hopefully we'll find Autumn before she's served," continued Gus. "Come on, let's try this way."

People bumped and jostled them, and Violet's skin prickled with sweat from the compacted heat of so many bodies. She couldn't fathom how warm Gus must be in his jacket. She scanned the crowd, hoping for a glimpse of fluorescent dreadlocks and a galaxy dress.

"There!" Gus yelled, pointing to the upstairs balcony.

Violet sighed in relief. Autumn was leaning against the balustrade, twirling a dreadlock with one hand and holding a drink in the other. She giggled as a guy circled his arm around her waist. A UV dragon snaked across the guy's ebony skin, from his face down to his neck.

Gus locked his arm tighter around Violet's and dragged her to the stairs.

They fought their way up, dodging the herd of people on their way back to the dance floor and bar. Violet had to hustle to match Gus's speed. Once at the top, they made a beeline to the balustrade, but the spot where they'd seen Autumn was now empty.

Gus growled in exasperation. "You've got to be kidding me!" He leaned over the balustrade and pointed to another staircase at the other side of the club. Autumn was at the bottom of it, being led through the crowd by the guy with the UV dragon.

"Look." Violet pointed out two other dark-skinned guys. They were following close behind, pushing and shoving people aside as they made their way through the crowd. A few seconds later, Autumn was led through a door with a STAFF ONLY sign, and the two other guys followed in after.

A tremor of adrenaline rushed through Violet's body.

She didn't like this. Her hands shook as she gripped her flamingo clutch tight, reaffirming the presence of her switchblade. She eyed the exit on the bottom level, opposite the door Autumn had gone through, and sucked in a breath. The stench of stale beer and strong spirits almost made her gag.

Gus took off, racing down the stairs.

Violet glanced at the exit again. Every instinct demanded that she run for it. Escape. Get as far away from this place as possible. But she couldn't leave. Not yet. Not without the others.

She swallowed her fear and forced her body forward after Gus.

They ran as best they could through the crowd, retracing Autumn's path until they reached the closed STAFF ONLY door. Gus yanked on the handle, but it didn't budge.

He cursed. "Of course, it had to be locked."

"Here, let me." Violet pushed in front of him. "Make sure no one's watching."

She removed the two pins holding her hair out of her face and placed one in her teeth, bending the metal and twisting the other hairpin into the shape she needed. She then slid both into the keyhole. She jiggled the hairpins, feeling for the subtle *click* of the tumblers falling into place.

Gus's jaw dropped when she opened the door.

"Come on." Violet grabbed his arm, and with a quick scan over his shoulder, she pulled him through.

"Where did you learn to do that?" Gus said in a hushed voice. The thundering club music had dropped to a muted beat as soon as the door closed behind them.

Violet shrugged. "You pick up a few skills in the foster system."

"That's so cool. The best skill I've picked up is macramé."

Violet quirked an eyebrow. "Seriously?"

He didn't respond. Instead, he scanned the low-lit concrete hallway they'd found themselves in. A fire extinguisher and an emergency evacuation map hung on the wall in front of them.

Violet looked down both lengths of the hallway. "Which way do you think they went?" Neither direction gave any visual clues.

"Let's try this way," said Gus, taking a decided step.

"Wait." Violet stopped him with a hand on his chest. "Do you hear that?"

A faint feminine giggle echoed from the opposite direction Gus had taken.

"Hopefully that's Autumn," said Gus, turning about-face.

They hurried to the end of the hallway and came to an intersection, then stopped to listen. A faint chatter of voices came from the left.

"This way." Violet linked her arm in Gus's, her heart pounding like a sledgehammer against her ribs. They followed the hall to an open doorway, which was emanating faint jazz music from within. The sounds of conversation and laughter grew louder as they moved closer.

"Maybe it's a private party?" Gus whispered.

"Maybe," said Violet, matching his volume.

They peered around the open door.

Relief washed through Violet when she spotted Autumn. She had her back pressed up against the opposite wall, standing nearly chest-to-chest with the guy from the club. He hulked almost a head taller than her, slouching just to look her in the eye. His fitted shirt—made from a transparent black gauze—was embroidered with a bold floral design of cerulean, navy, and black, and his ebony skin rippled and flexed beneath the fabric with every movement. The dragon body paint now shone garishly under the incandescent light.

"That guy's bicep is as big as my waist," whispered Gus.

Violet's urge to run intensified. This guy was a behemoth, a muscular powerhouse. She focused on keeping her quickened breaths silent.

Gus craned his neck a little farther into the open doorway. "I don't see the other two guys, do you?"

*The other two guys?* Violet had almost forgotten about them. She darted her gaze around the room. *Maybe they're not in there. Maybe—*

She twisted her head to peer behind her, checking both directions of the hallway.

"What's the bet they've gone to find their next hit of steroids?" whispered Gus.

A giggle from Autumn drew Violet's attention back inside the room. Autumn smiled, laying a hand on the guy's arm and murmuring something. Violet couldn't hear what over the music.

The guy smiled back.

"And like a moth to flame, another moron falls into Autumn's trap," said Gus in a low voice.

"What do you mean?" Violet asked. "What's she up to?"

Then, with a flash, the guy slammed his hand against Autumn's throat.

Violet gasped, then bit down hard on her lip to stop from screaming.

Autumn's eyes grew wide. Her mouth gaped as she clawed at the hand squeezing her windpipe.

*No, no, no! This can't be happening again.* A sob escaped Violet. Her legs went limp, and she collapsed against the wall, a surge of guilt and inescapable helplessness numbing every nerve in her body.

Gus rushed forward. "Hey! Get off her!" He jumped up and latched on to the mountain man's arm, his feet dangling off the ground. The guy looked down at him, making a face as if he were being bothered by a mosquito.

Gus yanked on the guy's arm, but he may as well have been tugging on the support beam of a bridge. The man released Autumn's neck to shake Gus off, and Autumn tumbled to the ground, coughing between gulps of air.

Violet scrambled forward—but yelped as she was wrenched back by an iron fist tangled in a hunk of her hair. As she grasped at the hand holding her, her flamingo clutch clattered to the ground by her feet.

"Get up, Autumn!" yelled Gus, still clinging to the man's arm. With incredible force, the man threw him hard against the wall. Gus *ooph*ed, his face scrunched in pain, before he crumpled to the floor.

Green dragon guy stood over Autumn, his face twisted with fury and his hands fisted at his sides. He barked at the guy holding on to Violet's hair, and they conversed in a clipped, guttural language Violet didn't recognize.

A cough from Autumn snatched Green Dragon's attention. He reached for her.

"No!" Violet yelled. "Leave her alone!" She squealed when the guy behind her jerked her hair with a warning.

Green Dragon paid her no attention. He crouched over Autumn, speaking once again in that rough, unknown language.

Violet squeezed her eyes shut, trying unsuccessfully to stem the flow of tears already streaming down her cheeks. She hadn't been able to save Lyla, and she couldn't save her friends now. Why was she so worthless? Why had she been the one allowed to live?

There was nothing she could do. There was nothing. *She* was nothing.

She held her breath.

*"Come on, kid. Just breathe." Nathan patted her on the back. "You've basically got it. All you have to do is try again."*

*Violet swatted his hand away and tore at the Velcro on her boxing gloves. In a frenzy, she snatched them off and hurled them at the boxing bag swaying from the ceiling.*

*"Aaargh! I'm never going to get this. I just can't." She slumped to the ground, dropping her head in her hands. "It's too late anyway."*

*After a moment came the* whoosh *and loud* crack *of a gym towel, followed by a sharp sting on her thigh.*

*"Ow!" Violet rubbed her leg and glared at Nathan, who was holding the offending towel in both hands.*

*"Stop blaming yourself for Lyla's death." His lips formed a stern line and his nostrils flared—an expression Violet could only guess was anger—but his eyes were soft. "We can't go back and change or*

95

*erase what's been done. We can only go forward. We have to learn from our mistakes and promise ourselves to do better. Stop letting the past control you."*

*Violet dropped her gaze to the floor. She blinked a few times, hoping Nathan would think her tears were just sweat.*

*The towel snapped again, and another sting flared across her thigh.*

*"Ouch!"*

*"Stop sulking. Get up. You know what to do."*

Violet opened her eyes.

She clamped her hands over the fist in her hair and pivoted her hips, stepping back and under her attacker's arm. The motion contorted the guy's shoulder and wrist into an unnatural, painful angle, and he grunted and doubled forward, trying to ease the tension.

In self-defense training, this was when she usually let go, and Nathan would explain the next few steps.

Not this time.

Autumn's raspy whimpers and Gus's slumped body pushed her into action. In two swift moves, she dislocated the man's shoulder and broke his wrist with an audible *pop* and *snap*. He shrieked, and Violet released him. The man collapsed to the ground, cradling his arm, and glared at her, shouting what she could only guess was a string of insults.

Her sights switched to the guy still hunched over Autumn. The behemoth's hand hovered just in front of Autumn's neck as he looked Violet up and down. With a sneer, he turned his attention back to Autumn. Either he didn't think Violet was a threat, or he didn't care what she did next.

Once again, he latched on to Autumn's throat, cutting off her desperate gasp. Tears glistened on Autumn's cheeks, and her gaze locked with Violet's, eyes wide and begging.

Violet spotted the flamingo clutch on the ground. She

retrieved her switchblade and crossed the room in three quick strides. Her thumb found and pressed the button. *Shnik.*

With her free hand, she grasped the man's chin and jerked his head up, pressing the blade right where the painted dragon's tail coiled down from his jaw. He froze, and Autumn's cries hushed.

"Let her go, or I'll slice you from ear to ear," Violet growled through gritted teeth. She tightened her grip on the switchblade; the black gemstones along the pearlescent handle bit into her palm.

Whether he understood her or not, she figured he at least knew the danger of her knife pressing into his jugular. She added some pressure, digging the tip into his flesh. He hissed and released Autumn.

"Autumn, get Gus. We're going," said Violet, not yet withdrawing her knife.

Autumn nodded, her eyes wide and a little bloodshot. Finger-shaped bruises were already blooming on her neck.

The green dragon guy flinched as Autumn moved away. "Zhivotza," he said, reaching for her again.

Violet dug in her blade a little more. "Don't move." But her warning landed on deaf ears as the guy tried to twist his head out of Violet's grasp. He repeated the foreign word again, this time more vehemently.

"I don't know what that means," said Violet, "but if you don't keep still, I'm going to spill your blood all over the floor."

He replied with a roar.

Before she could react, the man spun around with breathtaking speed. His heavy arm clipped her, and Violet toppled back onto the floor with a cry of agony, her eyes flinching closed on impact. Air whooshed out of her lungs. The simple act of sucking in air now sent sharp spikes of pain through her body.

When she opened her eyes again, panic gripped her chest, her shoulders, her throat. The guy loomed above, his enormous frame filling her entire vision. He pinned her shoulders to the ground, teeth bared and eyes bloodshot with fury.

She'd managed to keep her grip on her switchblade, but it felt puny and worthless. Everything Nathan had taught her about knife fighting fled from her mind. She cried, kicked, and flailed uselessly, swiping with her blade hand and punching with the other.

He caught both her wrists in a tight, inescapable grip and roared at her again, spittle flecking her face as he howled out the strange guttural words.

Tears stung Violet's eyes. She couldn't fight him anymore. Couldn't fight her panic or her fear.

Just as her strength was about to run out, something above her made a metallic *thunk*. The guy's face went slack, and his eyes rolled into odd angles before he slumped onto Violet.

Bessie's neon wig and butterfly-painted face came into Violet's view. She held a fire extinguisher over her head.

"Is he out?" Bessie asked.

Violet nodded, struggling to speak with the solid weight of the unconscious man on her chest.

Bessie dropped the extinguisher, her face white as a sheet. She kneeled down to help shove the heavy guy off Violet. "What . . . the hell? I was . . . Should I call the police?"

"No!" croaked Autumn. "No cops."

The four of them stumbled toward the exit. Bessie supported Gus, who'd nearly regained consciousness, and Violet leaned on Autumn, slinging her arm with the switchblade over her shoulders.

They'd just stepped into the concrete hallway when Autumn paused. "Oh, wait. I left my gold clutch in there."

"Forget it," said Violet.

"It's important. I'll be quick."

Violet winced as Autumn extricated herself from her arm. She tried to latch on to Autumn's shoulder before she stepped inside the room, but her friend twisted out of her grasp.

"What part of that psycho's death grip on your neck did you not take seriously?" Violet hissed after her.

The green dragon dude was still out cold, and Violet's heart thumped in her throat as Autumn tiptoed around him to retrieve the metallic gold clutch by his arm. The guy who had grabbed Violet's hair was nowhere to be seen, and who knew where the third guy was.

Relief washed over Violet like a tidal wave when Autumn snatched up her clutch and skittered back to them.

"Let's go," Autumn hissed.

Violet rolled her eyes. "Great idea. If only we'd thought of that before."

Autumn ignored the snippy remark and slung Violet's arm back around her neck. They tried their best to hustle down the hallway, glancing back frequently. Thankfully, no one was following them. Yet.

Violet hugged her body with her free arm and sucked in a shallow breath. Who knew how many ribs she'd cracked. The back of her head throbbed; even blinking was adding to the wave of aches in her skull.

They caught up with Gus and Bessie at the door to the club. With one last look behind, the four of them shoved through the door, the thunderous music enveloping them once again. Violet allowed Autumn to drag her through the crowd, close on Gus and Bessie's tail, toward the exit and back out to the alley.

"Whew, that was close," said Autumn when they rounded the corner back onto the main street.

Bessie instantly erupted with her freak-out vent. Gus was conscious enough to throw in a few snide remarks of his own, but his tone was a little slurred, whether from the alcohol or from hitting his head, Violet wasn't sure.

She didn't bother inserting herself into Bessie's hysterical outbursts or Autumn's blasé reassurances. She just wanted to get home and go straight to bed.

A dull ache in her hand surfaced, and she realized she was still gripping her switchblade. Bright orange liquid was smeared along the tip, glistening under the streetlights. Body paint must have rubbed off the green dragon dude when she'd held her blade to his throat. *Except . . .* She frowned. His paint was dry, and if she recalled correctly, there was no orange in the UV dragon design.

The back of Violet's neck prickled, and she cast another glance back toward the club.

A guy with skin as dark as midnight stood a few blocks away, near the entrance to the alley. He cradled one of his arms as he scanned up and down the street. Then his eyes met hers.

Panic roared in Violet's ears.

The man yelled and pointed at her, and a heartbeat later, the third guy from the club rounded the corner at a sprint.

"Guys, run!" Violet screamed.

Gus and Bessie hesitated only a moment, turning to see what was behind them before shouting in alarm and dashing forward. Violet was already dragging Autumn up the street.

Their shoes stamped against the pavement. Violet's lungs burned, and her ribs flared in agony with each frantic pant for breath. Autumn pulled ahead as Violet's pain caused her to slow down.

The thudding rhythm grew louder behind her. The guy was closing in.

"This way," exclaimed one of the others, whether Autumn or Bessie, Violet didn't care. The others darted across the road through a gap in the speeding cars, whose horns blared their annoyance. Violet chanced another look behind her before stepping out onto the road.

The guy was almost on her, his arm outstretched, his face contorted in a frenzied rage.

A scream caught in Violet's throat as she urged herself to run faster.

As she raced through traffic, Violet could almost feel the man's fingers brush against her back, his heavy breathing tickling her neck. And then—

*Crack. Thud.*

The sound of metal slamming into flesh seared itself into Violet's brain. Tires squealed as a car swerved and skidded to a halt, but Violet didn't stop running or even look back until she'd made it to the other side of the street. The guy's body lay unmoving a few yards away, surrounded by a small cluster of passersby.

Violet didn't hang around to see what happened next. Ignoring the few onlookers who called after her, she took advantage of the extra surge of adrenaline to catch up with Autumn, Gus, and Bessie. None of them stopped until they reached Violet and Autumn's dorm room, where they locked and bolted the door behind them.

## 10

## CINNAMON AND SALT

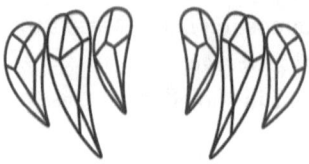

Nathan called out his thanks and goodnight to the owner of his favorite Chinese restaurant before stepping outside. Hot steam tingled over his fingers from the plastic bag in his hand, bringing with it delicious aromas of black bean chicken, ginger shrimp, and fried rice. His mouth watered. If there was one thing the Erathi were good at, it was cooking. He rotated through the cafés and restaurants in town several times a week, always trying something different on the menu. Since moving to Brookhaven, he'd been through the Chinese restaurant's entire selection at least three times. He no longer even needed to phone ahead for his takeaway order; the owner had caught on to Nathan's menu selection pattern and always had dinner ready for pickup on his Chinese takeaway nights.

Jude sometimes dropped him home after he picked up his dinner, but most of the time, he was more than content to walk the few blocks back to his place. It was a good excuse to bask in Venusian beams—to renew the Veniri energy stores that revitalized him to his very core.

He searched for the melodic hum that showed him the

direction of Venus's celestial position, acknowledging the gentle tug as it beckoned—never compelled—his Veniri side to the surface. Unlike what was so often depicted in fairy tales and teen novels, werewolves and other shifter species, such as his own, almost always had the choice to haze into their shifter forms or not. Their associated planet or moon was a source of needed energy, not a curse.

As Nathan cut through a park toward his street, his instincts abruptly pricked, along with the searing pain in his elbows.

Something wasn't right.

He hadn't survived this long, in either the Veniri or the Erathi worlds, by ignoring his intuition. He should reach for his gun—it was what an Erathi would do, especially an Erathi detective—but a strong impulse led him to raise his face to the inky sky and Venus's beams.

A tingle under his tongue intensified.

He flicked out his forked tongue once, then twice, tasting the night's air. The wind picked up. Leaves rustled from the trees, and a swing in the playground squeaked as it rocked back and forth.

He stifled a curse when he scented cinnamon.

*Not good.*

To basically the entire Erathi race, cinnamon was a pleasant flavor, but to every Veniri it was detestable and meant one thing: someone's intention to murder.

Nathan pulled out his phone and pressed a number on speed dial, the same number he'd called after leaving the Branstone's house. It rang twice.

A twig snapped. He swiveled to the right, and an electrical force punched directly into his face, snapping his head back. His body plummeted to the ground. The plastic bag of Chinese food scattered everywhere, seeping sticky juices into the dirt.

Nathan's face and neck were numb. His phone lay just out of reach, a faint voice emanating from the speaker.

Several figures came into view. From head to toe, they were clad in black, almost perfectly camouflaged against the darkened sky. They circled him, their silhouettes blanking out the stars above.

Nathan's tongue lashed out again, testing the emotions and intentions of his assailants. Cinnamon was still pungent, but he now sensed it was laced with salt. Interesting. Salt meant restraint. His attackers wanted to kill him, but for whatever reason, they were holding off for the moment. Maybe he could take advantage of that.

He released his crystal blades from his elbows and swung his arm at the nearest pair of legs. His blade caught fabric, flesh, and then bone. A muffled cry broke the quietness.

Nathan struck his blades out for another attack, but something sharp bit into his chest. He grabbed at whatever had punctured him, his fingers circling around a small glass dart tipped with a Diamantium needle.

One of the black figures removed its mask, revealing the face of a young male with white-blonde hair, his eyes a piercing pale blue. Nathan's vision blurred, but not before the youth's face contorted into a scowl that dripped poison.

## 11

## NO MORE PSYCHO CRAZY

*Damn it! Damn it! Damn it!* Violet swiped her student card once more at the front door of the library's photography wing. Again, the keypad beeped its angry red light and flashed an error code.

"What is wrong with you?" Violet growled. She'd only just picked up this new card from the student help desk after misplacing her last one a few days ago. She swiped again and the keypad beeped, *again!* "Why won't you let me in?"

In her periphery, someone leaned on the wall by the door. She didn't need to look up to know who it was.

Violet closed her eyes and drew a long breath, wincing as pain lanced through her still bruised ribs. "Go away, Autumn. I'm not in the mood."

"Come on, Vi. It's been three days. You can't ignore me forever."

"Don't underestimate my stubbornness."

"Can we please work this out?"

Violet ignored her and swiped her card again. Surely it would work this time. The keypad beeped; this time it asked for an authorization code.

"Damn it!" Violet kicked the door.

"Give me that." Autumn snatched the card, kneeled down on the ground, and pulled her laptop and another device out of her bag.

"Oh my gosh, Autumn. Do you seriously walk around with a card reader in your bag?"

Autumn cocked an eyebrow. "You'd be surprised how handy this thing is."

Violet huffed and leaned on the wall as Autumn swiped the card and clacked away on her laptop.

"Ah, there's your problem," said Autumn. "The looney who gave you this card forgot to activate it."

Violet groaned. "This can't be happening. I don't have time to wait in line for another half hour. And student services is all the way on the other side of campus."

"Chill, this won't take long," said Autumn, still typing on her laptop. "Aaaaaand done." She packed away her computer and card reader, then stood to give the card back to Violet. "Here you go. All activated and authorized to the highest clearance level. If you wanted to, you could have lunch in the faculty lounge. On Thursdays, they have a great spread of pastries and Danishes. Oh, and in future, if you're asked for an activation code, just type in your birthday."

"What?" Violet took the card from Autumn and frowned at it. "How do you know my birthday?"

"It's on your student file."

"How do you know what my student file says?"

Autumn answered with a smile.

Violet looked down at Autumn's bag with the laptop in it, then shook her head. "Unbelievable. You hacked my student file?"

"Please don't be mad. I only did it to find your schedule."

"Great!" Violet threw her arm in the air. "Now you're stalking me?"

"Only because you've been avoiding me like the plague."

"For good reason, moron. I'm pissed at you!"

"I know, and I'm sorry. Please, Violet, will you please, *please* forgive me? Gus and Bessie have."

"That's because they're idiots."

Autumn shrugged one shoulder. "Yeah, maybe. And I might have given them Katy Perry tickets and a new PlayStation game."

Violet rolled her eyes. "Is that why you're here?" She held up her student card. "To buy my forgiveness?"

"Well . . . no . . ." Autumn dropped her gaze to the ground, scuffing her shoe on the pavement. A few charms in her hair tinkled as dreadlocks fell over her face. "You're right. I screwed up. I should never have put you guys in that situation at the club. I do mean it when I say I'm sorry. You have no idea how sorry I am. I hate that you're mad at me." She peeked at Violet through her dreadlocks. "Please, Vi, tell me what to do to make you not mad anymore."

Violet was about to let out a sigh, then remembered her sore ribs, so she hugged her torso instead. "How about you start with an explanation. What the hell? Who the hell? And why the hell?"

Autumn winced. "Uh . . . You sure you don't want a box of cinnamon doughnuts instead?"

"Explain."

"I would . . . but I can't."

"Damn it, Autumn! If you don't start talking, I'm going to march over to student services and demand they switch me to a new dorm room."

"I'll just switch it back."

Violet gave her the filthiest look she'd used on the worst of her foster parents.

"Violet, I mean it. I *can't* tell you. As in, it's best that you don't know—"

"Don't give me that crap." Violet crossed her arms and narrowed her eyes. "You owe me way more than 'it's best you don't know.' And what about Gus? He's lucky he got away with only a mild concussion."

"Yeah, I know. But he's fine now. That campus doc did a great job treating him. I mean, let's face it, she's probably had a lot of practice with concussions from all the drunken frat guys."

"I'm not kidding. Someone could have been seriously hurt."

"I know, I know." Autumn fiddled with the end of one of her locks.

"I still think we should go to the cops, or at least—"

"No!" Autumn cut in. "No cops. Please, Violet. I'm serious. I just . . ." Her shoulders slumped. "I should never have dragged you guys along. I'm sorry. Just please, Violet, *please* don't go to the cops. Let me deal with it, okay?"

One thing in Autumn's expression Violet recognized clear as day. *Fear*. It contrasted completely with the confident, carefree rulebreaker Violet had come to know in the past few weeks.

"Believe me," continued Autumn when Violet didn't answer, "if I could tell you, I would."

Violet huffed out a sigh. "Can you at least tell me who that guy with the green dragon was?"

Autumn shook her head. "The less you know, the better."

Violet tutted and couldn't resist rolling her eyes.

"But seriously," said Autumn, "I had no idea that guy was going to turn psycho on me."

Violet's gaze fell to the fading bruises on Autumn's neck. Guilt rose in her chest. She'd been so angry for the last few days she'd forgotten Autumn might still be hurting from her attack. "How's your neck?" she asked, her tone soft.

"It's a lot better now," Autumn said, shrugging it off. "How about you? How's your head?"

"It's fine. I had a bit of a bump, but it's my ribs that are still sore."

Autumn winced. "Sorry to hear that."

Violet offered a small smile, and Autumn smiled back.

"So . . . are we cool?" asked Autumn, her eyes full of hope.

"Yeah," Violet answered after a moment. "We're cool."

"Promise me no cops?"

Violet snorted. "For now. But I swear if anything else psycho crazy happens, I will be calling Nathan in an instant." Although for her to tell him anything, he would have to start returning her calls. For the past few days, he hadn't even replied to her text messages. It was a little unusual. He was probably just getting super tied-up with work, but still, she was starting to get a little worried.

"I promise, no more psycho crazy." Autumn's grin lit up her whole face, and in a flurry of dreadlocks, she bombarded Violet with a hug. "Thanks, Vi. You're the best."

"Yeah, and don't you forget it."

"So," said Autumn when she finally released her, "should I assume you don't want these then?" She pulled a box of cinnamon doughnuts from her bag.

"You sneak!" Violet laughed and raised a finger. "Never assume I don't want cinnamon doughnuts. Give me one of those."

Autumn opened the box and they both took one. Violet bit into the soft dough, her teeth crunching on the sugar crystals.

"So, when's Bessie going to the Katy Perry concert?" Violet asked before taking another bite.

"The tickets were for Gus. Bessie's the gamer," said Autumn around a mouthful of doughnut.

"Seriously? Gus?"

"Yep. He's making a 'will you marry me' sign as we speak."

Violet laughed and reached for another doughnut.

"Uh, Violet?" said a male voice.

Violet turned to see who Autumn was gaping at. "Thane, what are you doing here?" She dropped the doughnut back in the box and dusted the sugar from her fingers. "I mean . . . Hi, how are you?"

He smiled and dug both his hands into his jeans pockets. "I'm fine. I'm sorry to bother you at college. I know you must be busy."

"No, not busy. Not busy at all," said Violet, wondering how her voice had suddenly become so squeaky.

"Okay, great." He flashed his gorgeous smile. "I just . . . um . . ." His eyes darted to Autumn.

Violet followed his gaze and cringed. Autumn's eyes were bugging out of her head, and if her jaw dropped any lower, it would be bringing back souvenirs from China.

"Oh, right." Violet gestured to Autumn. "Thane, this is Autumn."

"Hey," said Thane. "So you're the roommate Violet's been talking about."

"What? Me? She's been talking about me? To you?"

Violet struggled to hold back a facepalm as Autumn obviously checked Thane out, making no attempt to hide her appreciation for what she saw.

"What the hell, Autumn?" Violet said in a stage whisper.

"I think I should be the one asking 'what the hell?'" replied Autumn, also in a stage whisper. "How come you never told me about *him*?"

Thane cleared his throat, and both girls turned back to him.

"Sorry," said Violet, her cheeks growing warm.

He chuckled. "It's fine." He pulled something from his

pocket and held it out to her. "Here, this is yours. You dropped it last time at the café."

She recognized her old student card. "Oh, wow. Thanks," she said, hiding her new card behind her back and taking her old one from him. "You didn't have to go out of your way."

He shrugged. "It's no problem. I figured it was something you might be needing. I'm just sorry I couldn't get it to you sooner."

"It's fine." Violet's mind raced for something else to say— something light and relaxed, like the stuff they would talk about during their catch-ups at the café. But Autumn's ogling was setting her on edge.

Thane raked a hand through his hair. "So, uh . . . I can see you're busy." He pointed to the STUDENT PHOTOGRAPHY LAB sign on the door—the one Violet had kicked earlier. "So I . . . guess I'll see you around, Violet."

"Oh, okay," said Violet, hating this door even more now. Her shoulders drooped. The word *bye* was on her lips, but she didn't feel right saying it.

Thankfully, she didn't have to say anything. He waved at her and she waved back. Her gaze dropped to the ground as he turned to leave.

"Actually, there's something else," Thane blurted, swinging back to face her.

Violet's stomach flipped; the familiar sensation of angry pixies banging on her insides returned, much like the first day she met him. "Sure, okay. What?"

"I know we have kind of a 'you buy coffee, I buy coffee' agreement, but I came across this"—he reached into his jacket and pulled out a crumpled flyer—"and I was wondering if you'd, maybe, want to join me."

Violet took the flyer. It advertised the annual city carnival, promising various thrill rides, circus acts, live music, market stalls, showbags, carnival food, and "much, much more!"

"This sounds like a lot of fun," she said.

"Yeah?"

"Yeah."

He half squinted one eye. "It's not too corny for a first date?"

Violet gaped. "A what?"

Thane's mouth hung open for a moment, and his neck started to flush. "I mean, did I say . . . ? It doesn't have to be considered a date. It could just be, you know, two people going out at the same time, to the same place, and maybe doing the same things. You know, like . . ." His face screwed into a wince, and he rubbed the back of his neck. ". . . non-date-like things."

She looked down at the flyer again. *A date?* What would Lyla say if she could see her now? If there were such things as ghosts, then Lyla was likely poking her in the ribs and shouting, "Hurry up and say yes, Vi. What are you waiting for?" Although if Lyla's ghost wasn't heckling her, then there was a good chance Autumn was about to.

"I'd love to go with you," she said in a rush.

Thane's eyebrows shot up, and he dropped his hand from his neck. "Really?"

Violet nodded.

He smiled. "Great! How about I pick you up?"

Her cheeks grew warm at the sparkle in his eye, and for the first time in her life, she gave a guy her phone number and address.

After he left, Autumn's smirk was full of greedy curiosity. "Tell me *everything*."

## CHEAP-ASS STEAK KNIFE

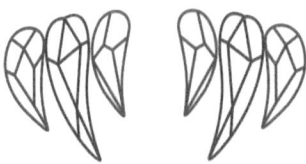

ACHES IN NATHAN'S SHOULDERS AND WRISTS DREW HIM slowly and excruciatingly out of unconsciousness. The more his awareness grew, the more the pain throbbed.

A boot scuffed on concrete. Instinct told him to keep his eyes closed and assess the situation with his other senses. Nearby, he could hear the subtle rhythm of someone breathing. Captor or captive?

He waited a few seconds, but other than his own thumping pulse in his ears, no other sounds became apparent.

He took stock of his body. A chill crawled up his arms, torso, and legs; he'd been stripped down to his boxer briefs. The weight of his body hung from metal cuffs around his wrists, which spread his arms wide above his head. His legs slouched beneath him, but thankfully, his feet were able to touch the ground.

How long had he been dangling like this?

He hesitated for a few heartbeats, reluctant to announce his return to consciousness by standing, but the pain was swiftly becoming intolerable. Finally, he flattened his feet on the ground and pushed himself upright, letting out a deep exhale of relief as the tension on his wrists and shoulders slackened. A chink and a rattle above his head confirmed his wrist restraints were attached to the ceiling with chains.

Boots shuffled on the concrete, followed by a high-pitched squeal of rusty hinges.

"Go tell the boss the slith's awake."

Nathan raised his head and tilted it from side to side, cracking his neck.

He opened his eyes, allowing his vision to adjust to the dim light as a group of black-clad males entered the room—making four in total. At the head of the group was Matthias Branstone. Sagan stood a foot behind his father, his intense eyes like shards of ice. His blond hair stood out starkly against the surrounding black of the group's attire and the darkened gray of the concrete walls.

Matthias took a few more steps. The *thud-thud* of his polished combat boots echoed off the walls.

"Matthias." Nathan stretched his face into a grin, then cast a look around the room. "Nice place you got here, although it's a little bland compared to your other place. Anyway, I apologize for the intrusion." He shook his chains. "It looks like I've got myself in a bit of a bind. If you don't mind giving me a hand, I'll get out of your hair and be on my way."

The corner of Matthias's mouth raised in a crooked smile. "Looks like we've caught ourselves a comedian, boys." He moved in closer until he was an inch from Nathan's face.

Nathan suppressed the urge to lean back, although he couldn't help a slight crinkle of his nose. The man's breath was heavy and foul.

"You know," said Matthias, "that day you came into my house, I just knew." He waved a finger in the air. "I saw the look on your face, and I knew. No one looks at a diamond necklace or a chandelier like that unless they know what it truly is." He placed his hands on his hips and gave Nathan that familiar shark grin.

A flutter rose in the base of Nathan's stomach, but he forced a smirk. "Yeah, you're right, I knew." He nodded. "I knew it was the sign of a truly whipped man who'd paid a fortune for a bunch of lousy rocks for his missus."

One of the guys behind Matthias sniggered, resulting in an elbow to his chest from the man with the gray biker beard standing next to him.

An emotion Nathan couldn't quite read flashed across Matthias's face before he smoothed it back into a smile. "Ah, again with the comedy. In that case, let's see how funny you think this is?" He raised a knife—a shiny serrated blade with a black handle.

The flutter in Nathan's stomach intensified, and his heart pounded against his ribcage. His elbows burned as if someone were holding red-hot pokers against the inside of his flesh.

He jutted his chin. "What's with the steak knife—?"

Blindingly fast, Matthias slammed the knife into Nathan's left pectoral muscle.

Nathan gritted his teeth and yanked on the chains.

Matthias's eyes flared, and his mouth curved into a crooked grin. "Looky, looky what we have here." He held up the knife triumphantly. The metal had curved and twisted out of shape, the tip mangled into a tiny concertina.

Nathan's breath hitched, and he looked down at his chest. Not a scratch, not even a bruise to suggest he'd just been stabbed. He clicked his tongue. "Looks like you got yourself some cheap-ass steak knives. I'd ask for a refund."

"Hmm," said Matthias. He dropped the knife, and it clattered against the concrete floor. "How about this one?" He held up his other hand, revealing an object that glittered in the weak light.

Several muscles in Nathan's face twitched.

Matthias leaned closer. "What? No jokes this time?" He twirled the Diamantium blade under Nathan's nose. Flecks of refracted light danced their rainbows over Matthias's face.

Nathan flinched away, rattling the chains overhead. The odor of the blade was overtaking his sensibility, crafting a furnace of rage deep in the center of his chest. He held his body back from hazing, but the searing pain in his elbows was nearly unbearable. He focused all his energy on stopping the sensation from piercing through his skin, but another searing pain soon flared to life in both his knees.

"Do you like it? This one's new." Matthias sneered. "And when I say 'new,' I mean, well . . ." His white teeth flashed as his grin grew. "I bet you can guess what I mean."

The muscles in Nathan's neck shuddered. He strained to control his labored breaths, but it felt as if his entire body were on fire. Every muscle twitched and shook.

Matthias chuckled, the sound deep and husky. He drew the Diamantium dagger back but paused. With his free hand, he gestured behind him. "Sagan, come here, son."

Sagan was hunching nonchalantly against the wall to Nathan's right, his arms crossed. He pushed off the wall to come stand beside his father.

Matthias put a hand around the back of Sagan's neck, pushing him directly in front of Nathan, and held up the dagger between their faces. Sagan's blond hair glowed like a halo in the incandescent light, the rainbow flecks skittering over his blank, stony face completing the angelic appearance.

Nathan's tongue all but vibrated in its eagerness to sense the boy's emotions and intentions, but he clamped his teeth shut with such force he risked cracking a tooth. He had no interest in giving these Erathi scum the satisfaction of seeing his true form, although he feared he wouldn't have a choice for much longer. A shudder racked through his body as his control began to slip.

Nathan's eye's flitted to Matthias, who was peering at him over Sagan's right shoulder.

"How about you do the honors, son?" Matthias held the crystal blade between Nathan and the youth. "Let's see what color this one bleeds."

An inscrutable emotion twitched across the younger man's face. Sagan looked at the dagger but made no move to take it. Just like that day in the Branstone's house, the tips of Matthias's fingers turned white against Sagan's neck.

Nathan laughed and shook his head. "Seriously, Branstone, I didn't think you were the type to make a child do your dirty work."

Sagan's gaze flew to Nathan's, and this time fire flashed behind the ice. Finally, an emotion Nathan understood. Without looking at the crystalline dagger, Sagan wrapped his fingers around the hilt and lunged.

Nathan roared.

The agony of the blade sliced through his left pectoral muscle and pierced through his back. Nathan's head rocked forward, giving him a clear view of the vibrant teal liquid streaming from his chest and coating Sagan's hand, which was still clenched around the dagger's handle. Either the boy had terrific aim and had carefully avoided both Nathan's heart and poison glands, which would have killed him instantly if punctured, or the boy had missed a fatal opportunity.

"Oooh, would you look at that pretty blue," crooned Matthias. He barked a laugh and slowly clapped his hands. "Nice work, son. Brecker, hit the light."

A scuffle of shoes on the concrete, then the room was bathed in darkness.

A dazzling blue glow pierced through the black. Nathan's

glowing blood trailed down his torso and dripped into blue splotches on the floor. Sagan released the dagger, streaks of teal leaving an abstract pattern on his hand.

Matthias chuckled. "I'll admit, this never gets old."

Nathan's body shuddered once again, the clatter of chains the only sound breaking the hush in the concrete torture chamber.

He no longer wanted to defy his inner monster. His body demanded he haze.

Drawing in a gulp of air, he raised his head. Sagan's features were illuminated in blue light. His face was still locked in a stolid guise, but some expression in the boy's eyes made Nathan pause. He couldn't quite work out exactly what it was, but it was raw.

Matthias ordered the light be turned back on, and yellow incandescence flooded the room again.

Sagan stood, statuesque, his blood-coated hand dripping a new puddle of teal onto the ground by his foot. Whatever Nathan had seen in his icy eyes a moment ago had completely disappeared.

Matthias put a hand on Sagan's shoulder and pushed him to the side.

Nathan dropped his gaze to his own bare feet, now splashed with blue. After a few heartbeats, Matthias's ugly mug pushed its way into his view.

"Don't pass out yet, slith. I wouldn't want you to miss what happens next."

"If it doesn't have anything to do with your Erathi face being kicked in, I'm not interested."

Matthias laughed lightly through his nose. "You know, I've always liked that word, *Erathi*, but only you shifters ever call us that." He crouched down and rested his forearms on his knees. "Here's a bit of trivia for you, slith. Do you know what *Erathi* means?"

Nathan grinned. "Of course I do, although most translations that come to mind include the word *anus*."

A flicker of annoyance flashed across Matthias's face before his features settled into a tight-lipped smile. "Hilarious. But no. It means 'unbound' or 'unfettered.'" He spread his hands wide to emphasize each word, like an enthusiastic storyteller.

"I think I like my translations better," said Nathan with a head tilt.

Matthias looked at him for a long moment, then stood up. "Brecker, Harold, I think it's time to bring in Aphrodite."

A squeak of rusty hinges penetrated the quiet room, and two pairs of feet shuffled out.

# HANDBOOK FOR GENTLEMEN

"So, I suppose now is the time I show off my superior masculinity and win you a stuffed toy." Thane grinned down at Violet as they weaved through the crowd.

Violet grinned back. "What makes you think I want a stuffed toy?" Oh gosh, her lips were still sticky from the cotton candy she'd eaten earlier. There was a high risk the sticky sugar would solidify her stretched lips in place, like Jack Nicholson's Joker.

"Come on," he coaxed, "you wouldn't want to deprive me of my role in this date, would you? This would be a failed date otherwise."

"Ah, so that's what's wrong with this date." Violet side-stepped a child covered in melted ice cream. "For the past twenty minutes, I thought it was the nausea from the Hurricane ride."

He laughed. "You're right. Maybe I should have suggested the deep-fried Oreos and the maple bacon funnel cake *after* the rides that make you puke."

Violet smiled; the sound of his laugh made *not* smiling impossible. "Well, lucky for you, the night is still young, so there's plenty of time to make it up to me." She stopped in front of a booth covered in balloons. "Let's see how good you are at darts."

"No, no. The first date handbook states, 'The gentleman gets to choose the game, and the lady gets to choose the stuffed toy.'"

"Oh, really?"

"Yes, really. These rules have been meticulously constructed over the centuries to ensure the gentleman makes a good first impression." He winked, linked her arm in his, and gently steered her away from the dart booth and back into the crowd.

The Hurricane ride must have started up again; a sudden burst of shrill screams drowned out the brassy chiming of the merry-go-round music. Cigarette smoke mingled with the aromas of hot popcorn and fried food.

She glanced at her hand resting on Thane's bicep. He'd placed his other hand on top of hers, the heat of his palm radiating over her skin. His hip gently bumped hers as they walked, and when an icy wind picked up, she couldn't help leaning into his side.

So this was what it was like to be on a first date—just like in those stupid romantic movies Lyla had always made her watch. Violet used to think the concepts were ridiculous— fairytales made up for all those suckers who wasted their money on movie tickets and romance novels. But now she understood how magical it was. Being here, with Thane, it was like a small spark had ignited in her heart.

"So," said Violet, "this handbook for 'gentlemen,' who supposedly wrote it? Mr. Darcy? Or—*Ah*!" She stumbled over a box of spilled popcorn, crunching scattered kernels under her shoes. Thankfully Thane gripped her arm tighter and avoided what could have been an embarrassing tumble.

Stupid shoes! Her cheeks burned. She never should have

let Autumn talk her into wearing these ridiculous wedge sandals. Who cared how much they suited her outfit? Her feet were freezing! If her toes fell off from frostbite before she got home, she was going to gift wrap them as a thank-you present for Autumn. It would also be payback for Autumn's ridiculous giggling and frequent mouthing of "He's so hot" when Thane had arrived at their room to pick her up. The worst part was when Autumn had shouted, "You two are gonna make beautiful babies!" down the dormitory hallway as Violet and Thane were leaving.

She bit her lip at the memory, once again catching the taste of that rebellious cotton candy.

Thane unlinked his arm from hers, then drew her into a closer, warmer embrace. "I don't think Mr. Darcy wrote this particular handbook," he said, continuing to guide her through the crowd. "That guy took too damn long to let a lady know how much he liked her."

She glanced up and met his brown eyes. He smiled, and something in her chest fluttered.

"Ah, now, this is a man's sport," he said, looking over at a shooting gallery booth. "Which toy is your favorite?"

Ten minutes later, Violet wedged three stuffed bears under her arm and two bunnies in her shoulder bag as they walked away from the shooting gallery.

"How are you feeling? Still nauseated?" Thane asked, wrapping his arm around her shoulders.

"No, I think I'm—whoa!"

A cloud of bubbles drifted across the path. They danced in the air, rainbow patterns swirling on their curved surfaces. A few brushed Violet's face, tickling her skin when they popped on impact. Young children were laughing and squealing in the center of the bubble cloud. They jumped and waved their chubby little hands to pop as many as they could.

Violet glanced up when Thane chuckled.

"Look at them," said Thane. "It's amazing that something so fragile can bring so much joy." He reached out an index finger to pop a bubble floating toward his face.

Violet took the three bears out from under her arm. "Here, do you mind holding these?"

Thane gave her a quizzical look but did as she asked. She reached into her shoulder bag for her camera and fiddled with the settings on the LCD display until she found the one she needed.

"Do you mind popping another bubble like you did before?"

Thane quirked an eyebrow but complied. Violet raised the camera to her eye, and the shutter clicked several times as Thane popped a few more of the soap globes.

"Perfect. I think I got it," said Violet. She scrolled through the photos she'd taken. "Check this out."

Thane leaned closer as she held the camera out for him.

She'd captured the bubble mid-pop. Half of it was still intact, glossy and rainbow, whereas the half closest to Thane's finger had shattered into a million tiny droplets.

"Wow," said Thane, his voice low.

"Do you mind if I get a few more shots?"

"No problem." He held up the three toys. "These guys will keep me company."

Violet giggled and stepped into the world of bubbles.

She took photo after photo, adjusted some settings, then took some more, taking careful note of the light, the color, the movement. She captured children in mid-jump and the babies in their parents' arms who tried to eat the bubbles.

Worried she was taking too long, she glanced back at Thane, but his attention was elsewhere.

A tiny girl bundled in a giant red jacket stood near him. Her eyes were red and blotchy, and her little hands were balled into fists as they wiped away an endless stream of tears. Thane had knelt down to her level. Violet couldn't hear what he was saying, but the little girl was nodding in response.

Violet crouched and raised the camera to her eye, adjusting the lens to focus past the bubbles around her. The shutter clicked, capturing Thane handing the little girl one of the stuffed bears. She hugged the toy close and smiled through her tears.

A moment later, a man and a woman came into view. By the relief on their faces, Violet figured they'd just found their lost child.

The man picked up the little girl, who held up her new toy and pointed to Thane. He and the girl's parents exchanged a few words, then the little family nodded and smiled before continuing on with their night. The little girl waved at Thane over her dad's shoulder right up until they disappeared into the crowd.

"That was a nice thing you did," said Violet when she walked back over to him.

He shrugged. "The kid was lost and upset. Anyone would have done the same."

"Not everyone," said Violet, childhood memories flickering through her mind. She switched her camera off and placed it on top of the two toys in her bag.

"Did you get what you wanted?" Thane asked, jutting his chin at the camera.

Violet looked up at him. "Yeah," she replied, "more than what I expected."

The gold flecks in his brown eyes were radiant. For several heartbeats, he just looked at her. No one had ever looked at Violet the way Thane was looking at her now. The longer she held his gaze, the more she felt it piercing through her barriers, glimpsing the delicate piece of her she'd tucked away long ago, out of everyone's reach. The part she hid away for fear of being shattered completely.

He reached out to stroke her cheek with the back of his knuckle, and his light touch sent shivers through her body. In that moment, she and Thane were the only people in the bubble swarm, the only people on the planet, the only people in the universe.

He took a step closer, erasing the gap between them.

A sliver of doubt cut through Violet's thoughts.

"Thane?"

"Yeah." His palm now rested on her cheek, and his thumb gently stroked her tingling skin.

"I, um . . . I've never done this before." Violet's words were barely a whisper. Her cheeks and neck blazed hot with embarrassment.

"Done what?"

"This," she said, gesturing a finger between them.

A small crease appeared between Thane's eyebrows. "Do you mean kissing?"

Another shiver trembled through her body. "I mean everything. This whole dating, flirting, romance stuff. And yeah, even . . . kissing." Her voice had dropped so low, the last word was almost inaudible. What was wrong with her? Why couldn't she say *kissing* like a normal person? He'd said it so casually. How could he say it so casually?

"In that case," he said, "there's something you should know."

Violet sucked in several shallow breaths.

"I've never done this romance stuff before either." The smile he gave her was so warm, so open, she felt some hard, defensive, unscalable wall inside of her melt.

Before she could reply, his lips met hers. Bubbles popped and tingled over her skin as they kissed.

The light in her heart sparked brighter.

## APHRODITE

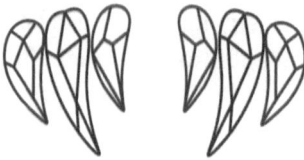

A RELENTLESS *DRIP, DRIP, DRIP* ECHOED OFF THE CONCRETE walls of Nathan's prison.

Matthias held a relaxed stance, checking his mobile phone at various intervals, while Sagan leaned rigidly against the wall. The boy's face remained impassive, but something intense, almost wild, glinted in his eyes.

Nathan gritted his teeth; the ache in his wrists had worsened. Even though his tough hide prevented almost anything, except Diamantium, from cutting his flesh, he could've sworn the metal cuffs were grinding into his bones.

A few minutes passed before the screech of rusty hinges announced the return of Matthias's minions.

A shudder racked through Nathan's body. He wasn't sure if it was from the fatigue of denying the haze or from the dread of whatever was coming through that godforsaken door. He dropped his head, feigning disinterest. The pool of blood beneath him continued to spread, but the blue flooding his vision was quickly joined by a pair of black combat boots. A hand grasped a chunk of his hair and yanked back. Nathan suppressed the urge to fight out of the strong grip.

"I told you not to pass out on me, slith. I have something to show you," said Matthias, his breath hot and humid on Nathan's ear.

The two men, Brecker and Harold, trudged into the room, dragging behind them a large object draped in black fabric. Nathan didn't recognize the silhouette. Whatever it was, he was probably better off not knowing.

"Ah, now, there's a pretty sight," Matthias crooned. "Allow me to introduce Aphrodite."

At a signal from Matthias, one of the minions removed the black fabric, revealing a medieval-like cannon with a futuristic makeover. The cannon's bulk—about the width of a man and half the height of one—sat on a wheeled frame. A touchscreen was on one side, and a long metallic barrel about the diameter of a soda can was aimed at the center of Nathan's chest.

The metal on the contraption had a green tinge—most likely Metallikite. He pitied the other species of shifter that had been forced to produce so much of the metallic byproduct. His own chains and shackles had to be made of the same metal; he could have broken through any other kind of standard steel or industrial alloy long ago.

Matthias released Nathan's hair and sauntered over to the cannon. "Isn't she a beauty?" he whispered, stroking the barrel as if it were a beloved pet. He leaned in, and for a moment, Nathan thought the man was about to plant a kiss on the contraption. Instead, Matthias rested an arm on the body of the cannon and swiveled to face Nathan.

"Aphrodite has the ability to project up to thirty thousand lumens of concentrated beams, equivalent to those filtered from Venus." He waved a hand. "Now, I don't know how many lumens you sliths need to shift. Some scientists in a lab somewhere did all the testing to figure that out."

Nathan's jaw clenched, imagining the types of "testing" that would have taken place.

"But whatever the number, these clever scientists came together to design and build Aphrodite to make our jobs easier." Matthias beamed, like a child showing off his new Pokémon cards. "Wanna take a look inside?"

He pulled a small flashlight from his coat pocket and shone a beam down the barrel. Nathan flinched as the reflected light flashed into his eyes. Once he adjusted to the brightness, he recognized the style of the refracted flecks of rainbow dancing around him.

Matthias stalked over and tapped on Nathan's pectoral muscle, just above the stab wound. "How ironic—that nothing can cut or penetrate your thick hides except the death of one of your own." He grinned, his pearly whites glistening.

Nathan thought of five different ways to bash the smirk off this Erathi scum's face.

Matthias studied Nathan, his scrutiny long and agonizing, as if his intelligent eyes were stripping Nathan bare, exposing every piece of him straight down to his soul.

Another tremble convulsed Nathan's body, and Matthias's eyes hardened. His nose crinkled and his mouth twisted into a sneer. "Damn prideful, ignorant creatures. You're all the same. You think I can't break you?" He whipped the back of his hand across Nathan's face. The crack of Erathi skin against Veniri hide echoed around the room. "You think I can't break you!"

Nathan's head snapped from side to side as Matthias landed several more blows. Despite the toughness of his hide, his skin still stung with each slap and throbbed with each punch.

Without warning, Matthias dropped his fist, breathing hard. He shook out his hand and broke into maniacal laughter. "You all think if you resist changing, we can't harvest your shards." He poked the flesh between Nathan's neck and shoulders. "Like the nice big ones that come from here. Or from here." He prodded the backs of Nathan's elbows. "And my personal favorites, here." He laid a finger on Nathan's knee. "With Aphrodite, I'll break you, slith. And you wanna know a secret?" He leaned in, his face about an inch from Nathan's nose. "Even if you die during the harvest, Aphrodite ensures you don't turn back to your human form." He groaned. "Lord knows how much of a pain in the ass it was to get a job done with you wretched things dying on us all the time. Of course, we could still use whatever was left inside. You saw that nice necklace my wife was wearing? I harvested the knuckle and wrist bones myself. But it's your large shards that are in high demand. Like most things in life, size matters."

Nathan glared at Matthias. "You done with your monologuing yet? I'd prefer you go back to the hitting."

Matthias's shark grin returned to its full dazzling glory. He shouted over his shoulder, "Brecker, fire her up," then took a few paces backward, never taking his eyes off Nathan. He winked. "Trust me, you're gonna love this."

Nathan smirked. "Whatever you say, sweetheart. Let's get this over with."

A hum resonated from within the cannon's barrel, growing louder and louder. Nathan recognized the melodic tune hidden beneath—the song of his connection with Venus, of his energy and the life that Venus gave his inner being. His body shivered as it serenaded his core. With all of his focus on the reverberation through his eardrums, he no longer understood why he resisted the haze. He *needed* to change. Needed to shed this Erathi form and embrace his true Veniri form.

A stab of pain in his shackled wrists brought him abruptly back to his senses.

He couldn't, wouldn't haze. Veniri shards were sacred to his race. The dishonor of one's shards being broken or severed often left one ostracized or even banished by their own family.

But his race be damned. He owed them nothing. He would remain strong to honor himself, and those he loved most. He would deny Matthias and his goons the pleasure of profiting off his corpse. Drawing on his dwindling energy stores, he fought back the desire to haze that was threatening to overwhelm him.

The humming grew even louder, and a blue glow from within the cannon's barrel came to life. A beam of blue light coated Nathan's skin like the warmth of the sun on a winter's day. The beam's energy restored his own inner energy. Blood in his muscles pulsed. His strength slowly returned, and fatigue began to slip away. The gaping flesh around his stab wound itched as the speed of healing increased.

"See, I told you you were gonna love this," Matthias yelled over the noise. "Just wait till you see what happens next." Matthias tapped a few buttons on the touchscreen.

After a moment, the humming rose to a scream. A piercing screech in Nathan's ears demanded every fiber and cell in his body change. The blue energy beams seared his flesh, turning from a soft, restorative force to fierce, undiluted energy.

A roar escaped Nathan's lungs as his body writhed and shuddered, desperate to escape the light and its shrill squeal. The need to haze overshadowed any coherent thought. He was on the verge of accepting defeat when the light and noise vanished.

The room switched from illuminated teal back to incandescent yellow. Blood—metallic and sweet—flooded Nathan's mouth as he choked on garbled breaths. He would have collapsed into a heap on the floor if his restraints had allowed it. The pain in his wrists was a relief compared to the torment from moments ago.

Nathan blinked. The afterglow of Aphrodite's beam hovered in front of his eyes.

Matthias's face moved into Nathan's view. "Hmm, not even a fang showing. I've never seen a slith with the extent of control you seem to have. They all turn within seconds of Aphrodite's light." His eyes squinted into slits. "How are you doing it?"

Nathan glared. "Just kill me and get this over with," he said, his voice hoarse.

A corner of Matthias's mouth curled. "Don't tell me you're giving up so easily? I know you've got more fight left in you."

Nathan closed his eyes and rested his chin on his chest. He would die soon, and he was done wasting his last few moments on these twisted games.

A woman's face flashed in his mind—delicate features, hazel eyes staring lovingly into his, a warm hand on his face and him turning into her palm to kiss it. The memories sent a stabbing ache through his heart. His usual reaction was to push them aside; the pain always became unbearable if he allowed his mind to linger. But in this moment, these memories were heaven.

"Fine," said Matthias. "If you won't fight for yourself, then how about for her?"

*Her?* Nathan's eyes flew open.

Matthias held out his phone, allowing Nathan to study the screen.

"No," Nathan breathed.

On Matthias's phone was a digital bounty order with a photo of Violet.

"No!" Nathan lunged. His chains rattled, jerking him to a stop an inch from Matthias's face.

Matthias's demented grin widened. "There, that's what I want to see."

"Stay away from Violet!" Nathan roared, as loud as his damaged vocal cords would allow.

A flash of movement against the far wall caught Nathan's attention. Sagan was now standing straight, his gaze fixed on his father.

"Please don't let him do this," Nathan said to Sagan. He didn't care if his tone was begging and desperate. "Don't let him hurt Violet. She was your sister's best friend. Please, don't do this."

Matthias chuckled. "*I* won't do this, but the man I've sent after her will. In fact, he's probably at her college right now."

"You're lying," Nathan hissed.

"Dad, is that true?" Sagan asked.

Matthias ignored him. "Don't worry. I'm sure my man will make it quick. It's likely she won't even feel it when he slices her throat in her sleep."

Sagan flew to his father's side and said in a loud whisper, "What happened to 'we don't kill our own'?"

Matthias glared down at his son. "I'm fully aware of the code, *son*." He leaned into Sagan's face. "And what do you care, hmm?"

"She . . . she was Lyla's friend," said Sagan, still in a whisper. "She was there for Lyla when she—"

"You mean she was there when Lyla was butchered?"

"But we don't kill—"

"Don't lecture me, boy!" Matthias roared, spittle spraying with each word.

"But, Dad—"

Matthias backhanded him. Sagan's head snapped to the side, and he sprawled back into the concrete wall. The force of the blow sent the phone flying out of Matthias's hand, and it hit the wall above Sagan's head. In any other scenario—one that didn't involve him being chained in a concrete room with psychotic hunters—Nathan might have been impressed with the shatterproof case that allowed the device to bounce off the wall and land unharmed at Sagan's feet.

"Brecker!" Matthias barked. "Turn that thing back on, and this time, make sure it's at double strength. We've got harvesting to do."

Sagan scuffled into a position that reminded Nathan of a cat about to pounce.

In a whirl of black, Matthias spun and threw his Diamantium dagger directly at Sagan. It sped through the air in a glittering blur, embedding into the concrete wall next to his son's head. Sagan's blue eyes glazed in shock. He raised his hand to his ear and inspected the crimson blood smeared on his fingertips.

Matthias pointed at him, his jaw set in an expression of pure arrogance and victory. "Stay down, boy, or the next one goes through your throat."

Nathan fixed a glare on Matthias. Surely the guy was bluffing. But something in his expression suggested otherwise.

The boy fisted his bloodied hand and resumed his slouch against the wall.

"It's ready," said Brecker.

"Good." Matthias rolled his shoulders back. "Now. Where were—"

A man burst into the room and ran over to Matthias.

"What did I tell you about interrupting me," Matthias hissed.

"But, boss," said the newcomer, "he's here."

Matthias held up one hand to Brecker, who paused. "What do you mean he's here?"

"I mean he's actually *here*. He says she found them and wants to set up a meeting."

Matthias's whole countenance lit up like a kid on Christmas morning. "Take me to him."

"But, boss, what about the slith?" Brecker asked.

"Start without me." Matthias strode out of the room without a backward glance.

Nathan sized up the three remaining men. Sagan had slid to the ground, an image of defeat, his arms crossed over his chest. A trickle of red made a path down his neck and over the black chain visible above his shirt collar.

Brecker lounged on the cannon and smirked at Nathan, his hand poised over the touchscreen. "Oi, Harvey, get the crystal cutter ready."

"Hold up, I've got 'em here somewhere." The man disappeared behind the cannon, and a clatter of bangs and clangs ensued, followed by the reverberant ring of metal being dragged across concrete. Harvey brought out what looked like massive bolt cutters, the tips caked in dried Veniri blood.

Dread pulsed through Nathan's chest. He needed to get out of here. His wretched Aphrodite experience had given his body a small surge of restoration, but he was over-buzzed, as if he'd just been pumped with a hefty dose of caffeine and methamphetamines.

He tugged on the chains—definitely Metallikite. There was no point attempting to break them. His best chance was to take out these hunters before they hit the switch, but he was out of reach. Even a kick would only hit air. Swinging might gain him a few inches, but they would guess what he was up to before he achieved enough momentum to do anything.

They would have to come to him.

Of course, if he succeeded in incapacitating these three, there was still the problem of breaking free of the chains. But forget that for now. One problem at a time.

Nathan flexed his tingling fingers in a useless attempt to get the blood recirculating. Wincing, he grasped the chains just above the cuffs, then tested his numb hands' ability to hold up his body weight. Brutal pain shot from his shoulders straight down his spine, but it was nothing compared to the impending onslaught of Aphrodite's light.

Once he confirmed he could hold himself up, he stood on one foot and kicked at the puddle beneath him. A gush of blue splattered over Brecker.

The hunter bellowed and held his arms out like a scarecrow. Trails of Nathan's blood trickled down his face and dripped from his beard, and his features twisted into a look of pure revulsion. He tried wiping his mouth on his sleeve, then realized the fabric was also coated in gore.

Harold rushed out from behind the cannon. Upon seeing the state of Brecker, he barked out a laugh. Brecker turned to him, lips pursed, as Harold continued to point and jeer.

Nathan kicked at the puddle again, this time aiming for Harold.

The laughter died, cut off by a gargled outburst. Harold stood frozen, his gaping mouth displaying a tongue that was now a solid shade of teal.

It was Brecker's turn to bellow with laughter.

"Why, you filthy—!" Harold spat and sprayed gore and saliva, punctuating a furious string of profanities. "Ugh, who knows what kind of diseases are in that filth?" He fixed his gaze on Nathan, his nostrils flared and his jaw jutting forward. "You're gonna pay for that, slith."

A corner of Nathan's mouth twisted into a sneer, and he kicked the puddle again. Harold roared with rage, then rushed him.

"Oi, now, Harold!" Brecker stepped between them and shoved a firm hand against Harold's chest.

"Outta my way! I'm gonna gut him!"

Harold tried to push past him, causing Brecker to slip back slightly on the slick ground.

*That's it*, thought Nathan. Just a few more inches and he'd be able to—

Brecker punched Harold in the face. "Pull yourself together! He's baiting you."

Harold stumbled back, moaning and clutching his nose, and Brecker grasped the front of his jacket. "Stop mucking about. You can gut him after he's been harvested."

Harold glared at Nathan.

Nathan grinned back.

A tinkling melody echoed around the room. All eyes turned to Sagan. Matthias's phone was still on the ground at his feet, vibrating softly.

"Oi!" Brecker called over to him. "You gonna sit there and sulk all day, or you gonna make yourself useful?"

Sagan ignored him and picked up the phone.

Brecker *tsk*ed and shook his head. "Useless kid," he mumbled.

Panic began to surge through Nathan as Brecker repositioned himself back at the touch pad of the Aphrodite cannon. His dirty trick with the blood hadn't worked, but he chanced another go and kicked another spray of blue.

Fury and disgust raged on both Harold and Brecker's blue dripping faces, yet neither made any movement toward him. Instead, Brecker stabbed his finger at the touchscreen. "Oh, you're gonna get yours."

Before Nathan could react, the Aphrodite beam engulfed him; the strength of both light and sound that raced through his body ignited into overdrive.

This time he had no chance of refusing to haze.

Shards of crystal sliced through his insides and punctured his skin, spearing up from his collarbones and sprouting along his shoulders and neck. Blades burst from his elbows, extending all the way to his wrists. Protrusions from the center of each knee grew to a quarter of the length of Nathan's thighs, and smaller crystals spired out of the rest of Nathan's body in his own unique pattern. His flesh rippled and molded into iridescent teal and dark gray scales, which glowed—as if from an inner illumination—at the bases of the larger spikes. His feet and toes elongated several inches, morphing into prehistoric raptor feet armed with glittering Diamantium talons.

Nathan's inner eyelids shuttered open and closed, adjusting to the intense exposure of the condensed Venusian beam. A tingle in his skull intensified into painful vibrations as smaller shards of Diamantium sliced through his scaled head, adorning his brow bones, cheekbones, and chin. His canines and premolars lengthened and sharpened. After a moment, his forked tongue slashed out between a triple set of protruding fangs.

Nathan's jaw locked open in a long guttural roar. His body writhed and flayed, the chains his only tether to the world.

At last the transformation ended.

Nathan waited for the relief that usually came after his body hazed, but the onslaught of evil continued, promising no end to his suffering. The world became nothing but a blur of pain. Excruciating pain. He wished and prayed it would all end. That *he* would end.

Then, miraculously, Aphrodite flicked off.

Nathan sagged against his bonds. A glitter of rainbow light reflected off his crystal spires and onto the blue puddle below.

Although his closed inner eyelids fogged his vision, his

tongue fumbled outward instinctively to taste and assess his surroundings. His mind, however, repelled any comprehension beyond a vague sense of movement before him—two blurry figures.

He blinked a few times at the pair of grinning faces speckled with blue liquid.

They were speaking, but to Nathan's ears their words were unintelligible. He shook his head, then immediately regretted it as a wave of nausea collided into him

He strained his remaining concentration until he understood some of the words.

". . . gonna start with this one."

The speaker held up what looked like enormous scissors. Or were they oversized nail clippers?

Odd sounds issued from both figures—some kind of gurgling. After a moment, Nathan realized it was laughter. The smaller figure clamped the oversized nail clippers on a Diamantium shard jutting from Nathan's collarbone.

A stab of pain jolted through Nathan's body. His eyes widened, and the world crashed back into focus.

"That's it, Harold, get a good grip on it."

Harold tugged on the spike. A hoarse groan escaped Nathan.

"Careful now, you don't want to cut into it yet. What you want to do is yank hard and see if you can get a few more inches before you break it off." Brecker tapped the center of Nathan's torso. "Put your foot up here for some leverage."

Nathan grunted as Harold adjusted his stance without easing his hold on the spike. A cold, slick boot pressed into Nathan's stomach.

"Ready?" said Brecker.

"Yup."

"Now yank as hard as you can."

Harold grunted with the effort, his boot ramming into Nathan's diaphragm.

Nathan's scream was futile, almost soundless. It may as well have been a gust of wind or an unseen ghost crying out to the living. Pure agony radiated from the shard in Harold's grasp, the pressure unendurable. The shard's hold on Nathan's internal skeleton was on the verge of breaking.

Harold's laborious grunts ended abruptly, interrupted by the dull *thud* of metal hitting flesh.

Brecker collapsed in a heap.

"What the . . . ?" Harold didn't have time to turn before Sagan struck him across the back of the head with a metal bar. Like a marionette with cut strings, Harold's limp form joined Brecker's on the floor.

Sagan stepped over the bodies, retrieving the cutting tool from Harold's hands. Nathan blinked sluggishly.

Sagan raised the cutters. In quick succession, he cut both of Nathan's wrists free.

Nathan's arms fell to his sides, and his fingers flared torturously as the blood rushed back into his hands. He eyed Sagan, trying to read his expression.

Sagan held up Matthias's phone.

Relief washed over Nathan after he read the text message on the screen.

## 15

# GREEDY WITH THE "CRAZY" TITLE

Violet pulled her blanket off the bed, jumped onto the window seat, and threw it over the curtain rail. The room dimmed to a sepia glow, soft beams of sunlight still creeping in at the edges of the window frame.

"Thanks for agreeing to this," she said. "I would have asked one of the others, but they're all busy today."

"No problem," said Thane, "happy I could help. So, what's your class project again?"

Violet tugged on the edges of the makeshift drapery until all sunlight was blocked. "It's about capturing emotions in photos."

"Cool. So all you need me to do is smile and frown and cry, right? Fair warning—I can't make any promises on the crying part. Unless you're planning to kick me in the groin or something."

Violet laughed and jumped down from the window seat. "No plans for any groin kicking."

"Great."

Warm incandescent light bathed the room when she turned on the desk lamp. "I need to put together a folio of different emotions. The idea is to capture the feelings in ways other than just facial expressions. We need to incorporate elements like posture, lighting, hands, and props to create an emotional story." She pointed to the floor in front of the window seat. "I'll need you to stand there for me, please."

When Thane was in position, she turned to rummage in the top drawer of her desk, pulling out some scissors and a necklace with a vintage pocket watch pendant.

"What's next?" asked Thane.

Violet clipped out an image from a department store catalogue. "I just need to finish making this prop. And then I'll need you to . . . um . . . I'll need you to . . ." Her voice dropped to a mumble.

"Sorry, I didn't catch that last bit. You need me to what?"

Violet tore off some tape and rolled it sticky side out as she gave an uncomfortable cough. "I need you to take off your shirt."

She refused to look at him, training all her focus on attaching the tape to the back of the catalogue clipping, but she swore she could feel Thane's amused expression boring into her back.

"The lady hasn't even bought me dinner, and she's already asking me to undress." He chuckled.

Violet bit her lip to hide a grin. When she was satisfied with her improvised prop, she turned back to Thane.

"Here. We'll start with this." She held out the necklace. The pendant dangled down from her fingertips, the embossed filigree pattern on the watch cover capturing the light as it gently swayed.

She hated having to use her desk lamp. It was tacky compared to the better, more expensive lighting equipment available, but at least it could still create the light and shadow contrast for what she had in mind.

Thane eyed the watch as he undid the last few buttons on his shirt. The light from the lamp washed over his bare skin from the waist up, creating shadows that accentuated the rippled muscles on his arms and down his abdomen.

Violet sucked in a breath. *Keep cool, Violet. Don't go making a fool of yourself.*

He took the pocket watch and inspected it, tracing a finger over the filigree. "This is amazing. Where did you get this?"

"Um, it was . . ." Violet shifted a little on her feet, avoiding eye contact. "A friend gave it to me."

He pressed the button that released the cover, revealing the watch face. On the inside of the cover was a baby photo she'd clipped out of the baby clothes section of the department store catalogue. After a pause, he said, "Hmm, interesting. So, do you want me to put it on or hold it? How do you want this to go?"

She let out a breath of relief and smiled at him. "Here, let me."

She reached out for his right hand and entwined the chain around his fingers, leaving the watch to dangle a few inches from his wrist. Then she rested his hand on his chest, just above his heart, and positioned the pendant so that both the watch face and the image of the baby were visible.

Thane kept quiet and pliable, allowing her to form the vision in her mind.

She took a few shots with her camera on the tripod, then tried a few close-ups. The regular clicking of the camera shutter barely drowned out the pounding of her pulse in her ears. The angry pixies in her chest were *raging*.

"What kind of emotion are you trying to capture?" Thane asked.

"I'm not totally sure yet," Violet confessed. "I had this

image in my mind when I was given the assignment, and I just thought I'd run with it and see how it turns out."

Thane nodded. A few more clicks of the shutter filled the short silence.

"Do you mind if I make a suggestion?" he asked.

Violet looked up from the viewfinder.

"I mean, only if you want me to," he quickly added. "I don't mean to take over or anything."

Violet smiled. "It's fine. What do you have in mind?"

He reached for her hand, and she let the camera dangle from the strap around her neck as he drew her closer. Spicy hints of his aftershave hovered in the air. Unlike the heavy musk of those typical spray-on deodorants, his scent was earthy and rich.

"This may or may not work, but I'm happy for you to be the judge of that." He laced his fingers in hers and hugged her hand to his chest.

She sucked in a breath, trying desperately to ignore the intense fluttering in her ribcage and stomach and—

"What do you think?" he asked.

She cleared her throat. "This is actually pretty great." With her free hand, she took a few shots, then scrolled through the photos she'd taken. Her eyes widened at the stunning images on the digital display screen. Thane had terrific instincts for this kind of thing. She imagined the final photos in black and white. Or was that too cliché? Maybe sepia?

"So, this friend of yours, the one who gave you the watch. Does she go to college here too?" asked Thane.

Violet paused her scrolling. "No, she, um . . . she . . . passed away a few years ago."

*Passed away.* Violet hated that term. It made it sound as if Lyla had just slipped off peacefully in her sleep. She may as well say something like "An angel flew gracefully down from the heavens and enveloped Lyla in a holy embrace to escort her to the hereafter."

Yet, words like *died* or *death* were just too brutal, too callous. Too *final*.

She shuffled her feet, gluing her attention on her sneakers, waiting for the questions. *How did she die, Violet? Why can't you remember what happened, Violet?*

"She was special to you. Wasn't she." He said it like a statement, not like a question. His thumb stroked small circles on the back of her hand.

"Yeah," she said, the word nearly a whisper. "She was my best friend in the whole world. I know it sounds cliché, but she saw me when . . . when I was invisible."

Thane edged closer. She could almost taste the sandalwood in his aftershave. He placed a hand on her cheek, and she sucked in a breath, averting her gaze.

"Violet, look at me," he said, his voice low and flowing like liquid silver. He tilted her chin up. The flecks of gold in his eyes were mesmerizing—holographic against the brown of his irises. "You're not invisible to me."

A flutter stirred in her chest, and she bit her bottom lip and closed her eyes. His thumb stroked her cheek, then moved down, tracing the corner of her mouth, the edge of her bottom lip.

When she opened her eyes, his gaze was locked directly onto hers. She could drown in the molten gold of those eyes.

His hand stilled. "Are you all right?"

She nodded, her gaze once again falling to the ground. "Yes. It's just . . . I've never . . ."

He angled his head, trying to recapture eye contact. "It's okay, you can tell me."

She looked up. The glow of his eyes had intensified—almost as if it were radiating out and around him.

"Whoa," she said in a soft voice. "You look . . ." Even after

144

rubbing her eyes, the golden light was still there. It started to dance around him like an aura of glitter, like fireflies.

She unlaced her hand from Thane's and took a few steps back, her gaze swiveling around the room. "You can see this too . . . right?" Maybe this was all in her head. *Great!* She was in her room with the hottest guys she'd ever met, and she was going crazy. Was this her way of fleeing from the first sign of commitment? She *had* developed a knack for switching foster homes back in the day.

Thane's brow furrowed, his confusion clear. But the bafflement wasn't directed at her, Violet noticed with a flood of relief. He craned his head around, also looking at the light.

"Yeah." He gave a slow nod. "I can see it. Is this some kind of fancy lighting effect? I thought that was done in the editing stage."

Violet shook her head and glanced at her desk lamp. "It's not me."

So many questions raced through her mind. Her head was freaking out—yet she didn't *feel* in danger. In fact, the lights seemed almost calming. Reassuring.

Thane was looking down at himself, inspecting his arms, his chest, and the air around him. "It can't be . . ." he murmured.

"What? What is it?"

"I . . ." He glanced at her and grimaced. "To be honest, I don't really know."

One of the tiny flecks was hovering a few inches in front of Violet's face. The closer it got, the more she wanted to reach out and touch it. What would happen if she did? Would it burn her? Zap her? Would it hurt at all? She didn't think so. Again, her instincts told her it was safe.

The little light flickered and sparked as it drifted closer.

"Wow, it's so pretty." Violet reached out a hand.

"Wait," said Thane. "Don't touch it. I don't know what it

does." But before he'd finished speaking, the golden fleck landed on her palm and soaked into her skin.

He rushed forward and grabbed her hand, inspecting where the fleck had landed. The other lights trailed after him.

"It didn't hurt," she assured him.

"What is going on?" Thane said, more to himself.

"Have you seen anything like this before?"

Thane shook his head, eyes wide. She smiled at his expression of wonderment, his awe toward what was happening.

If there was one thing Violet could tell for sure about the lights, it was their source. Thane. The tiny luminous particles kept multiplying, appearing like small halos against his bare skin, then gently drifting off to hover around them both, much like the swarm of bubbles from their first date.

She looked down at the camera still in her hands. "Hmm, I wonder . . . Stay still for a second."

Violet stepped back, then snapped a few shots. She alternated between looking at Thane through the viewfinder and over the camera, trialing and testing a few angles and perspectives.

After a few more photos, she noticed Thane start to twitch and rub at his skin.

"Are you okay?" She lowered the camera. "What's wrong?"

He scrubbed at his face. "I don't know. I feel kind of tingly."

Violet tilted her head. "Tingly how?"

"Well, I may have noticed something in the last few minutes." As he spoke, his hands were still scratching at his face, his hands, his abdomen. Eventually, he settled for massaging the area around his eyes. "I may be at risk of sounding a little crazy, but I think I can feel you looking at me. Like, actually feel your gaze on me."

Violet raised an eyebrow. "Umm . . . what?"

Thane chuckled sheepishly. "I know, crazy, right?"

Violet shrugged. "Maybe? There's an easy way to find out." She put a hand over her eyes. "How do you feel now?"

After a few heartbeats, Thane clicked his tongue. "Believe it or not, it's stopped."

"What? No way." Violet dropped her hand. "You're totally playing me."

Thane shook his head and started running his hands over his face again. "Ha, if I was playing you, this would be a totally weird prank to pull."

She couldn't argue with that. "Okay then. Cover your eyes."

"What? Why?"

"Just do it."

Thane laughed and did as she said. "Okay."

"Good. Now, tell me if you can feel this." She fixed her gaze on the hand covering his eyes.

"Yep, pretty sure I can feel it."

"Where?"

He pointed to the back of his hand.

*Hmm. Lucky guess.* She looked at his chin.

"It's here now." He scratched at his chin with one finger.

Violet frowned. She looked at his elbow. He pointed to his elbow. Next, she looked at his shoulder, and without hesitation, he pointed to his shoulder, right at the spot where she was focusing.

*You've got to be kidding!*

"You're totally peeking," she said.

"I swear I'm not," he said on a laugh.

She frowned, then a smile tugged at her lips.

Violet slowly moved her gaze from his shoulder along his collarbone. He traced the path of her eye with his finger, following it to the hollow of his neck, then down the center of his torso.

"Violet, what are you doing?"

She noted the mild amusement in his tone, but she refused to lose focus or change direction. Her eyes trailed lower, lower. The rise and fall of Thane's chest quickened as his finger continued to trace the line she was leading—down and down his sternum.

Violet's heart thudded in her chest, and shivers raced up her neck.

His finger was almost at the waistline of his jeans.

Then, in a flurry, she flicked her gaze back up to the hand over his eyes.

He threw the hand down and laughed. Violet covered her mouth, her own giggles mixing with his deep chuckles.

The firefly lights around him had begun dancing and glowing with more vigor. A cloud of them drifted toward her, too many to dodge. Before she could react, they'd landed on her and, as before, soaked into her skin.

"Whoa! Tingly." Every place they touched her exposed flesh seemed to vibrate. She sucked in a breath and held it. Intense joy and extreme sadness washed over her in an overwhelming wave.

Thane took her by the shoulders. "Violet, what's wrong?"

"What? What do you mean?"

"You're crying."

She touched her face, feeling the warm dampness on her cheeks.

"Violet?"

"I'm okay. I'm fine. I just . . . Well, I feel weird, actually. It's kinda hard to explain. I don't have anything to compare it to. I feel really happy. Like, it's the happiest I've ever been in my life."

He smiled.

"But then I also feel extremely sad at the same time."

His face fell. "What do you mean?"

"I don't know. Mixed with the joy is this really intense sadness. But it's kinda like a good sadness. Almost a complement to the happiness. You know, like, the sadness is totally worth it, because of the extreme happiness." She screwed up her face and put both hands on her head. "I'm sorry. I sound like a crazy idiot."

Goodbye to getting to know this guy any further. Hello to dying alone.

"Violet, we're standing in the midst of unexplained light that seems to be coming from me, and you think you're the crazy one." He arched an eyebrow.

She laughed. "Good point. I suppose I can't be greedy with the 'crazy' title, especially after you thought you could *feel* me looking at you."

"Actually, I'm pretty sure that's still happening."

"What?" Before she could stop herself, her eyes did a quick scan of his bare torso.

A corner of his mouth tugged up, and her cheeks burned. He took a few steps forward, closing the small gap between them. At the same time, the glowing lights seemed to brighten, sharpen.

"Thane, what are you—?"

The chance to finish her sentence was lost as Thane pressed his lips to hers.

She froze for half a heartbeat, then drew closer, twining her arms around his neck. In response, his strong arms wrapped around her lower back and lifted her off the ground. She hitched her legs around his waist, molding her body against his, desperate to deepen the intimacy. The desire for more raged through her core. Her skin burned wherever it touched his.

All sense of time, place, and being stood still, trapped in

Thane's bewitching kiss. She couldn't even guess how long they remained locked together.

With an abrupt *thud*, the dorm room door burst open, letting in a stream of harsh light from the hallway.

Violet and Thane broke apart as Autumn, Gus, and Bessie strolled into the room. Gus's eyes bugged and his jaw dropped open. Bessie smirked, and Autumn grinned as though she'd just won the jackpot.

"See, Bessie," Autumn said in a stage whisper, "I told you he was hot."

Bessie nodded. "Yep. These two will definitely make beautiful babies."

Gus cleared his throat. "And clearly we've interrupted the baby-making process." He rubbed the back of his neck. "Sheesh, Violet. Put a sock on the door handle next time."

## 16

## I'D RATHER BE A PIÑATA

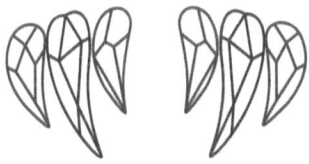

NATHAN WAS THANKFUL, NOT FOR THE FIRST TIME, THAT HE wasn't an average human. The amount of blood pooling around him and Sagan was enough to drain a horse.

Ironically, the rays from Aphrodite had sped up his already inhumanly fast healing process. Not only the wound on his chest but every cell and fiber of his body were being rapidly restored, including his blood supply. He was almost grateful for Aphrodite.

Almost.

He winced. The condensed Venusian rays still shuddered through his core. His vision was blurry and he felt light-headed, as if he'd just stepped off a roller coaster. A film of sweat coated his body, accompanied by an icy chill, and various muscles in his legs, back, and arms twitched with the sensation of electricity sparking under his skin. He shook and flexed his hands and fingers, which screamed as blood refilled their starving veins.

A particularly strong wave of dizziness crashed into him, and he tumbled to the ground, splashing blue liquid.

"Get up, slith," Sagan hissed.

Nathan snorted. "Give me a minute, kid."

"We haven't got a minute. We gotta go *now*."

Nathan raised his head, trying as best he could to bring Sagan into focus—the white-blond demon with an angel's face. He managed to get himself upright and take a few stumbling steps, his vision still spinning, but he had to throw out an arm to catch himself on the laser cannon when he neared the doorway.

"Hurry up. I'm not carrying you." Sagan's features contorted into a sullen frown, and he marched out the door, not checking to see if Nathan followed.

Nathan cursed as he pushed himself off the vile contraption. Damn these Erathi hunters and their talents for torture.

He staggered the last few steps out of the door and hustled, half limping, to catch up to Sagan. The boy guided him through a labyrinth of concrete hallways and chambers, some of which were still slick with the remnants of their most recent occupants. Nathan's stomach flipped; for a moment, he was glad his vision wasn't clear enough to identify the details.

After taking another turn, Sagan stopped short and glared at him. At least, Nathan assumed it was a glare; his eyes were still having trouble focusing.

"What are you doing? Why haven't you changed back into human form yet?" Sagan hissed.

"Huh?" Nathan looked down at himself. His crystal shards and scaled skin glittered under the brighter lights of the stark hallway.

Sagan pointed to the ground behind Nathan. "Damn it, slith. Could you make our escape any more obvious?"

Nathan winced. Even with his blurry vision, his trail of blue clawprints was painfully apparent on the concrete floor. He rubbed at his eyes, willing his sight to clear and for the spinning to stop.

Sagan let out a guttural sound of frustration and kept walking.

Hazing back into Erathi form was usually only a slightly more difficult process than changing into Veniri form. Yet this time when Nathan went to haze, nothing happened.

He tried again. Still nothing.

"Hurry up and change back," whispered Sagan over his shoulder.

"I can't."

"What do you mean you can't?"

"Uh . . . how long until the effects of Aphrodite wear off?" he asked in a low voice.

Sagan shook his head. "I don't know. No one's ever . . ."

Nathan didn't need him to finish to realize no one had survived long enough to find out. A muscle twitched in his jaw. He didn't quite fancy the idea of being at Sagan's mercy to escape this godforsaken place. The thought drifted through his mind that this could be some sick prank—a psychotic ruse for whatever Sagan and his father had planned for further torment.

He flicked his tongue at the young hunter and analyzed the influx of flavored emotions.

*Hmm, interesting.* Sagan's emotions were a little unstable, but at least there was no hint of cinnamon. Whatever Sagan was up to, he didn't plan on killing him. He would trust him for now.

They took another turn and stopped at the entrance of a cavern. The low ceiling of the passageway opened up into a cave half the size of a football field, with floodlights suspended from the rocky canopy a few hundred yards above their heads. Nathan squinted. Cars, trucks, and piles of what he guessed were ropes, chains, weapons, and crates of who-knows-what-else were scattered throughout. Based on the lack of sound, he and Sagan were the only ones present.

"There." Sagan pointed to a vehicle, a matte black Land Rover Defender, parked about a hundred yards away.

They'd almost made their way to the Defender when Nathan spotted sunlight beaming through a large entrance at the other side of the cavern. Relief flooded through his tense muscles, but in an instant, the flicker of hope switched to a burst of terror.

It wasn't sunlight.

Sagan shoved Nathan behind a stack of crates, out of the line of the approaching vehicle's headlights, which were growing brighter by the second. The growl of an engine reached an echoing crescendo as a black box truck drove in.

Nathan and Sagan crouched low to the ground, peering through gaps in the crates as the truck stopped a few feet away from their chosen getaway vehicle.

Sagan hissed out a breath.

The engine cut off, and two men jumped down from the cab, laughing and joking about a recent football game. Their voices reverberated around the cavern. Distinct amulets swung on black chains from their necks, but Nathan couldn't make out the number of colored vials through the blur.

An Erathi hunter with a gray biker beard reached into the truck and pulled out a crystalline trident. Nathan growled through his fangs, earning a quick glare from Sagan.

The hunters kept up their banter, meeting up at the side of the truck. After a few moments, another roar of an engine preceded a black SUV, which drove in and parked beside them. More voices followed the click and bang of car doors as five more hunters exited the SUV.

"What took you so long?" said Gray Beard with the trident. "Let's get this over with. I've got a game to catch."

"Yeah, yeah. You've always got a game to catch, Axel," said one of the newcomers, waving an indifferent hand.

The seven of them assembled on one side of the truck. All

were equipped with some kind of glittering Diamantium weapon.

"Whose turn is it?" asked one of the younger hunters. Nathan guessed him to be in his late teens.

This question earned a guffaw from a few of the others.

"Haha! Nice try," said Axel, clapping a hand on the back of the young hunter.

"Come on, Axel, can't we just—"

"Nope. You know the deal."

Ignoring the young Erathi's stammered protests, the other hunters shoved him away from the group and toward the truck. Axel bashed his trident on one of the vehicles shiny rear doors, and the truck convulsed as if startled from slumber. The Erathi kid tried to step back, his head shaking with furious intensity, but the others jeered and pushed him forward.

"Ready?" said Axel, taking hold of the latch.

Before the boy could answer, the door was flung open, and in a blur, a creature pounced out and onto the youth.

Chaos ensued. The hunters laughed or cheered, urging the youth to fight back.

Nathan's fury boiled. The creature was a preadolescent Veniri—about eleven or twelve, judging by the fur that was yet to shed from the young male's forearms, shoulders, and calves.

The Veniri growled, thrashing and clawing. It was becoming clear he had the upper hand over the inexperienced hunter. With one swipe, the Veniri gouged three angry red lines into the hunter's face. One of the other hunters made a move to intervene, but Axel held him back.

Nathan frowned. This must be some kind of sick initiation.

The youth started to scream and yell, begging for help and begging for the Veniri to stop. Nathan couldn't bear it anymore. He didn't have it in him to watch either the young Veniri or the Erathi die.

He stood up.

Sagan grabbed his wrist and yanked him down. "Don't you dare."

"But it's just a child! They both are!" Nathan hissed.

"You can't go out there, especially while you still look like *that.*"

An anguished nonhuman wail echoed around the cavern. The sound pierced and shuddered through Nathan's core. He snatched himself out of Sagan's grip and lunged out from behind the crates.

Sagan kicked a foot out, entangling Nathan's ankles and sending him face-first into the rocky ground. Nathan rolled and pushed into a kneeling position, but Sagan was ready for him, Diamantium blades in both hands and a fierce, determined scowl on his face.

"You go over there and you'll die."

Nathan scoffed but made no further move, hating the reality of Sagan's words. He could easily take down three—possibly four—of the hunters, but the odds were severely against him, especially against weapons that were designed to stun and incapacitate. He pounded a fist into the ground, the dull thud barely audible over the shrieks and cries of the Veniri child and the hunter. "You expect me to do *nothing?*"

The scowl on Sagan's face faltered. "I expect you to live. I expect you to help me save Violet."

Nathan's neck throbbed with tension; his teeth ached from the severe clench of his jaw.

Violet was in danger. She needed him. He wasn't sure how much time they had before another attempt was made on her life. The text message Sagan had shown him earlier on Matthias's phone blazed into his mind.

*I made a mistake. Killed the wrong girl. Need to leave. Too many cops near Violet.*

Nathan released the tension in his body and hung his head. He needed to find Violet, but being unable to also save the Veniri child tortured him. He didn't fear death, but dying would be futile if he couldn't guarantee the child would be safely returned to his family. Assuming his family was still alive.

The child called out in his language. Begging for his mother, begging for somebody, anybody, to save him.

Nathan squeezed his eyes shut. He hung his head between his arms, his palms pressed flat on the cold ground.

The hunters' success in containing the child was evident in their laughter and cheering. Clinks of chains joined the begging, followed by the sound of something being dragged along the stony floor. Gradually, the cries of the doomed child and the raucous chatter of the hunters faded into a side tunnel, leaving only Nathan's ragged breaths growing louder in his ears.

He shook his head. He hated this. He hated himself. He hated Sagan, a hunter of all things, for showing reason— reason to ensure their own survival, and perhaps even Violet's.

Nathan opened his eyes and stood up. "Lead the way, hunter." The sneer in his voice was noticeable even to himself.

A muscle in Sagan's cheek twitched. He pointed with a dagger. "Put those away first."

Nathan lifted and rotated his arms. "It's funny you're concerned with these when you have a pair yourself." He eyed Sagan's glittering daggers.

"I mean it, slith. Put 'em away."

A corner of Nathan's mouth curled up. "Why not you first?"

Sagan glared with icy ferocity; Nathan's smile widened. He held his palms up, the blades along his forearms in full view, and Sagan watched intently as the blades retracted into his arms.

"Now the rest. Change back to human."

Nathan hesitated for a moment. If he was able to sheath his elbow blades, then perhaps Aphrodite's influence was wearing off. Once again, he tried to haze, and with sweet relief, his body transformed. His crystal shards melted back into his flesh, and his scales rippled back beneath the surface of his smooth skin. He shivered as the cavern's cool air grazed his body, reminding him he was only wearing his boxer briefs.

He resisted the urge to cross his arms to retain body heat. Instead, he pointed to Sagan's daggers. "Your turn."

Sagan hesitated, maybe waiting to see if Nathan was planning to change back, but after a few moments, he put the daggers away.

Nathan sucked in a heavy breath and followed Sagan to the Defender. While the Erathi loaded a few crates into the back of the vehicle, Nathan kept an anxious eye on the tunnel the hunters had disappeared down.

Finally, a black briefcase in hand, Sagan gestured toward the car. "Get in."

\* \* \*

They drove in complete silence for hours.

Sagan sped over dirt roads and ploughed through bushes and creeks. They had yet to pass a town or a road sign indicating their whereabouts. Nathan had tried to keep track of the directions they traveled—maybe there was a chance he could backtrack and attempt to rescue the Veniri child—but it wasn't long before he lost his bearings.

At this stage, Nathan wouldn't put it past the young hunter to purposefully leave him in the dark. Keeping a victim disoriented and hopeless was a typical kidnapper method. But then, Sagan could also be sticking to the back-roads for security reasons, avoiding areas with traffic cameras and witnesses. The matte black Defender wasn't exactly inconspicuous.

He closed his eyes and leaned back on the headrest. His body still thrummed. Whatever the lingering influence of Aphrodite's beams was, they still echoed through every muscle, nerve, and vein. The eerie sensations carved deep into his bones. He winced. How long were these effects going to last?

"I gotta hand it to you for putting up with that father of yours, kid. He's the most sadistic sociopath I've ever met." An echo of Matthias's feral laugh quaked through Nathan's thoughts. "I fail to see what your mother sees in him."

"She's not my mother," barked Sagan.

Nathan's eyes flew open, and he swiveled his attention to the scowling hunter's profile. "What?"

"She's Lyla's mom, *not* mine."

Interesting that he volunteered that bit of information, although judging by the rigid posture and white-knuckled grip on the steering wheel, this was a common misconception Sagan didn't approve of.

Nathan's brow furrowed as he thought back to the investigation of Lyla's murder. Not once had any of the Branstones mentioned Sagan and Lyla were half siblings. How had he missed that?

He clicked his tongue. "So . . . no disputing how much of a sadist your father is then?"

Sagan didn't answer. The silence dragged out, only this time it was a little heavier.

Nathan cleared his throat. "So, what's the plan? After we find Violet, you go back to harvesting me?"

Sagan scoffed. "I need you alive, slith."

When Sagan didn't elaborate, Nathan said, "Don't I get a hint why?" He made a show of tapping his chin. "Hmm . . . is it . . . you've found a client who's willing to pay double for a home butchering?"

No response.

"No? Hmm . . . Ooh! I think I got it. Some bratty hunter's kid wants to hit a real live Veniri with a stick instead of a piñata for his birthday?"

The leather creaked as Sagan adjusted his seat.

"Come on, kid—"

"Stop calling me 'kid,' slith," growled Sagan.

"Sure," replied Nathan, "only if you stop calling me 'slith.' And why do you hunters insist on calling us that, anyway? If it's a reference to snakes, then you're confusing us with the European Veniri. We don't all look the same, you know."

Sagan shot him a glare before veering the vehicle off the dirt road and dodging through the forest. Once they'd reached a thick clump of trees, he turned off the engine.

"Why are you stopping?"

Sagan switched off the headlights, plunging them into darkness. "We're at least a half hour away from the mountain pass, and this is the safest place to stop."

"Then I'll drive."

Sagan let out a derisive snort.

"Just give me a map and I'll get us there."

"Not likely."

The interior light blinked on and off as Sagan opened his door, jumped out, and closed it behind him. Silence rang in Nathan's ears. He wound down his window and leaned his arm on the opening. The nightlife of the woods chirped and twittered within the rustling wind.

The interior light switched back on as the driver's door opened. Sagan held an indistinct bundle of black in his hands. "Here. Put these on."

The bundle landed in Nathan's lap. Without another word, Sagan shut the door, and darkness flooded the car once again.

An amused smile twitched a corner of Nathan's mouth up as he unraveled a long-sleeved shirt and jeans. A few minutes later, he hopped out of the vehicle dressed in the all-black outfit. The clothes were a little tight, but they were better than nothing but boxer briefs.

He found Sagan lying down on one of the side-facing bench seats in the rear of the Defender.

"You may as well make yourself comfortable," said Sagan. "We've got a few hours to kill before daylight."

"I was serious when I said I could drive. We're wasting time. Violet needs us."

"The mountain range isn't far away, and it's too risky to drive it at night. We leave at first light."

Nathan sighed and rubbed his eyes with the heels of his hands. He climbed into the back, dodging the crates and bags, and lay down on the spare seat. The leather upholstery creaked under his weight.

He looked over at Sagan. The young hunter was twirling a dagger in his fingers. Moonbeams streamed through the windows and reflected off the glittering blade, sending rainbow specks dancing around the vehicle.

Nathan was about to close his eyes when Sagan began speaking.

"Do you . . . I mean, I've always wondered . . . can you tell who this belongs to?"

Nathan eyed the Diamantium blade, blinking a few times as he processed the question. He turned away and looked out the window on his side. "You spill your secrets, little hunter, and maybe I'll spill mine."

Venus, the brightest star, twinkled against the inky sky. He felt far from safe, but the planet's celestial glow sparked a peacefulness that spread through his core. He was fortunate to even be looking up at the night sky again. He closed his eyes and breathed in the sweet, earthy air.

"This was hers, you know. Lyla's," continued Sagan, his voice soft. "All she wanted for her birthday was a pair of rollerblades. Not nail polish or hair accessories like every other girl her age. Just rollerblades. And you wanna know what my father got her? This dagger. She didn't care that this was a sign of her family legacy or about the custom handle and emblems. She hated it. But my father hated it even more when I traded my old pair of rollerblades for it. She skated every single day until she was halfway through high school."

He expertly flipped the blade through his fingers, increasing the speed of the disco ball effect around the vehicle. Then, without warning, he caught the dagger, and the flurry of light stilled.

Sagan sat up, and after a moment's hesitation, he held the dagger out to Nathan, handle first. "You should have it."

Nathan's eyebrows shot up. Never in his life had anyone, Veniri or Erathi, presented him with a Diamantium fragment. "Keep your shard of Venus," he said after a few heartbeats. "Keep it to remember your sister."

"But . . . shouldn't it be buried with your people?"

Nathan shook his head. "We don't bury our dead."

"So cremation then?"

"No, we don't do that either."

"Oh. What do you do?"

Nathan was about to reply with a smart-ass comment, but something in Sagan's tone made him hold back. "Why do you want to know?"

Sagan didn't answer.

Nathan cleared his throat, then started talking before he could stop himself. "We don't do things the way you Erathi do. Instead of individual ceremonies, we hold one big ceremony during Venus's inferior conjunction." He paused, expecting Sagan to begin asking questions. When none came, he decided to explain anyway. "The inferior conjunction is when Venus's orbit passes between Earth and the Sun. It happens every nineteen and a half months. Between those times, all of our deceased are stored in . . . I suppose you could call it a tomb of sorts, and they are overlooked by what would be equivalent to priests. Leading up to each inferior conjunction, the deceased are ground up into dust and taken to the ceremony chamber, where the center of the room contains a wind vortex that channels up and out of a hole in the ceiling. Family and friends gather around the vortex as the priests transfer the dust of their loved ones into the whirlwind."

Moments of silence passed. He must be crazy, revealing such a sacred ritual to none other than a hunter. He doubted Sagan could do much damage with the knowledge, especially considering no hunter had ever successfully discovered a Veniri hive—at least, not in this country. Still, exposing that kind of information was pretty stupid. Maybe he'd been holding back his Veniri side for too long, and it was starting to burst out on impulse. If he was honest, it was nice to divulge something true about himself for a change.

Nathan sat up and swiveled to face Sagan, his movement making the leather creak again. "So, what's your plan, kid? Why'd you help me escape?"

"Because I need you to help me rescue Violet."

Nathan shook his head. "You can do that on your own. You didn't need to drag my sorry ass along for your rescue mission. So, what do you need me for?"

Sagan dropped his gaze to the dagger in his hands. The moonlight cast half of his face into black shadow, but the expression on the illuminated half grew fierce. "I knew you'd help me find Violet, and . . . I need you to take me to your *queen*." He spat out the last word as if it tasted bitter.

Nathan was dumbfounded. "Do you have any idea what you're asking? Trust me, it'd be easier to get you face-to-face with the Queen of England. Forget it. Even if I could, I'd rather be a piñata." He paused for a few seconds. "But for curiosity's sake, why do you need me to take you to her?"

The atmosphere in the Defender turned heavy, almost sticky.

"I'm going to kill her."

Nathan threw his head back and laughed, and Sagan's expression turned furious. "I'm serious, slith. I am going to kill her. And you're going to help me."

Nathan stared at the young hunter's half-lit features. "Why me?" he finally asked.

"What do you mean?"

"Well, surely I'm not the only Veniri you've come across recently. You could have snatched any one of us from your father's lair to help you with your suicidal idea of killing the Veniri queen. So, why me?"

Sagan shifted. "Because I was there," he said in a low voice.

"You were where?" A slight pressure began to build in Nathan's chest; he had a pretty good guess what Sagan was about to say.

"I was there, in the forest, the night Lyla was . . . when she was killed. When my sister went missing, I knew something bad had happened to her. And when I couldn't find Violet either . . . By the time I had tracked them down, it was . . . I was too late."

Nathan didn't know how to respond.

"I arrived just as you found Violet, and I saw what you did."

Nathan rubbed the back of his head and barely suppressed a groan.

"Don't worry," said Sagan. "I haven't told anyone about it, especially not my father."

Nathan narrowed his eyes. "Good." He lay back down. He couldn't process this right now. His thoughts were muddled, overlapped with the resurfaced fears and emotions of that night. He closed his eyes and placed his forearm over his face. "Wake me up when it's time to leave."

A few moments of silence passed. Nathan peeked out from under his arm.

Sagan still sat staring at the dagger in his hands.

Nathan took advantage of the darkness to chance a small flick of his tongue, and a wave of flavors engulfed his senses. Sagan's need for vengeance was evident by the burning sensation of chili on Nathan's palate, and it was fueled by his unwavering determination, which had the earthy flavor of dark, dark chocolate. But one flavor captured Nathan's interest the most: the murderous taste of cinnamon. It was rich and black, as if charred on a raging fire.

## DANCING TREES

VIOLET HEAVED HER BAG OF BOOKS ONTO HER SHOULDER AND stood just inside the glass door of the library, watching the sway of the trees silhouetted against the streetlamps. They looked as if they were dancing, caught up in a melody only they could hear.

*Music that only trees can hear?* Violet giggled to herself, imagining trees with ears. Not dainty ones reserved for mythological dryads descended from goddesses of ear envy, but big dopey ones the size of dinner plates that stuck out on either side of their trunks.

Violet sighed. She must be beyond overtired if her mental images had stooped to the level of tree ears. She didn't bother looking at her watch. It was late. Well, actually, it could be considered early. The last member of her study group had left a good half hour before she'd even thought about packing up and heading back to her dorm.

When she'd signed up for this course, she'd assumed she would be spending the majority of her time going on photographic adventures with the class, discussing lens and lighting preferences, color techniques, blah blah blah. But apart from that one shoot with Thane, her assignments had mostly been heavy in theory and research. Currently, the focus was on world events—past, present, and predicted—and the involvement of photographic journalists. This was their time to "learn from the masters" and take note of what worked and what didn't.

So where did aspiring photographers start to "tread in the footsteps of those before them"? Out in the field at public events? Photographic art galleries? A third-world village? Syria? Nope, they started at the library. All the aforementioned were extracurricular and only expected from those with rich parents who wanted to give their darling child's dream a little extra nurturing.

Another sigh escaped her. This internal whining was getting redundant; there was no point sulking over her neglected past. Plus, if she was honest, mentally cataloguing her woes was just a way to delay stepping outside into the cold and trekking all the way to the other side of campus to her dorm room.

She tightened her jacket and adjusted her scarf. For a moment, she was tempted to just curl up on one of the library couches, but all she really wanted was her own bed.

*Pillows. Blankets. Comfy.* Great, now she'd reached that sleep-deprived stage where her thoughts had been reduced to single words. *Come on, Vi, stop procrastinating.*

She swiped her student card to unlock the after-hours security door, then pushed out into the night, snuggling deeper into her scarf as the expected icy gale billowed around her. The rustling canopy of leaves reached a crescendo before dying down to a lull. A few leaf escapees twirled down in a graceful dance to join the rest of the leaf litter on the ground.

She rounded a corner and cut down a narrow path between two buildings, temporarily shielded from the cold breeze. For a few steps, all she heard was the padded sound of her sneakers hitting the pavement. Then came the scuff of a boot and the rattling *click-clack* of a kicked stone. The heavy boots' rhythmic thudding continued to follow along the pavement behind her.

She sucked in a deep breath, trying to shut away the sudden torrent of anxiety. *It's all right, Vi. It's just another student up late like you, making their way back to their dorm.*

She took a premature turn. A few moments later, the same heavy boots did the same.

Her breaths came a little quicker. *Don't panic. It's just a coincidence we're going the same way. It's late, and it's dark. You're freaking out over nothing.*

She took another turn. Again the footsteps followed.

Violet started to shove her trepidation down with more voice-of-reason arguments—until she realized the buildings and gardens around her were unfamiliar. Everything looked different at night. *Crap!*

She picked up her pace, a shudder of adrenaline coursing through her veins. What was she doing? She was going to get even more lost. All she had to do was turn around and back-track to familiar territory.

*Thud. Thud. Thud.*

No way. Backtracking meant coming face-to-face with whoever was following her. And she *was* being followed; she was sure of it. The voice of reason had been locked and barred away, freeing up extra room for panic. She pulled out her switchblade and clutched it to her chest.

Another turn was up ahead, about twenty steps away. She walked faster.

*Thud. Thud. Thud.*

Ten steps to go.

*Thud, thud, thud.*

Was it her imagination, or had the person behind her adjusted their speed as well?

*Thud-thud-thud.*

Two steps. One.

Once around the corner, Violet took off at a sprint. Her bag bounced awkwardly, stabbing a corner of one of her books into her hip with each step, but she ignored the pain and kept running. She gripped her switchblade so tight an edge of the handle cut into her palm.

The thudding behind her turned the corner as well. It sounded farther away than before, but then it picked up speed.

*Thud-thud-thud-thud-thud.*

Violet forced herself to run faster. She flew around another corner, nearly losing her balance from the sudden turn.

All the while, her mind chanted. *Faster.*

Another turn, and her breath hitched. She found herself in an open garden, a few evenly spaced ancient trees lining either side of the path. The next building ahead was about a hundred yards away.

The orchestral sound of the wind and leaves returned, drowning out the thudding boots behind her. Gone was her impression of trees dancing gracefully to their own night-song. They shook with wild force, branches waving in frightful warning of the threat behind her.

Panic squeezed her throat. Her lungs burned with the icy air she dragged in with each breath.

She darted off the path and behind one of the trees, her back against the trunk, and strained to hear the heavy boots. The wind had died down. Her heavy breathing was loud in her ears, and her hands flew to her mouth, the switchblade sandwiched between them. With all her might, she forced herself to silence her panting, even as her heart bashed against her ribcage. Her eyes darted around as she analyzed every sound.

*Rustle. Whoosh. Crick.*

*Thud . . . Thud . . .*

The thudding stopped.

She held her breath. Lowering her hands from her mouth, she gripped the handle of the switchblade in both hands. Her thumb found the button and pressed.

*Shnik.*

Gravel ground, as if a boot was pivoting to change direction. She bit her lip, praying the direction was away from her.

Then she noticed a glowing light from between the cracks of her fingers. *What the . . . ?*

The light was coming from one of the black gemstones embedded in the switchblade's handle. But it was no longer black. It was glowing a vibrant teal.

The thudding had stopped. The person must be taking precautions, silencing their steps. The slight scuff of a boot farther down the path was all that indicated the person was moving at all.

With each passing moment, the gemstone shone brighter. *What kind of switchblade did Nathan give me?* Violet hid the switchblade under the ends of her scarf, fearful the light was going to give her away.

A slow crunch of gravel came from behind the tree. Too close. Far too close.

*Crack!*

The sudden sound pierced through the night, followed by chatting voices. Students were spilling out from one of the nearby building's wooden doors, which had smacked hard into the brick wall behind it. Relief washed over Violet like a tidal wave as she recognized the entrance to her dormitory building.

A fresh pulse of adrenaline flooded her body. She would have to leave the sanctuary of her hiding spot to run across the grass and reach her dorm.

*On the count of three.*

A slight scuff. Closer again. She hardly heard it over the chatter of more students swarming out into the night.

*One—*

A shrill, piercing series of beeps cut into her eardrums as a cellphone behind her rang. A masculine voice hissed a curse—not loudly enough for Violet to decipher who it was, but she wasn't going to stick around to wait for more clues.

She pushed off the tree and sprinted.

The ringtone was cut off. Either the call was answered, or the phone was switched to silent. Violet didn't care which. She focused all her attention on the door of her dormitory building.

*Faster!*

Only a few steps to go. She could have cried with relief as she flew through a gap in the students, ignoring their confused expressions.

Up the staircase. Up to the floor of her dorm room. Once on the landing, she finally allowed herself to pause and catch her breath, heaving enormous gasps as the burning in her chest and legs subsided.

When she at last stepped out into the hallway, it was her turn to be confused.

Instead of the area being deserted, as it normally would be at that time of night, all the doors were open, and a crowd of students were huddling about halfway down the hall. Violet racked her brain. Had she missed the memo for a social? By the looks of everybody's attire, it must be some kind of pajama party.

She weaved her way through the crowd, no one paying

her much attention. The throng of people was condensed around one door in particular. Her door.

The closer Violet got, the more her chest tightened. She picked up the pace, elbowing her way through the barricade of bodies until she had a full view of what had captured all her classmates' attention.

A hand flew to her mouth. *No! Oh, please, no!*

Several paramedics and police officers, the dorm supervisor, and the dean were gathered in a tight knot in the entryway of Violet's room. One of the police officers was trying to clear a path through the crowded students, making way for a paramedic wheeling a stretcher.

On top of the stretcher was a zipped-up body bag.

A roar in Violet's ears drowned out the chatter and noise in the hallway. Blotches of white light speckled her vision, and a black fog clouded her periphery.

*Lyla . . .*

Just as her body was about to give way, someone slammed into her, and steady arms wrapped around her shoulders. "Violet, there you are."

Violet blinked, recognizing the deep voice. "Thane?" She staggered but managed to steady herself against him. "Thane, what are you doing here?"

"Violet!" exclaimed a female voice. Autumn and Gus pushed their way through the crowd.

Thane released her, but his hand trailed down her arm and took hold of her hand.

The cousins rushed in to envelop her in a group hug. Autumn was shuddering, but Gus stood solid, almost rigid.

"Where the hell have you been? You had me worried sick." He looked angry, but Violet could feel the concern in the tight grip of his hand on her shoulder.

Both Autumn and Gus were standing before her. Alive. Autumn's cheeks were stained with two black trails of mascara. She was in a faded band T-shirt, the one she usually slept in, and her dreadlocks were sticking out in uncontrolled directions.

Violet opened her mouth, attempting and failing to articulate any of the questions spinning through her confused mind. She looked beyond their faces, in the direction the stretcher had been escorted. The only word she could form was "Who?"

Autumn burst into tears, and Gus's expression turned pained.

"He killed her, Violet. She's dead." Autumn paused, taking in a few hiccupy breaths. "He killed Bessie."

"What?" Violet's eyes grew wide. "No . . ."

Not Bessie, the girl with the Irish lilt who could laugh and party like no other. The avid gamer and Hello Kitty enthusiast. The bubbling brunette who was a key member of Violet's little group of college friends.

*This can't be happening. This can't be real. Why? How?*

Through her tears, Autumn plunged into a rambling story of how Bessie had come over to study and, after a few hours, fallen asleep on Violet's bed. "It was late, and you hadn't come back yet, so I didn't think it was a big deal. So I let her sleep because I knew how exhausted she was, and I figured you wouldn't care. And then I fell asleep—" Autumn took a few ragged breaths, then bit into her fist, her eyes clenched shut.

Gus put an arm around her shoulders.

"And then I woke up," continued Autumn, "and . . . and . . . he was there."

"Who was it?" They all turned at Thane's question. He was still holding Violet's hand, his warm closeness providing a slight comfort.

Autumn shook her head, her expression anguished. "It was dark and I didn't see." She grasped Violet's upper arms.

"But, Violet, he said *your* name. Right before he . . . right before Bessie—"

With her free hand, Violet pulled Autumn into another tight hug as her friend shook with a new onslaught of sobs.

Thane lay a hand on Autumn's quaking back, but his attention was trained on Violet. His strong hand gripped hers tighter.

## 18

## VENUS DIMPLES

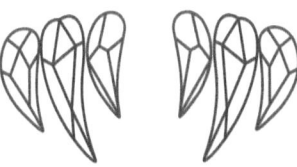

A FEW SUNBEAMS PIERCED THE DARKENED SKY. THE MORNING star shone in its dazzling glory, casting subtle beams through the windows of the Defender.

Nathan rolled onto his side for what might have been the hundredth time in who knows how many hours. He should have fallen asleep easily based on how exhausted he was from almost being harvested and enduring the evil onslaught of Aphrodite's beams, but his mind was wide awake. Along with the usual worries, concerns, and suppressed memories of his past, his small conversation with Sagan was also getting its fair share of replays.

"*. . . I saw what you did.*"

Nathan shifted onto his back. The memory of the night he first met Violet Chambers returned with vivid clarity.

\* \* \*

*Nathan hung his head, covering his face with his hand and wearily rubbing his temples. He reached down to her neck to look for a pulse; a faint beat tapped against his fingers. With an instinctive* flick of his tongue, he latched on to Violet's essence, and his eyes grew wide.

How was this possible?

An Erathi's soul-scent changed over the course of their childhood and puberty. It could be frustrating for the Veniri, but for the Erathi, the shifting scent was a benefit, especially if they happened to find themselves in a situation where a Veniri was tracking them. Violet's missing person's file stated she was sixteen, not yet fully matured, but her pubescence was already fading, revealing hints of her permanent soul-scent underneath—a scent that was eerily familiar.

A memory of a woman from his past snapped through his mind.

He lashed out his tongue again, and Violet's essence reignited on his palate. His insides turned to granite. There was no mistaking it. The scents were almost identical.

Violet was definitely her daughter.

A low groan cut through the night, but it didn't come from Violet. Nathan shone his flashlight in the direction of the man in the hoodie lying nearby, who had begun stirring. A teal blotch gleamed against the dark fabric of his torso. Based on the location, the wound didn't appear fatal.

The face of the Veniri in human form rolled into view. Cold, piercing eyes glimmered in the beam of Nathan's flashlight.

With slow, calculated movements, Nathan stepped away from Violet. A torturous burn sizzled in his arms as his crystalline blades sliced from his elbows.

The Veniri's features hardened into a menacing glare, which Nathan returned with his own scowl. He hated everything about why this Veniri was far away from the safety of his hive, why he'd risked crossing other shifters' territories and risked hunters picking up his trail. He hated that dozens of human families would be contacting the police and would spend countless hours searching for their missing teenage daughters.

He clenched his fists. What he hated most was that he'd once been a part of these kidnappings of innocent human girls. Killing this Veniri scum wouldn't right his own wrongs or the wrongs his race had inflicted, but it would be a start.

The Veniri lashed out his forked tongue.

Nathan grinned. He knew exactly what the Veniri was tasting; rhubarb for Nathan's initial surprise, and chalk laced with cider vinegar for his long-lived resentment and grief. But the most offensive flavor would be cinnamon; there was no way he was going to let this Veniri live.

The Veniri's eyes darted from Nathan to a small Diamantium dagger by Violet's hand. The blade was smeared with luminescent blue.

Before the Veniri could act, Nathan swooped and plunged one of his crystal elbow shards into his victim's neck. A startled gasp escaped the Veniri right before his vocal cords were severed.

Nathan shunted back out of reach of the Veniri's own elbow blades.

The doomed shifter clutched his throat, and his eyes shot skyward in panic and desperation. His face shifted as his human features hazed into Veniri. Flexing scales of iridescent teal rippled to the surface of the exposed skin of his face, neck, and hands, and small hornlike crystals lined his eye sockets and cheekbones, glittering under the moonlight. Fabric tore as crystalline spires sliced through the hoodie and jeans.

Nathan scoffed. His aim had been true; the wound was fatal. The healing energy of Venus's beams would be ineffective in healing him. The useless creature was only prolonging his excruciating and inevitable end.

The Veniri looked back at Nathan, reaching toward him with a gurgled plea.

Nathan glared. The scum deserved far worse. He turned his back, not bothering to watch the creature's final moments. Instead, he focused on the frail girl among the leaf litter.

He shook his head, mentally sifting through the contents of her *case file. This kid had already been through hell within the foster system, and now she'd been dragged into a different hell by Veniri kidnappers. If she survived this, she'd never be able to explain who or what she'd seen. Even if she could, and even if people believed her story, it would bring even more danger, not only to her world but also to his.*

*Regardless, her scent would forever make her a target. The fact that she'd been constantly shuffled around in the Erathi foster system, as well as her unstable childhood scent, had kept his people from discovering her so far. But Violet's mature essence would soon become a beacon. Who else knew of her existence? Did the queen know?*

*He narrowed his eyes. He definitely couldn't let the queen, or anyone else, track Violet. There was too much at stake.*

*He pressed the tip of his elbow blade against Violet's flesh, right above her windpipe. This was likely the most mercy anyone had ever shown her. He would not only end her misery but also keep her away from whatever tortures would be inflicted upon her if she were caught again.*

*Then a thought crossed his mind.*

*What if he shielded Violet? His father had done it.*

*Nathan flexed his fingers. The procedure would be difficult, and he only knew the theory from what his father had explained to him long ago.*

"Yes, it is possible to shield an Erathi from being soul-tracked. The poison glands around our heart produce a protein just for that purpose, believe it or not. If one were to transplant two glands into an Erathi host, the small amount of poison wouldn't harm them. They might get symptoms of what the Erathi call a 'cold,' but once their immune system clears away the poison, the glands will still produce the protein to shield them."

*Nathan flicked a glance back toward the shack. So far, no one had followed him out, but he needed to act fast. A spike of adren-*

*aline shot through his body at the thought of what he was about to do. This was not going to be pleasant for either of them.*

*He threw off his jacket and removed his shirt. Raising his face to the heavens, he hazed, making sure the change was isolated to his hips up; he'd rather avoid his leg shards slicing through his pants. He selected a shard on his torso and hacked it off with an elbow blade, then knelt down and carefully rolled Violet onto her front.*

*A pang of guilt stabbed through his chest. This plan was really risky, not to mention highly invasive, but the alternative of her being killed or caught was much worse.*

*He lifted the hem of Violet's shirt, uncovering the two Venus dimples on her lower back. Following his father's instructions, he used the hacked shard to gouge a hole in the center of each dimple. Liquid crimson pooled on either side of her spine, then streamed down her hips. Violet stirred a little but, to Nathan's relief, didn't regain consciousness.*

*He sped up his actions, praying she wouldn't wake up or lose too much blood. He needed to get this done before he lost his nerve.*

*After cleaning the broken shard on his shirt, he placed the tip at the base of his ribs on his left side. He heaved a few quick breaths, gritted his teeth, and—before he could back out—sliced into his hide. Teal blood seeped down his torso as he dragged the shard through his flesh, carving out a gash several inches long. With an agonized grunt, he dug his fingers into the wound.*

*Every logical part of his mind screamed at him to stop, but he pushed his fingers farther, up along the inside of his ribs. After a few moments, his fingertips reached what he needed. Going by feel and with as much care as he could muster, he removed two small glands from near his heart.*

*Remembering the rest of what his father had told him, Nathan transplanted the glands into each of Violet's dimples.*

*Once again, he cleaned the shard on his shirt, then turned his focus to Venus. The Venusian beams were invisible to his human eyes, but with the aid of his Veniri inner eyelids, he could perceive* them easily. He held the shard under one of the beams and fiddled for a moment with the angle. Much like a sunbeam caught in a magnifying glass, the Venusian beam condensed into a small dot of light, which Nathan focused onto each of Violet's wounds. She moaned and shifted as her flesh began to sizzle, but he didn't stop until both wounds were cauterized shut.

He needed to seal this procedure with a mind block, not just for her safety but also to erase the horrors she'd witnessed over the past few days. His focus returned to Venus, and he raised his hands, circling them within a beam until the subtle light became tangible in his hands, fluffy like cotton candy. He gathered what he could into a loose ball and placed it over Violet's head. Her whimpers and cries of pain became more anguished as the bundle glowed a vibrant blue.

After a few heartbeats, Violet's whimpering ceased and her body relaxed.

With a sigh, Nathan removed the cottony beam from her mind and released it into the air, where it disintegrated and fused into another nearby beam of celestial light. He retrieved the Diamantium spike, stood up, and with his free hand, pinched the gash beneath his ribs. To cauterize his own wound, he'd need to make sure—

"Nathan? Is that you?"

He froze, his skin crawling at the familiar, delicate voice.

"Oh, it is you!" A feminine giggle followed, like raindrops on a crystal cup.

He turned, making an immense effort to prevent the raging turmoil from showing on his face.

A smoky blue apparition hovered over the Veniri on the ground, its vaporous wisps flowing and undulating into the shape of Idalia, queen of the Veniri, in human form. Her goddess-like appearance was enhanced by her avant-garde crown and stunning dress molded to defy gravity around her neck and shoulders. The neckline plunged almost to her navel.

Horror pinched Nathan's throat and chest. Her appearance could not have come at a worse time. He cursed himself for not ending the Veniri's life swiftly; he should have foreseen this possibility.

Nathan glanced at the Veniri male on the ground, the source of the phantasm. He still clutched at his throat, his body heaving in its desperate attempt at retaining life. Eyes wider than ever, the creature clutched in vain at the wisp above him. He may as well have tried grasping a tendril of smoke.

Idalia giggled and clapped her hands, ignoring the dying Veniri. "My dear Nathan. I thought I would never see you again. You've been truly wicked to me."

Nathan gritted his teeth at the irony of her choice of words.

She reached out her hand as if she expected him, her loyal servant, to kiss it. His lip curled into a sneer. She knew full well he couldn't touch her in the form she was in, but that wasn't the reason he didn't make a move. He remained still as a statue, his crystal shard suspended over the gash he was still pinching closed.

A hardness crossed her features. She scanned the scene, her gaze alternating between Nathan's wound and Violet's back, and raised a delicate eyebrow. Her expression dripped triumph and curiosity as she pointed at Violet. "Nathan, my sweet, who is that?" she asked, her tone light yet commanding.

Nathan didn't, couldn't answer. It was too late to hide what he'd done. Idalia's wisp glided closer to study Violet's unconscious face.

"Whoever she is, she's none of your concern," said Nathan.

He didn't miss the slight twitch at the corner of Idalia's mouth before her features dropped into a dramatic pout. "You're not still sulking over our last encounter, are you?"

Nathan ignored the question. He turned his back and focused on angling the shard to concentrate a Venusian beam, on searing his wound shut. He winced and bit back his cry of pain at the sizzling burn.

"Nathan, Nathan, Nathan. What are you doing to yourself?"

*Nathan scoffed. Once his gash was sealed, he pocketed the crystal shard and reached down for his shirt, cursing himself as he gave in to temptation and glanced back at the figure in the blue mist.*

*"Come home, my sweet, and I'll have my personal physician tend to you." Her words rolled over him like honey.*

*He glared at her. "And then what? Once I'm healed and healthy, you'll have me prepped for execution? I bet your cousin Kronan would eagerly volunteer to remove all my shards and my head. How is that coward, by the way? Make sure you send him my ill will."*

*She tilted her head back and laughed. "Oh, you are holding a grudge. What if I said I missed you and wanted you back?"*

*"I'd say, 'What's the catch?'"*

*Her expression turned to mock hurt. "You would question my sincerity?" She put a hand on her hip. "Are you not yearning to come home? To have everything back to the way it was?"*

*Nathan didn't answer straightaway. He knew this tactic of hers. She wasn't concerned with what he wanted; she was reminding him of what he'd once had. She was toying with him, like a child toys with an insect right before they rip off its wings.*

*"Back to the way it was?" Nathan shook his head. If he was honest with himself, yes, a part of him did miss the hive.*

*A corner of Idalia's mouth twitched up in triumph. "Why don't you tell me where you are, and I'll—" Her brows suddenly drew together, and her gaze locked on Violet.*

*Nathan's insides clenched. Idalia's wispy blue face looked as if she'd just discovered a deep, dark secret. Her eyes narrowed. "Who is she?" Steel had replaced all evidence of the previous sweetness in her tone.*

*"None of your concern."*

*Idalia turned her severe expression on Nathan.*

*She'd figured it out. Either Idalia had recognized Violet's features, or catching Nathan shielding a young girl was enough for* her to piece together the puzzle. The latter was more likely. Idalia's manipulative intellect was second to none.

"If that is who I'm guessing it is, then I demand you kill her and bring her to me." She enunciated every word with authoritative power.

"No," said Nathan.

"I command you to—"

"No," repeated Nathan with his own edge of authority. "I am no longer your plaything to command."

Idalia's eyes blazed. "What? You would allow the spawn of one of those rebel slaves to remain alive—those slaves who persist in threatening and terrorizing our existence?"

"And what about us? What about what we've done?" Nathan gestured to Violet. "How many more Erathi have we terrorized? We have kidnapped thousands of innocent Erathi girls and forced them into slavery. We shouldn't—"

Idalia threw her head back in a condescending laugh. "You speak as if it's something I choose to do. Tell me, my sweet, what do you propose as an alternative? Do you want our race to die out? Hmm? In our hive alone, I am the last female to have been born in almost fifty years. We need these female slaves to breed—"

Nathan growled. "Do you seriously think I still believe that? Have you forgotten who you're talking to, or is there someone in your chamber with you that you need to keep spinning these lies?"

A few moments passed in which the queen's posture and expression turned statuesque.

"Kill the girl," she said. "Remove the glands and bring her to me, and I will restore your honor. By my side."

His chest heaved as the weight of her last three words barreled into him. He had disgraced his family and his people. He had disgraced her. There was no way he could ever return. How could she offer such a thing? Allow him to return, not just alive but—

"By my side."

*Nathan almost crumpled to his knees. He had lived his entire life to hear her say those words.*

*Instead, he shrugged on his shirt, cringing a little when the movement tugged at his injury, and looked up at her. Her features were serene, as if she had just woken from a peaceful sleep. He knew that expression, had seen it countless times when she was scheming for a coveted prize. Or announcing an execution.*

*"I would rather die," he spat.*

*Her expression sharpened; the hard edge in her eyes promised murder.*

*Nathan's ingrained logic screamed at him to apologize, yet something gave him the confidence to continue. Maybe it was his festering hate and resentment, or maybe it was the knowledge that a blue wisp couldn't punish him for the blatant disrespect. "To answer your question, no, I don't want our race to die out." He stabbed a finger at her. "I only want you to die. I wish for nothing more than your severed head to be mounted on my wall."*

*All expression fled Idalia's beautiful face, and for a few excruciating heartbeats, the slight breeze in the trees and the Veniri's dying gurgle were the only sounds. If luck was on Nathan's side, death would finally take the Veniri and end all communication with Idalia.*

*"Kill that girl." Her face twisted with fury. "If you don't do as I demand, I will double your death price and end your pitiful existence."*

*He chuckled deep in his throat. "Don't flatter yourself. You'd have to find me first." He did up his last button and rolled his sleeves up above his elbows.*

*"Turn your back on me and I will not only hunt you down but destroy every last thing on this god-awful earth that you hold dear."*

*Nathan's heart hammered in his chest. He sneered. "There's nothing left for you to destroy."*

*The phantasm drifted closer until it was a mere inch from his* face. "You are mine, Nathan. I will break you." The vehemence in her promise was tangible and sticky.

For several moments, Nathan stared into Idalia's eyes. Then when he couldn't take it any longer, he walked through the blue mist and, with a swipe of his elbow blade, cleaved off the dying Veniri's head.

The queen's furious shriek was instantly silenced as her apparition effervesced into nothing.

## 19

## BLOOD, BREATH, AND . . . BONES?

Violet adjusted her hold on her suitcase as Thane unlocked the door and held it open for her.

"Thanks so much for doing this," she said, stepping into his apartment.

"It's no problem."

She placed her suitcase on the floor next to the three-seater sofa. The lounge and dining room were adjoined, small but cozy. A kitchen lined the apartment wall to the right, and an island with a sink divided the room. At the end of the kitchen and dining area were floor-to-ceiling glass doors that opened onto a small balcony.

Thane picked up her suitcase. "Your bed's through here."

She followed him into a room with a double bed, an en suite bathroom, and a small walk-in closet. A desk at the end of the room overlooked the balcony view through more floor-to-ceiling windows.

Thane set her suitcase down on the bed. "It's not much," he said with a slight wince.

"This is great. I'm just sorry for imposing."

"No, not at all." Thane waved one hand. "You're welcome

to stay as long as you need. I think it's great your college sent you guys home to recover." He shook his head. "Poor Autumn."

"Yeah, I can't imagine being her right now. At least she has Gus with her." Violet grimaced. "And Bessie. I can't believe that she's . . . she . . ." There was no good way to end that sentence. Hastily wiping away her welling tears, she unhitched her camera from around her neck and placed it on the bed before pulling out her phone to check for messages.

*We're about to get on the plane. Autumn's still a mess. She'll be better when she sees her mom.*

*Did Nathan get back to you yet?*

"Anything?" asked Thane.

"Just Gus checking in. Still nothing from Nathan." She rubbed the heel of her palm on her forehead. "Look, I really appreciate you allowing me to stay here, but maybe I should just drive back to town and let myself in at Nathan's place. I'm sure he won't mind."

Thane's nose crinkled. "I'm gonna be honest, I don't like the idea of you driving all that way by yourself right now. It'll be dark soon, and you've had a rough day with the cops and meetings with the dean and all. How about you take it easy? Rest up. Get this crappy day over with and start fresh tomorrow."

After a short pause, Violet nodded. "Okay, sounds great."

"Great." He gave her a reassuring smile and gestured around the one-bedroom apartment. "There are spare towels in that cupboard and blankets if you get cold. The TV remote's over there, and help yourself to anything in the kitchen."

"Thanks, but you know, I'm more than happy to sleep on the sofa. I don't want to disrupt your life. I know you work from home, so I promise to get out of your hair as soon as possible."

Thane held up both hands and gave a sharp shake of his head. "If there's anything my mother taught me, it's how to treat a lady right. The bed is all yours. I insist."

Violet opened her mouth to object, but instead, she relented. "Okay. Thanks."

"Don't mention it. How about I put the kettle on and order us some dinner?" He glided into the kitchen and rummaged through some cabinets.

Violet followed him out of the bedroom, weaved through the living area, and stepped out the glass door. The balcony overlooked the apartment complex and the city beyond. The late afternoon sun dipped close to the skyline, and a subtle orange had begun to encroach on the blue sky.

She adjusted her stance against the balustrade; the switchblade in her jeans pocket dug into her thigh. Reflexively, she laid her hand on it, suddenly hit by a flood of anxiety and doubts. She did a mental check of her surroundings. Only one way in and one way out. Unless . . . She looked over the edge of the balcony and judged the distance to the ground below.

She blanched. What the hell was she doing? She wasn't in any danger. She was with Thane.

But still . . .

She shot a quick glance at him. A few weeks ago she would have assessed Thane's apartment the moment she walked in, checking for exits and orchestrating a potential plan for escape. But lately she'd been letting her guard down, especially when it came to Thane.

A few interactions at the coffee shop and one date didn't mean she knew the guy all that well.

*Stop it. I have nothing to worry about.* Honestly, she was grateful Thane had offered her a place to stay. He didn't know her all that well either and didn't have to open up his home to her.

And even if she wanted to, she couldn't go back to her dorm room. The fact that her bed—

Violet shuddered, not wanting to continue that train of thought.

She sighed. What she needed was to focus on something else for a little while. Returning to the bedroom, she retrieved her camera from her small pile of belongings and took it back out to the balcony. Twilight was starting to work its magic as a few stars twinkled into existence.

"I see you're taking advantage of my view," said Thane, stepping out to join her.

"Yeah, that's one way of putting it." She peered through the viewfinder of her camera and took a few shots. His shoulder grazed hers when he leaned on the balustrade.

Violet's cheeks flushed.

They stood for a moment in silence, taking in the view of the skyscrapers with their backdrop of indigo, violet, pink, and burning reds, the final remnants of the setting sun.

The familiar scent of Thane's earthy aftershave—sandalwood, cedar, and peppermint—drifted in the air. Violet bit her lip. Her heart pounded, and memories of working together on the photography assignment raced through her mind.

"The place is a matchbox, but you have to admit the view is spectacular," said Thane, cutting into her thoughts. He leaned against her and pointed. "See that bright star over there?"

Violet followed the direction of his finger.

"It's not actually a star," he continued. "That's Venus."

"Really?" said Violet.

"And that one there"—he pointed to another star—"that's Mars. And that one over there is Jupiter. Aaaaand . . ." He scanned up and around. "Hmm, it doesn't look like Saturn is visible tonight."

"Are you an astronomy nerd or something? Am I going to find a telescope somewhere around here?"

Thane chuckled. "Sadly, no telescope. It's just something my mom taught me when I was a kid. Looking at the night sky was one of our things."

"Your mom sounds amazing. I'd like to meet her one day."

"She . . . um . . ." Thane dropped his gaze; his knuckles on the balustrade turned white. "She passed away."

Violet sucked in a breath. "Oh, Thane. I'm really sorry to hear that."

He gave a half shrug. "Thanks, but I'm sure she's in a better place."

"Still," said Violet, "I bet she misses you."

He looked down at her. The golden flecks in his eyes glimmered.

Violet's heart skipped a beat.

He edged closer, reaching out a hand to lay his palm on her cheek. His fingers laced into her hair, and his thumb stroked her cheekbone, her lips, her chin. Shivers ran down Violet's spine and up her neck. Her chest fluttered and her knees grew weak.

"You are so beautiful," he whispered. "Tell me this isn't a dream."

"If it's a dream, it's definitely not mine," she said.

"How do you know for sure?"

"Because . . ." She hesitated, her body trembling again as his thumb slid across her bottom lip. "It's not my dream because I don't feel scared."

The hand on her cheek froze. Thane's gaze sharpened,

and the molten gold began to cool. "Scared? As in, nightmares?"

Violet's cheeks grew warm. "No, more like just the one nightmare."

His brow creased. "What do you mean?"

"I just have this one nightmare that I've had for a few years. It's . . ." She winced. "Actually, never mind. It's stupid. A girl from college has been murdered, and here I am complaining about my own issues."

She shook her head and tried to turn back to the cityscape, but his hand on her cheek wouldn't allow her to turn away.

"Look at me, Violet." He angled her face so she had no choice but to look at him. "I want you to know that you don't have to be afraid anymore. I'm here for you, and I will . . . I'll . . ." It was his turn to look away. A series of emotions flickered over his face too quick for Violet to decipher.

After a moment's hesitation, he locked eyes with her. He took hold of her hands and clutched them to his chest. "Violet, will you accept my steadfast protection?"

Violet blinked a few times, and her mouth fell slightly open. "Umm . . ."

The gold in his eyes burned fierce.

This conversation had taken an intense turn. Any sane person would be running for the hills by now, but the words *steadfast* and *protection* had grabbed her. From her own mother abandoning her at the hospital to every lowlife foster parent and burned-out social worker abusing and ignoring her, not one person in her life had been willing to remain "steadfast."

"Yes?" she replied uncertainly. What if Thane's question wasn't as sincere as she hoped?

"Then I pledge my soul to you. My flesh is your flesh. My

breath is your breath. My blood is your blood. My bones are your bones."

Violet's eyes widened as he spoke. His tone was rigid and formal but filled with a deep underlying passion. Was she supposed to respond with the same type of formality? "Is that, like, a poem or a quote from a movie or something?"

A corner of Thane's mouth twitched up, and his posture relaxed a little. "Yeah, something like that." He let out a nervous laugh and took a step back. "I'm sorry. That was totally weird."

Violet immediately regretted her awkward reaction. "No. It wasn't weird. It was . . . um . . ."

A whistle came from the kitchen, announcing the kettle was done boiling. "Oh no," said Thane, running a hand through his hair. "I've just realized, I don't have any chai." He heaved a dramatic sigh.

Violet placed a hand on her hip and shook her head. "That's it. I'm leaving. How do you expect me to stay here without any chai?"

"If you like, I can duck down to the store and get some."

Violet waved a hand. "No it's fine. I'll just pretend I'm normal and have a coffee like everybody else."

"If coffee makes you normal, then I don't think I'm drinking enough of it."

Violet leaned against the balustrade and laughed, glad the mood was no longer uncomfortable.

A bell chimed, and they turned their attention to the front door. "That's probably dinner," said Thane.

They made easy small talk as they ate, much like the conversations during their meetups at the café. The aromas of spicy red curry, tender duck, crunchy bamboo shoots, and moreish coconut and turmeric rice had Violet's olfactory senses and taste buds singing. After they'd eaten, Violet helped Thane clear the table.

She leaned on the island as he rinsed the dishes under the tap. The muscles in Thane's arms flexed as he rotated a plate under the stream of water, his cotton button-up shirt rippling with the movement. The top two buttons were undone, and Violet's gaze fixed on the small exposed patch of skin. Her heart began to pound as she recalled the photo shoot—the sculpted form of his bare shoulders, chest, and abdomen.

Her eyes trailed up his neck, chin, and then to his mouth as she remembered the taste of his lips on hers, his hands pressing on her back, her legs—

"I think I can feel it again," said Thane.

Violet blanched. "Um . . . what?"

He turned the tap off and grabbed a towel, dragging out the silence as he dried his hands. "I can feel you looking at me."

Violet's cheeks burned, and yet she couldn't stop herself from shooting another glance at his mouth.

Thane's eyes glinted with amusement, and his mouth twisted into a half smirk.

"Oh no." Violet's hands flew to her face. She turned away with an embarrassed whimper.

Thane chuckled. "Violet, don't. It's okay." He took hold of her shoulders and pivoted her back to face him. He gently tried to pull her hands from her eyes, but she held firm. "Violet, let go."

She gave a sharp shake of her head. "No, I can't."

"Violet." His voice was low, almost a whisper. "Look at me."

It wasn't a command, or even a plea, but an invitation. He was asking her to trust him. Whatever she decided to do next was her choice, and he would respect it.

After a few heartbeats, she allowed him to remove her hands, but she kept her eyes shut, not yet ready to look at him. His warm palms rested on her cheeks. With delicate strokes, his thumbs brushed back and forth across her eyelids, each touch easing the weight of her humiliation. Finally, she had enough courage to open her eyes.

Her gaze met deep brown irises, flecked with gold. Glowing lights like little fireflies hovered close by.

She sucked in a breath. "The lights are back."

Thane kept his hands on her face as his eyes tracked the tiny drifting lights. "I still don't know what they are."

"Have you seen them since . . . you know, since the other day?"

He shook his head. "No. They only seem to appear when I'm . . ." He returned his attention to her. ". . . when I'm with you." The golden flecks in his eyes glowed brighter just as the dancing lights in her periphery became more radiant. He heaved a deep breath. "Violet, I . . . I know you've had a rough day, and I don't want you to feel like I'm taking advantage of you, so it's okay to say no. I just . . . can I . . . kiss you?"

Her eyebrows inched up. The last time they'd kissed he hadn't asked her permission; there was no need.

Instead of saying anything, she raised up on her toes and pressed her lips to his. Every trace of embarrassment and uncertainty melted away as she wrapped her arms around his waist.

His response was instantaneous. He took a step closer—eliminating the gap between them—and cupped one hand around the back of her neck. Shivers ran up her spine as he deepened the kiss. His tongue traced her bottom lip, then the top, before reaching inside to find her own tongue.

Violet moaned and her knees buckled. She leaned into him, clutching at the fabric of his shirt as his hands trailed down her back. He took hold of her waist and lifted her onto the island, and she eagerly hugged her legs around his hips. Her skin tingled where his lips brushed against her cheek, teased along her jaw. She tilted her head and arched back, inviting him farther down. The feather kisses traced her collarbone, lingered at the hollow of her neck, followed an achingly slow path back up to her throat.

Violet tangled her fingers in Thane's hair as his lips found hers again. The scent of sandalwood, cedar, and mint engulfed her with each breath. His defined muscles were evident even through the barrier of his shirt, and she ran her hands over his chest until she found and unhitched a button. She moved on to the next, and then the next, inch by inch revealing his toned body. Their kiss grew more fervent as she explored his perfect contours.

He reached under the hem of her shirt, and shivers raced along her spine as he stroked his hands over her ribs and back. He paused when he reached her bra strap, resting his forehead against hers, his eyes closed. His heavy breaths mingled with her own. For a few heartbeats, he just held her.

"What's wrong?" Violet asked.

"Nothing's wrong. Everything's perfect." He took a few more breaths before continuing. "I just . . . I want to make sure . . . I don't . . . want to do anything you don't want to do."

"I want what you want," she said after a few ragged pants. "I want you."

"Are you sure?"

She placed her hands on his cheeks and stroked his closed eyelids, just as he'd done to her moments ago. "I'm sure."

He smiled. When he opened his eyes, they were more golden than brown. He lifted her from the bench and carried her into the bedroom, leaving a trail of dazzling lights behind them.

* * *

A gentle caress against Violet's cheek brought her out of the realm of sleep. It continued over her jaw and lips, up over her cheekbone and brow, then down her nose. The light touch feathered over the lashes of one closed eye and then over the other.

*Thane.*

At the thought of his name, her soul sang with an echo of last night's euphoria.

His fingers brushed over her lips, then pulled away all too soon. She opened her eyes just as Thane shifted off the bed and headed into the en suite, closing the door behind him. A few seconds later the shower turned on.

Violet rolled onto her back and stared at the ceiling, her fingers retracing Thane's gentle caress over her lips. She smiled. The memories of last night lingered against her skin: the feel of his hands, his mouth, his body. What it had been like to fall asleep locked in his embrace.

She'd never expected to experience such a profound connection—with *anyone*.

Her whole life had proven she couldn't trust anyone but herself, especially not at the level an intimate relationship required. Long ago, she'd decided love wasn't for her. It only ever exposed your heart to abuse, betrayal, and deep, deep loss, as it did for every bickering foster parent who couldn't figure out how to love their own flesh and blood, let alone an orphan left at their doorstep by child services.

But Thane was different.

He knew how to reach her, on her level. To unravel her layer by layer, exposing feelings, dreams, and desires she'd never known. With him, she felt . . . complete. How was that even possible for someone as broken as her?

Her brow creased. Clearly there were a lot of things she had yet to understand about herself, about Thane and this relationship with him. She still didn't know what to think about what he'd said on the balcony. What was with that pledging stuff—blood and breath and . . . *bones*? It was a little weird, and yet it was the most sincerely anyone had ever spoken to her.

A sudden stab of grief pierced through her thoughts, followed by a rush of guilt. *Bessie.* Her eyes squinted shut. Her friend had been killed just over twenty-four hours ago, and here she was having the time of her life with Thane.

*No.* She couldn't stand to dwell on that. Not yet.

Hissing out a sigh, she flopped onto her belly and snuggled closer into the pillows. A smudge of makeup stained the pristine white pillowcase in front of her face. With a frown, she propped her head up to get a better look. *Damn it!* It hadn't even crossed her mind to wash off her makeup before falling asleep, but how had she managed to get *so much* of it on Thane's pillow? Ugh! She'd just have to apologize and try to clean it later.

The shower turned off. Rolling out of bed, Violet got dressed in one of Thane's white button-up shirts. The en suite door was slightly ajar, and she nudged it open, revealing Thane standing at the vanity wrapped in a towel.

"Morning," she said. "For breakfast, I was thinking—"

Thane spun, knocking items from the vanity onto the floor.

"Oops! I didn't mean to scare you," Violet said, covering her grin with her hand. She bent down to pick up a tube that had rolled up to her foot.

Thane gave a lopsided grin. "It's all good." He picked his way over the scattered items to wrap his arms around Violet's waist and kiss her. "I just can't believe you're really here."

Tingles rippled through Violet's core, spreading through the rest of her body. She circled her own arms around Thane's neck and tilted her chin up for a deeper kiss, losing her breath when he responded by pinning her body against the door frame. For a few seconds, or perhaps an eternity, Thane's hands moved over her, reexploring her curves.

Just when Violet was sure the events of last night were about to be reenacted, her stomach made a very loud grumble.

Thane smiled against her mouth. "I'm sorry, you were saying something about breakfast?"

"Nope. Don't know what you're talking about."

Another audible growl. *Curse you, stomach.*

Thane raised an amused eyebrow. "How about we get some breakfast first, and then we can pick up where we left off."

She heaved an overly dramatic sigh. "Fine. If you and my stomach are going to gang up on me, then I'd like to suggest we go to that little café I saw down the road."

"Sounds like a plan. And sounds like we'll need clothes." He eyed his shirt, the only covering Violet had on at the moment.

Violet pouted. "Fine. But only because I don't want to be arrested for indecent exposure."

He chuckled.

She remembered the tube in her hand. "Here's your . . . makeup?" Squinting at the label, she read: *Movie Magic Concealer, Great for covering birthmarks, scars, and tattoos. Lasts for twelve hours.* Confused, she looked up. "Why do you have . . . ?"

Then she noticed his neck. A tattoo that hadn't been there the night before. A tattoo that had haunted her every day since she was sixteen. A tattoo of a crystal scorpion.

Where the hell was her switchblade?

## 20

## I'M VERY PERVABLE

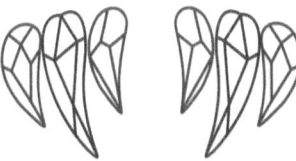

ALL TOO SOON, SAGAN ANNOUNCED IT WAS TIME TO START driving again. Nathan groaned, unsure whether he'd managed to sleep at all.

The young hunter navigated the Defender through the forest like an expert rally driver, only slowing down when they reached the mountain pass. It became clear why Sagan had insisted on journeying up the range by daylight. Many sections of the dirt road had washouts and fallen boulders, and in places, the road was barely wide enough for the Defender. Nathan gripped the door handle tight, trying his best to avoid looking down the sheer drop outside his window. He only relaxed once the Defender left the mountain pass and was back on asphalt, winding through another forest.

Nathan gave a slight shake of his head. How had he ended up here, riding shotgun with a hunter who had rescued him —from the kid's own father, no less? He leaned his elbow on the door and rested his chin on his hand, scanning the trees as they whipped past.

"So, I've been meaning to ask," said Sagan, cutting through Nathan's thoughts, "what's so special about Violet?"

Nathan glanced over at him.

"I mean," Sagan hastily added, "why is the queen trying to kill her?"

Nathan shifted in his seat. "Well, that's a bit of a long story."

"We've got two hours until we reach the next town."

"Oh." Nathan turned his attention back to the forest, contemplating whether to respond or not. "How about this? I'll answer your questions if you answer mine."

"Fine, but that depends on the questions."

"Okay, what about this one: why are *you* trying to help Violet? I thought you hunters were all about spilling blood to fill the vials in your amulets, not rescuing people."

"Because I . . ." Sagan let a few moments pass before continuing. "Because I owe it to Violet for being there for my sister, when I . . . I wasn't there for her."

"Oh," Nathan said, a little taken aback. He tried to come up with something better to say, but thankfully, Sagan kept going.

"Lyla was bullied in high school, and as much as I tried to be there for her, my father kept dragging me along on all his hunting missions. When Violet befriended her, it was like her whole world changed. She was happy, confident. I'll always be grateful to Violet for that.

"When they were kidnapped, my father and I were out of town. I was sent home early, and when I found out what happened, I immediately searched for Lyla. But . . . I was too late." Sagan's quiet voice turned sour. "Your queen sent those Veniri slavers to snatch my sister, and I'm going to make her pay for it."

"Hmm" was all Nathan managed to say. He'd fully

expected Sagan to hedge around any question he asked, not answer with his heart on his sleeve.

"So, why does the queen want Violet?" Sagan asked. "I've spent enough time with Violet to know she's not Veniri, and the queen wouldn't hire my father to track down a simple human girl if something else wasn't going on."

Nathan quirked an eyebrow. "Pretty sharp." He blew out a heavy sigh. "You're right, there is something else going on, but it's not Violet the queen wants. Violet is just a means to an end. She's the key in tracking down her mother and sister."

"*What*?" Sagan's head snapped to him. "Her mother and sister?"

"Yeah." Nathan had never expected he'd be having this conversation with anyone. He'd meant to take the secret to his grave, to ensure not only Violet's safety but also her mother's and younger sister's. If he was to spill this to anyone, an Erathi hunter should've been at the bottom of the list. Even so, a deal was a deal.

Plus, he'd kept all this pent up for so many years. Maybe this was an aftereffect of opening up about the Veniri funeral rites last night. If so, the floodgates were truly open now.

"Violet's mother was kidnapped from the hospital right after Violet was born. She was taken by the Veniri and enslaved as a breeder."

"A breeder? Is that . . . what I think it is?"

"It's precisely what you think it is."

Nathan ignored Sagan's snort of disgust and continued. "Over the last century, there's been a rapid decline in the birth of Veniri females. No one knows why, but it's gotten to the point where only one female is born for every one hundred males.

"Long before I was born, one of the early queens decided something drastic needed to be done to avoid our race's extinction, so she introduced the breeding program, where young Erathi females were kidnapped and forced to breed with our males. It was meant to be temporary, but unfortunately, the program hasn't helped much."

Sagan shook his head. "Surely there's got to be a better way to preserve your race than kidnapping our kind."

"Like what?" Nathan put on a pompous accent. "Excuse me, Mr. President, our shifter race is dying. Please give us your females to make more shifter babies."

Sagan rolled his eyes. "Point taken. But what about the forced breeding stuff? I highly doubt your elitist males would be over the moon about shacking up with Erathi girls."

"Yes, the breeding program is vulgar for Erathi and Veniri alike, but the Veniri are aware it's a necessary evil."

"Definitely evil," sneered Sagan. "So what about the babies then? I'm assuming you're a product of an Erathi-Veniri combo? Is that why you guys can shift?"

"As far as I know, our race has always been shifters."

"So, one thing I've always wanted to know, how did the Veniri originate on Earth?"

Nathan shrugged. "How did werewolves originate? How did the Yranum originate? Or the Djiovis and all the other shifters?" He shot a pointed look at Sagan. "How did the Erathi originate on Earth?"

"Hmm..."

"I don't know, kid. I haven't been schooled in the origins of the Veniri, but we tend to only shift when we leave our... ah, colony. There's no need to be in human form otherwise.

"And yes, my mother was an Erathi breeder. Erathi DNA is more compatible with Veniri than that of any other shifter race. The Veniri gene is very dominant, and every baby born in the breeding program has been practically a full-blooded Veniri. However, there's a tiny dilution with each generation, and I've been told that if the breeding program continues, within a millennium we'll be virtually human."

Sagan snorted. "And that would be a bad thing?"

Nathan shrugged. "Who knows? I won't be around to find out."

"Okay, so, what's the deal with Violet? Why does the queen need her?"

"Idalia needs Violet, or even her mother, to track down her sister. Her sister is Veniri, which means she can one day challenge Idalia for the throne.

"The Veniri are matriarchal. We're ultimately ruled by an empress, but every colony is led by a queen under the empress's command. And because of their rarity, every female Veniri born becomes royalty by default. When a female comes of age, she can challenge the current queen for power."

Nathan paused. As much as his mind kept shouting that he shouldn't be sharing any of this, especially with the likes of an Erathi hunter, finally speaking the straight, untainted truth about himself and his race filled him with undeniable relief. But up to this point, the conversation had basically been a Veniri history lesson. The next part was where things became more personal.

"Unfortunately, because our culture holds our females in such high regard, bitter rivalries and resentment can form between the females. A queen's law is ultimate—that is, until a new queen comes of age and challenges her.

"In my colony, Queen Idalia was the only female to be born in almost fifty years. At least, that's what we'd all been led to believe. Just before I left, I found out Idalia was actually slaughtering any female babies being born. Once I found that out, I helped Violet's mother and infant sister escape."

"Hmm." Sagan frowned. "But aren't the Veniri the best

trackers in the whole shifter kingdom? Won't the queen just get one of her minions to track her down?"

"No. My father managed to put a shield on them before he—" Nathan cleared his throat. "They can't be tracked with a shield. But unfortunately, there's a loophole. If a Veniri can get a taste of a close family member's scent, it reignites the shielded person's scent, and the shield becomes void."

"But I'm assuming you've already put a shield over Violet. In the forest, I saw you put some sort of bright light thing on her head. Was that the shield?"

Nathan gave him a sidelong glance. "Just how close to us were you that night? And how come I didn't pick up your scent?"

Sagan's features remained placid, not giving anything away. "Wouldn't you like to know."

"Well, yeah." Nathan narrowed his eyes. "It'd be nice to know if a sneaky hunter was perving on me."

Sagan scoffed. "Don't think too highly of yourself."

"Why not? Haven't you noticed? I'm very pervable."

Sagan just shook his head. "So was the light thing the shield or not?"

The subject change didn't escape Nathan's attention, but he had the feeling if he pressed, Sagan would clam up. Regardless of their tentative agreement to give answer for answer, Nathan had every right to clam up himself and cut the conversation short, but his instincts told him Sagan was worth allying with. And having another ally to back him up against Veniri and Erathi enemies certainly wouldn't be a bad thing.

"Not," said Nathan, deciding to keep up his end of the "honesty" bargain. He turned his attention to the scenery out the window. They'd passed through the forest a while ago. Lush greenery had been replaced by farmland—vast grassy fields for cattle and sheep, and crops in neat rows stretching to the horizon. Nathan recognized wheat, sugar cane, olive trees, and sorghum.

"The shield requires a gland implant in the subject's back," continued Nathan. "If you remove the glands, you remove the shield."

"Oh, that's what you were doing with Violet's back? But hang on, where are Violet's mother and sister now?"

"I have no idea. I might've helped them escape, but they didn't trust me. We parted ways shortly after. It was safer for all of us to separate anyway."

"But surely you of all people can track them down with Violet's scent? Didn't you get a whiff of it before you put the shield on her?"

"Violet was still going through puberty back then, and her permanent scent was underdeveloped—not effective for tracking."

"Hmm." Sagan paused before asking the next question. "So . . . does Violet know about any of this? About her mother and sister?"

Guilt punched Nathan in the gut. "No," he said in a low voice.

Sagan sucked in a breath through his teeth. "Aw, man. That's brutal."

"It was better for everyone if she didn't know."

"I doubt Violet will see it that way. Are you planning on telling her?"

"Maybe." The moment Violet found out, she'd want to track down her family, and the only way to do that was to remove her shield. Once the glands were removed, the procedure couldn't be done again. Not only Violet but her family would be exposed to Veniri trackers. If by some miracle the queen forgot about all of them and they were no longer in danger, then, maybe, he could tell Violet the truth.

But for now . . .

He recalled what Sagan had said the previous night. *"I'm going to kill her."*

If Sagan truly planned on killing Idalia, there was no way he could accomplish it alone. The queen was a royal power-house who ruled the country's Veniri in whatever way suited her. She was a genius manipulator who had her followers eating out of her hand and her enemies kissing her feet.

How did Sagan think he could pull it off? Was he planning to blast through the hidden city's gates, waltz on up to the queen, and just put a Diamantium dagger in her heart? Even the Veniri resistance hadn't been successful in any of their assassination attempts—though they were admittedly small in number, lacking in equipment and skills, and mainly composed of Erathi slave runaways.

Pulling off such a mammoth mission would require someone who knew the right people to bribe. An in-depth understanding of Idalia's labyrinthine personal quarters and daily schedule would be a must, along with a solid idea of how and when she deviated from that schedule. Nathan had spent enough time with her to know there were only a handful of places she deviated to ...

Before he knew it, he had a rough plan for how to bring a successful end to Idalia's tyranny. With her dead, he would be safe. Violet and her family would be safe. Young Erathi girls would be safe from abductions. With Idalia gone, his hive could reach out to hives in other countries and work together to raise female births without extensive kidnappings and bloodshed.

His race deeply needed to cleanse itself of the corruption that had spread through their culture like a poison.

"Okay," said Nathan, "I'll do it."

"Do what?"

"I'll help you kill the Veniri queen."

Sagan gave him a sidelong glance, and Nathan swore he saw the corner of the hunter's mouth curve up.

Nathan leaned back against the headrest and closed his eyes. "You'll need to make a detour to my place. We're going to need some supplies."

## 21

## SLIVERS OF GLASS

Violet shuddered. She needed to get away, escape, but instead she froze, unable to peel her eyes away from the crystal scorpion tattoo on Thane's neck.

Thane stretched out his hands. "Violet, don't—"

She cut him off with a knee to the groin. He collapsed forward, groaning in pain. Violet lunged toward the bedroom door, but Thane recovered enough to reach out and trip her. She stumbled and fell face-first among the discarded clothes on the floor by the bed.

She screamed and kicked as a hand latched on to her ankle.

"Violet, stop!"

She momentarily stopped screaming—not because of his command but because she spotted her crumpled jeans.

They were just out of reach.

She tried to scramble toward them, but strong hands flipped her onto her back to face the man of her nightmares. Except the man with the neck tattoo was no longer faceless.

"Don't touch me! Let me go!" she sobbed. "It was you! This whole time it was *you*!"

Jeans. Jeans. She needed her jeans! But no matter how hard she thrashed, her struggles were useless against Thane's ferocious strength.

"Calm down!" he yelled, catching her wrists in a vicelike grip, but her screams and tearful sobs drowned him out. The tattoo was clear and unmistakable now. Definitely not a figment of her dreams.

"It was *you!*" She gasped in horror as retrieved pieces of her forgotten memory assembled into place. Her mind seared with agonizing pain, as if slivers of glass were piercing every inch of her skull.

Everything came flooding back—

*She and Lyla, bound and shoved into the trunk of a car.*

*Who are these men? One has a scorpion tattoo on his neck.*

*Lyla has a secret, a dagger made of crystal. "They're not human, Violet. We have to escape."*

*The man with the tattoo picks her up. Takes her to a locked door with bars.*

*Days. Nights. How many have passed? So hungry. So cold.*

*"Time to go to your new home, girls."*

*Lyla has a family. She will be missed.*

*"Please. Just take me and let Lyla go home."*

*A man with a hoodie grabs her. She tries to get away. Pain, so much pain.*

*Lyla lunges. So fast. She's fighting Hoodie, who has a monstrous face.*

*Hoodie is too strong. Lyla is dead. So much blood.*

*She screams. Hoodie and Scorpion Tattoo argue.*

*She sees the crystal dagger in Lyla's pocket. She takes it.*

*Hoodie throws her over his shoulder. So much pain.*

*She stabs. Hoodie roars. Bright blue liquid.*

*Darkness.*

.  .  .

The stabbing pain in her skull subsided. Acid burned the back of her throat, and she covered her face with her hands, choking on her ragged breaths. Tears streamed down her cheeks. The returned memory still burned hot and brutal in her mind.

"Violet? Can you hear me?" Strong hands shook her shoulders.

She opened her eyes. Thane loomed above her, straddling her. Thane, one of the kidnappers from her memory. The tattoo was as vivid as she remembered.

"*You*," she growled through clenched teeth. "I remember *you!*"

"Violet, I—"

She bucked her hips, shifting Thane's center of gravity and rolling them both to the side. With a grunt of surprise, he tumbled to the ground, and she flung herself on top of him.

Before he could recover, Violet punched him as hard as she could in the face. She landed blow after blow, using a mixture of her fists and elbows. In an attempt to block her assault, Thane managed to take hold of one of her arms.

Violet's eyes darted to her jeans, now just within reach. She thrust her free arm forward.

"Violet, stop!" Thane roared, his iron grip on her arm tightening; she needed to act fast. Just as he reached out to take hold of her other arm, there was a subtle *shnik*.

Violet plunged the switchblade into his chest.

Thane's eyes grew wide. The guttural roar that escaped him was unlike any human sound Violet had heard before. She yanked the blade free, grabbed her jeans, and ran for the bedroom door. Thane yelled after her, calling her name between gasps and groans of agony.

She snatched up her bag with her keys and phone and dashed to the exit. Thane's harrowed roars echoed behind her, all the way down the stairs of the apartment complex.

## 22

## DON'T GET ANGRY, OKAY?

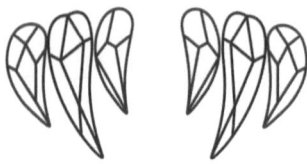

SAGAN VEERED THE DEFENDER INTO NATHAN'S STREET.

"Pull in 'round the back," said Nathan, pointing to a side road. He'd spotted Jude in a patrol car when they'd entered town. If she drove by and spotted a vehicle in his driveway, she'd certainly investigate, and that was the last thing he needed. He wasn't quite sure how long he'd been MIA, but regardless, Jude must be worried about his disappearance.

*She can worry a little longer*, he thought.

"You wanna come in?" Nathan asked when Sagan parked in the rear gravel driveway. "It's possible there's something edible in the cupboard."

Sagan shook his head. "I also have supplies I need to pick up from home. Be ready when I get back."

Nathan quirked an eyebrow. "I think you've missed your calling as a drill sergeant."

Sagan responded with a scowl as he shifted the car into gear and tore back out onto the road. Nathan shook his head with a chuckle and headed straight to the shower.

A few minutes later, he towel-dried his hair with one hand and rummaged through his closet with the other. He put on a pair of dark gray jeans—a much better fit than the black hunter's jeans Sagan had given him—and selected a shirt, pausing when he caught his reflection in the mirror on the closet door.

With a frown, he rubbed his fingers over the smooth flesh of his pectoral muscle. *Interesting.* There was no trace of the stab wound. Not even a hint of a scar. His hide was tough, but the long scar below his ribs proved Diamantium blades left their mark.

The memory of his time in the hunters' lair flashed through his mind, reigniting his anger. His fear. His—

His eyes widened. A subtle gleam of turquoise scales rippled over his bare torso and up his neck. When it reached his face, it washed over his features, revealing for a moment his true appearance.

He raised a hand to his cheek and, with a jolt, noticed a crystalline spire jutting out of his elbow. In a rush, he checked his other arm, then hissed a curse under his breath. The startled movement had caused the second protruding blade to slice through some of his clothes hanging nearby. The severed pieces of fabric fluttered to the carpet.

He rotated his arms, inspecting his elbows. How could this be? There hadn't been any pain. No burning. No *warning.* He tested the blades, drawing them back into his arms, then out again—without any of the usual resistance. He marveled at the smooth and painless action. This was . . . *bad.*

How would he be able to restrain the blades if he couldn't feel them? In public? At work? With Jude? There was no way he could—

A soft *thud* came from one of the outer rooms. He narrowed his eyes and checked his watch. Sagan couldn't possibly be back already. His house was on the other side of town.

Taking care not to make a noise, Nathan crept toward the

direction of the sound. He leaned against the wall by the open bedroom door, waiting and listening. There it was again: soft footfalls on the floorboards in the hallway, gradually getting louder the closer they came to Nathan's room.

Then silence.

Nathan braced himself; he could almost *feel* the intruder just on the other side of the hallway wall, one step out of Nathan's view. He bent his knees, waited half a second, then sprung.

Nathan slammed into the intruder just as he stepped into the room. A voice *oof*ed as Nathan pinned a pair of broad shoulders to the wall, but he paused when he caught sight of the crystal scorpion tattoo on the intruder's neck.

"Thane! What the hell?"

Thane held up both hands. "Geez, old man. What's the big deal?"

"I thought I told you to stay away. Or did you forget Erathi hunters are after me?"

"No, I didn't forget"

"Then why are you here?" Nathan gritted out.

Thane hesitated. "Are you going to let me go first?"

Nathan inclined his head to Thane's elbow blades, which glinted in his periphery. "Are you going to put those away?"

"Are you?" Thane retorted.

Nathan frowned. He dropped his gaze and realized his own elbow blades were out as well. He sheathed them, still without any pain, and took a step back. This was starting to really concern him.

After a heartbeat, Thane withdrew his own blades and rolled one of his shoulders. "Geez, you can pack a punch. Have you been weightlifting or something?"

Nathan scoffed. "Not quite."

"Well, whatever you're doing, it's working."

"That's the first time I've seen you haze in a long time."

Nathan jutted his chin at Thane's elbows. "I thought you said you were done being Veniri and would never haze again."

Thane winced and rubbed his shoulder. "Yeah, well, when someone jumps out of nowhere and pins you to a wall, I suppose instinct kicks in."

"This is my house." Nathan pointed an accusing finger. "You're the intruder here. Which brings me back to my original question: why are you here?"

"I just . . . I was hoping . . ." Thane rubbed a hand on the back of his neck and looked around the room.

Nathan didn't like the expression on Thane's face. He narrowed his eyes. "What's going on?"

Thane continued to avoid eye contact, his gaze flicking down the hallway. "Well, I, um . . . don't get angry, okay?"

Nathan folded his arms.

With a heavy sigh, Thane asked, "Is Violet here?"

Nathan blinked. "What?"

"Is Violet—"

"I heard what you said. Why would she be here? She should be at college."

Thane half squinted an eye and sucked in a breath through his teeth. "No. She's not . . ."

"What do you mean she's not?" Nathan dropped his arms to his sides. "And how would *you* even know?"

"Well . . ." Thane began cautiously, his words gradually speeding up as he spoke. "I've kinda been keeping an eye on her since you dropped her off at college, to, you know, make sure she's safe. Which was just as well, because there was an incident yesterday. She and a few other students got sent home. But when you didn't answer any of her calls, I offered for her to stay at my place and—Whoa!" His eyes widened and he held his hands up. "Come on, Nathan. There's no need for those."

Nathan followed Thane's gaze down to his gleaming

elbow blades. Again, no pain and no warning. He took a step forward, and in sync, Thane took a step back.

"Nathan—"

"Where is she?"

"I . . . I don't know. Things were fine. She was fine. But then she . . . Nathan, something happened to the memory block you put on her. She remembered who I was, and she—"

"What?" Nathan spat the word out through clenched teeth. "Do you have any idea what you've done?" Violet's memories returning—not to mention her already delicate mind processing them all—would have been utterly excruciating. The onslaught of horrors could potentially crush her. Nathan trembled, every muscle in his body taut. "*I told you to stay away from her!*"

Lunging, he crashed into Thane. They ricocheted off the wall and thundered to the ground, Nathan's hand fisting tight around Thane's shirt collar. Eyes huge and frightened, Thane latched on to Nathan's wrists, but the older man didn't budge.

"I didn't spare your life so you could ruin hers! I should have killed you that night, like I did your brother. Why didn't you stay away from her?"

"Because"—a flurry of emotions crossed Thane's tormented face—"I was trying to protect her."

"NO! *I was already protecting her!*" Nathan raised Thane's shoulders off the floor by his shirt, then slammed him back into the ground.

"Someone had to look out for her!" Thane retorted. "There's more than just Veniri out there that can harm her!"

"And what could *you* possibly do?" Nathan spat. "Considering all you've done is bring her harm!"

Thane's expression instantly switched from defeat to rage. He bucked his hips, toppling Nathan to the floorboards with a heavy *thud*. Taking advantage of the momentum,

Thane drove his forearms up between Nathan's arms and forced him to release his grip. He seized Nathan's biceps and pinned him to the ground just as his own blades sliced, glittering, from his elbows.

"I didn't harm her!" he roared through bared teeth; his nostrils flared and his eyes burned golden. "I would never harm her! *I love her!*"

Nathan paused, inspecting the determined face of the man who held him down. Despite the adamancy of Thane's declaration, Nathan's instinct still drove him to test his words with a lash of his forked tongue. A pungent mixture of bleach and pine needles washed over Nathan's senses. The undiluted flavor of bleach proved Thane spoke the truth. The pine needles represented Thane's love, not false or fleeting but evergreen.

Nathan wasn't sure how he felt about that. What did this mean for Violet? Did she know? And if Thane loved her, he should know better than anyone that the best thing for Violet was to keep her away from the Veniri world.

"Then why?" Nathan asked, his tone laced with anguish. "Why couldn't you just leave Violet alone? Why couldn't you stay away from her?"

After a few moments, Thane's pressure on Nathan's arms slackened. "Because of my mother," he finally said. "And because of what she told me before she died."

Nathan was taken aback. Thane was eight when his mother died. What could she possibly have told him?

"She said—" Thane's voice cracked. He released Nathan and slid back to lean against the wall. "She said, 'Real strength and real power don't come from tough hides, crystal shards, or even crowns. They come from within. They come from getting up when you've been beaten down, from fighting for what's right when everyone else has embraced what's wrong. They come from committing yourself to the ones you love with such devotion you'd sacrifice everything for them.'"

Thane covered his face and heaved a few deep breaths. Grief crushed Nathan as he remembered just how much Thane's mother had sacrificed for her son.

Thane dropped his hands and continued, his voice tight. "My mother was the strongest and the bravest in that whole goddamned hive, and she was just a frail Erathi. When they killed her, I had nothing left. I followed orders like an Erathi slave and waited for my father to finally kill me. There were so many times he came close, and there were so many times I wanted—*needed* him to just end it all. And then something changed in me. The first time I saw Violet."

Thane closed his eyes. Nathan didn't need to taste Thane's emotions to confirm the self-loathing written all over his face. He stayed silent, allowing Thane the chance to proceed.

"Every day I regret being involved in Violet's kidnapping. But at the same time, I can't regret finding her. She . . ." Thane raised his eyes to the ceiling, searching for his next words. "I saw in her the same strength and courage my mother had. We'd been holed up in that shack for two days, waiting for the other Veniri to return with some more girls. Violet's friend was on the verge of breaking down. Violet had begged for us to let her friend go and just take her instead. When it became clear neither of them were going home, Violet was strong for both of them, right up until the moment her friend snapped. Violet got hurt in the process, and by the time I turned back to her friend—it was too late. My brother had killed her."

Thane crossed his arms over his folded knees. "Violet reminded me that there's more to this world than just myself. It was what my mother was trying to teach me when I was eight, but I didn't understand it then. Violet showed me that even when you're on the verge of losing everything, you still give everything."

Thane turned his attention to Nathan. "Both you and Violet gave me a second chance, and I made sure I did my best to turn my life around—to make amends for what I'd done, to right my wrongs. And I tried, Nathan, I really tried to stay away from her, to give her the space to live her life. But some part of me keeps drawing me back to her, and I no longer have the strength to fight it."

Nathan quietly processed Thane's words, a melancholy heaviness in his chest. He still didn't regret killing Thane's brother in the woods. Thane's three older brothers were cut from the same cloth as their monstrous father, and all were wrapped tightly around the queen's little finger. The less of those Veniri scum in this world, the better. But he'd never realized the weight Thane had been carrying all these years.

"Why didn't you tell me any of this?"

Thane lightly snorted. "Would you have listened? You were so concerned that I stay away from Violet. You weren't ready to hear my side."

Nathan was about to rebut when, with a flood of shame, he realized Thane was right. "I'm sorry," he finally said.

Thane quirked a corner of his mouth. "It's fine. I knew you were focused on Violet's best interest."

Nathan slowly nodded, absorbing this new feeling of humility.

"I didn't hurt Violet," Thane said again. "I've been looking out for her, making sure she's okay. I know you think her shield will keep her safe now that she's reached maturity, but it didn't stop a guy from attacking her at a night club. I had to ram him with my car so she and her friends could get away."

Nathan *humph*ed. "You said Violet remembered. What happened after that? How did she take it?"

Thane shook his head. "Not well. She started screaming, as if she was in severe pain. And when she looked at me, she ... she remembered who I was. I tried ... I tried to explain. I tried to tell her she wasn't in danger, but she kept screaming and didn't hear me. And then she pulled out a knife and stabbed me."

"She stabbed you?"

"Yep." He pulled down the collar of his shirt, revealing an ugly wound. The bluish-black center was ringed by uneven, bubbled flesh that looked burned, as if from acid. Knotted lines of raised skin coursed out from the center to form an irregular star shape. "I'm assuming it was you who gave Violet a star-blade." Thane's expression was a mixture of indignation and amusement.

Nathan arched an eyebrow. "Serves you right. I warned you to stay away from her."

Thane chuckled and shook his head. "Where did you even find a star-blade? Does Violet know what else it can do?"

Nathan released a heavy sigh. "Unfortunately, there are a lot of things Violet doesn't know. And I'm starting to question my wisdom in keeping it all from her."

Thane nodded. After a beat, he asked, "So is she here?"

Nathan shook his head. "No, I haven't seen her."

"Why didn't you say that earlier?" Thane let out a frustrated groan and jumped to his feet. "We have to find her. Can you try calling her?"

Nathan rubbed his eyes with his finger and thumb. "No. I, um . . . lost my phone during my time with the Erathi hunters."

Thane's eyes bugged. "They caught you?"

Nathan nodded.

Thane swore under his breath. "Damn. That's . . . Wait." His eyes narrowed. "How is it that you're here then?"

"It's a long story. I'll tell you about it later." Nathan stood to retrieve his shirt and tan suede jacket. "How about you fill me in on why Violet was sent home from college? And make it quick, I'm heading out." He glanced at his watch; Sagan was due any moment. The only things Nathan still needed to grab were some food and his survival go-bag, which was in the cupboard by the front door. It contained enough supplies to last him about seventy-two hours—along with a pretty extensive stash of weapons.

While Thane spoke, Nathan headed into the kitchen to rummage around in the cupboard, but all he found worth eating was an unopened bag of beef jerky. He really needed to restock his groceries.

"I just knew something was wrong that night," said Thane, recounting the details of the murder. "I can't explain it, but I knew something bad was going to happen. I could taste it on the wind. Cinnamon. It was so strong. Violet was up late, studying at the library. She was the last to leave, and I had to make sure she was safe, so I followed her back to her room. When we got back, everything was in chaos. A girl was killed. She was a friend of Violet's, and her only crime was falling asleep on Violet's bed." Thane ran a hand through his hair. "Nathan, the killer made a mistake. He was after Violet. We need to find her."

"I will find her," said Nathan around a mouthful of jerky. He checked his watch again and frowned. Sagan should've been back by now.

"Great," said Thane. "Let's go. I'll drive." He took a step toward the back door.

"Hold up, Romeo." Nathan blocked his path. "You're staying here."

Thane's brow creased. "What? No, I'm not. I'm—"

Nathan shook his head. "Thane, I'm sorry if you don't want to hear this, but you're the last person she needs to see right now."

"But I . . ." Grief, hurt, then understanding chased each other across Thane's face.

"Just give it time," said Nathan. "She's been through a lot. At least give her the space to process."

Thane dropped his gaze to the floor, and his shoulders slumped. He took a few steps back, only stopping when he bumped into the dining table. Unable to find words to ease the heavy atmosphere, Nathan folded and unfolded the empty jerky packet in his hands. The plastic crackled, filling in the lengthening silence.

Then a body barreled into him, and arms wrapped around his waist.

"Nathan! Where have you been?"

"Violet?"

Tears streamed from her red, puffy eyes and dripped down her cheeks. She buried her damp face in Nathan's shirt. "I'm so sorry," she finally said. "I didn't know where else to go. A girl died at college, and we got sent home. I tried calling and calling you, but you didn't pick up." She looked up at him. "Why didn't you return any of my calls?"

Nathan stared at her, frozen. His mind raced, trying to figure out what to do or say.

"I'm sorry, I didn't mean to cry on you." She wiped her cheeks with her sleeve. "Ugh! The last few days have been *awful*, and—" She choked on a sob.

Nathan put his arms around her. "It's okay, Violet."

She snuggled against his chest. Nathan tried to surreptitiously catch Thane's attention. Clearly, she hadn't seen him yet. But the younger shifter's focus was fused to Violet.

Thane shifted, his shoe softly squeaking on the floorboards.

Violet's sobbing paused, and she twisted to look behind her. Every ounce of color drained from her face as her body turned to stone in Nathan's arms.

## 23

# TWISTED GAMES

Violet's stomach lurched.

Thane stood by the dining table with his palms held out, his fingers spread wide. Her gaze flicked to the scorpion tattoo on his neck. Ice splintered through her veins, tingled down her spine. Her throat tightened and she tasted acid.

She screamed.

Nathan's arms locked tighter around her. "Violet, it's okay."

"Violet." Thane took a step toward her. "I—"

Violet pointed, her finger trembling. "It's him! Nathan, it's *him*!"

"Violet, please. Let me explain," pleaded Thane.

She shrunk back against Nathan as Thane moved closer.

"Thane. Stop. Now is not the time." Nathan stepped between them, blocking Violet's view, but that didn't stop the image of the crystal scorpion from continuing to scald her vision. She huddled against Nathan's back. Between nightmares and her reality, she couldn't get away from the man with the tattoo on his neck.

"Violet, please, you've got to believe me—"

"Thane. Stop," warned Nathan again.

Thane's voice grew louder. "Tell her, Nathan. Tell her I would never hurt her."

Shock gripped Violet, then a severe, sickening dread. She pushed away from Nathan and bumped against the counter, scrabbling for her switchblade. The two men halted and turned to her when they heard the subtle *shnik*.

She pointed the knife at Nathan, her teeth bared. "You know him?"

Nathan's eyes widened. He squared his body to face Violet, one hand held out in a placating gesture. "Violet, give me the knife."

She shook the blade once but made sure it was out of his reach. "Do you know him?" Her voice cracked.

Nathan's mouth opened and shut, and he started to shake his head.

"Don't lie to me!" she shrieked.

The impending sobs jolted her chest. This couldn't be happening, couldn't be real. It was another version of her morbid nightmares. Nathan couldn't, wouldn't know the man that had haunted her for the past three years. A man that had kept his identity hidden in order to play twisted games with her feelings, deceived her for his perverted amusement.

"How long have you known him?"

Nathan's shoulders drooped. "Violet, I . . ."

"Did you know he was one of the men who kidnapped Lyla and me?"

Nathan dropped his eyes to the floor and heaved a deep breath. "Yes, I knew it was him."

She squeezed her eyes shut and pressed the heel of her free hand to her forehead.

*This isn't real.*

The pain in her throat and chest convinced her otherwise. If Nathan had hidden this from her . . . then what else was he hiding?

"Come on, Vi. How about you give me the knife and we can talk about this."

Out. She needed to get out.

She locked a hard gaze onto Nathan. "If you come near me again, I will *kill* you." Her low voice dripped venom.

She edged her way to the dining room exit, switchblade still extended, her eyes never leaving Nathan. His pained face sent a stab of guilt through her heart, but she pushed it aside; he was a traitor.

She turned and ran, ignoring the pleading exclamation from Thane. When she was a few feet from the back door, something heavy crashed to the ground just behind her. She whipped her head around. Thane was sprawled on the floor with Nathan on top of him. Violet didn't pause to watch the scuffle. She sprinted out the front door and down the driveway to where she'd parked her jeep.

The engine roared to life, and she tore out of the driveway and headed for the outskirts of town, checking the rearview mirror every second. No one followed her even as she reached the THANK YOU FOR VISITING BROOKHAVEN sign and continued into the forest.

A shrill tune startled her. She glanced down at her ringing phone on the passenger seat. Gus's name flashed on the screen.

She pressed the answer button. "Gus—" A lump constricted her throat and her eyes blurred with tears.

"Hey, Vi. I just thought I'd check and see how you're doing. Autumn and I are home now and . . . Violet? Are you okay? What's wrong?"

"I'm just . . . I'm—" Her sobs claimed her. She wiped her eyes with the back of her hand.

"Where are you, Violet? Are you driving?"

Her gaze flicked back to the road ahead, then she slammed on the breaks.

A person was standing in the middle of the road.

She screamed as the jeep swerved.

## COME AT ME, SLITH

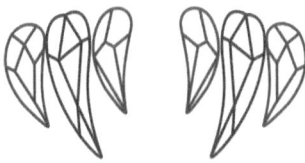

"GET OFF ME!" BARKED THANE, THRASHING. "I HAVE TO GO after her."

Nathan's grip slackened and Thane bucked him off. The older shifter allowed his body to slump into a heap as Thane thundered out the back door, the floorboards reverberating after him.

*"If you come near me again, I will kill you."* Violet's words echoed in his mind like a chant.

Nathan winced and rubbed his eyes, but it couldn't wipe away the image of Violet's betrayed expression. His hands fell to his sides, and he stared at the wood-paneled ceiling, the last of his energy leaking away. The fatigue from the past few days had caught up to him—although even the evil rays of Aphrodite had been easier to endure than Violet's stinging words.

*". . . I will kill you."*

She had been broken and beat down when he first met her. He'd helped her put the pieces back together, but now she was broken again, and this time it was his doing.

And all for what?

For Thane?

He shook his head. Should he regret tracking Thane down the night he'd found Violet? He'd had every intention of killing him. Thane represented all that was corrupt and repugnant in Nathan's own race. He'd wanted to destroy every Veniri in existence, starting with Thane, the pathetic Veniri with the tattoo on his neck. When Nathan had raised an arm for the fatal blow, Thane hadn't fought his impending death, had begged for Nathan to end his life.

But Nathan stopped. He couldn't bring himself to follow through with the death strike. The last time he'd seen the boy, right before Nathan had fled the hive and his race, Thane had been about eight years old. Despite Thane's matured features, he still held a stark resemblance to someone Nathan had broken a promise to long ago, an Erathi woman, also kidnapped when she was a teenager and forced into slavery. Thane's mother.

She'd done her best to protect Thane from the abuse of his father and three older brothers, but there had come a time when she could no longer look out for her youngest son. Her words from long ago rang clear in Nathan's mind. *"Please! Promise me you'll protect my son."*

He'd spoken truth in that moment: *"I promise."* But he'd later ignored his oath for the purpose of his own selfish gain.

Grief and self-resentment had flooded him as he'd stared at the dispirited Veniri who couldn't face what he'd become. Nathan was looking at a younger version of himself, at the pivotal time he realized he didn't want to be Veniri anymore.

Nathan's forked tongue lashed out and sampled every flavor of Thane's self-loathing. But there was more beyond the heavy, bitter tastes of desperation and grief. A sea breeze hint of longing, hope like fresh-plucked mint, and love. Deep binding love, cool and cedar sharp.

For a moment, Nathan wondered if his race could be

redeemed after all. That night in the woods, he decided to follow through on his promise.

But a few days later, he discovered Thane's deep infatuation with Violet. Nathan had warned him to stay away from her. Hell, he still remembered the exact phrase he'd used: *"You go anywhere near her and I'll impale you with your own shards! Got it?"*

Nathan hammered a fist on the timber floor. Why hadn't that damned imbecile listened to him? If Thane had stayed clear of Violet, then she—

A muffled yell came from outside. Nathan turned to the open back door, an image of Violet struggling to get away from Thane flashing through his mind. Grinding his teeth, he flipped himself onto his feet and lunged toward the door. In a few long strides, he was outside.

Grinding gravel caught his attention, and Nathan's stomach dropped. Three men clad in black had Thane pinned to the ground at the end of the driveway. All three wore distinctive amulets hanging from their necks and held weapons with glittering Diamantium trained on Thane.

Nathan was about to step in and claim that Thane was just an Erathi, a simple human, but then his hopes for Thane sunk. Even from where he stood, he could make out the faint rippling of scales over Thane's furious expression. The young Veniri was trying his hardest not to haze.

"Go on, slith." A hunter leaned into Thane's face. "Show us those pretty spikes." He placed the tip of his Diamantium machete on Thane's chest. "If you won't show us those spikes, then I'll just have to find them myself."

"Hey!" barked Nathan. All turned to look at him.

"Well, well," said the hunter who'd threatened Thane. He stood up and rested his machete on his shoulder, his amulet swinging against his chest. Of the ten vials in the amulet, five were filled. Five types of colored blood from five shifter species slaughtered by this hunter. The man looked Nathan up and down with casual triumph. "I believe this is our runaway, boys."

Nathan's pounding heart beat against his ribcage. How on earth had the hunters tracked him down so fast?

The hunter chuckled. "You should see the look on your face. Not only were you stupid enough to think you could escape, but you were also stupid enough to take a car with a tracking device on it. Not so smart, eh, slith?"

Nathan clenched his fists by his sides. Sagan was the one who'd chosen the car. Why would Sagan help him escape only to see him captured again? Unless Sagan didn't know about the tracking device.

"Let him go." Nathan jutted his chin toward Thane. "You're not here for him. I'm the one you want. So let him go."

"What? And miss out on a nice little bonus with this month's paycheck? Not likely." The hunter's face twisted into a menacing glare. "You're *both* coming with us." His gaze lowered, and he grinned wide and pointed with his machete. "Now, that's what I like to see."

Nathan glanced down. Both his elbow blades were extended, glittering in the sunlight. Once again there had been no warning, but this time he didn't care. He glared back at the hunter.

"Come on, slith." The hunter's grin dripped with malice. "Let's play."

Nathan leaped, soaring into the air with startling speed. The hunter's eyes widened, his cocky grin vanishing. Before the man even had a chance to raise his machete, Nathan sliced his own Diamantium blade clean through the hunter's forearm. The severed hand and crystal machete landed on the ground at the same time as Nathan's feet.

Agonized screams filled the air. The hunter's knees buckled, and he toppled to the ground, clutching the remainder of his arm. A shower of red covered his face and remaining hand.

Nathan held himself back from gaping at the scene. He'd never heard of anyone, Erathi or shifter, moving with the speed and agility he'd just shown. He glanced up. Thane and the other two hunters wore similar stupefied expressions.

For several heartbeats, no one but the screaming hunter moved.

Nathan grinned, hazing the remainder of his body into Veniri form. His scales rippled into existence, and his numerous Diamantium spikes glittered specks of light over the hunters' faces. Their expressions twisted into scowls, and as one, the last two hunters dove for Nathan.

Thane kicked out a leg, tripping one of the hunters; Nathan braced himself for the other.

The hunter slashed and swiped his two Diamantium tomahawks, but not one of the strikes landed anywhere near its mark. Nathan weaved around the aggressive attacks, just as fast and nimble as before. Or was he faster now? He had always felt more natural and capable in his Veniri form.

He smiled. Despite the situation, he was enjoying himself. His grin aggravated the hunter even more, and the man's attacks sped up, sloppy with desperation and rage.

Nathan would have loved to continue teasing this hunter with his newfound abilities, but an anguished cry from Thane brought him back to their dire reality. He blocked the tomahawks with his arm blades, then came in with a counterstrike, driving his knee into the hunter's abdomen. His knee spike sliced up and into the man's heart.

Life faded from the hunter's eyes as he crumpled against Nathan's knee. The crystal tomahawks clattered to the ground.

Nathan shoved the hunter off, then turned to Thane, who

towered above their remaining enemy. Thane's victim writhed on the ground, clutching a gaping wound in his neck. Though Thane remained in human form, his scales hazed in and out of view, rippling up his arms and under the sleeves of his dark gray T-shirt. His chest heaved as he clutched at one of his shoulders; rivulets of teal blood seeped out from between his fingers.

"You okay?" asked Thane.

"Never mind me," said Nathan. "Where's Violet?"

Thane shook his head. "Gone. She drove off before I could catch her. She headed down the main road out of town. These beasts showed up just as she left."

A branch snapped behind Nathan, and he swiveled. A figure was lurking in the trees on the other side of his yard. Despite the foliage, there was no question it was a Veniri in full shifted form. Nathan's eyes widened with recognition, and his stomach lurched.

"Kronan." The name was a whisper on Nathan's scaled lips.

"What? Are you sure?" Thane moved to stand next to Nathan.

Nathan slashed his tongue out. "I'm deadly sure. I'd recognized his stench anywhere."

The air was pungent with cinnamon, a remnant of the hunters' and his own lust for murder. But the other flavors on the wind confirmed what Nathan suspected. Every Veniri from Nathan's hive knew the soul-scent of Kronan, Queen Idalia's cousin. It still held the flavors of malice and cowardice.

Nathan hadn't seen Kronan since escaping the hive. And for years Nathan had evaded detection from his race. Yet, here at his house . . .

The Veniri intruder hissed, and his own forked tongue

whipped out. Then, in a flash, Kronan scurried over the fence, cutting through the neighbor's yard and out of sight.

Nathan narrowed his eyes. If Kronan was here, then the queen had sent him. And that meant . . .

"Get him," said Nathan. "He's after Violet."

Like twin bullets, they shot across the yard after Kronan, but a second before they reached the fence, Thane suddenly disappeared out of Nathan's periphery. Before Nathan could register what happened, pain sliced through his leg. He bellowed. His leg was yanked out from under him, and with a resounding *thud*, he landed hard on the ground. A Diamantium-tipped barb attached to a wire line had pierced straight through his calf.

He and Thane were dragged backward by their tethers, directly into a new group of hunters.

Nathan gritted his teeth as the barb tore into his leg. Thane grunted and thrashed in his own agony, sending up clouds of dust.

They came to rest a few feet away from the hunters. Relief flooded Nathan as the tugging ceased, but the barbed bolt still sent spasms of torment through his leg. Two men—one with a brown goatee, the other with red hair—controlled the devices that had reeled them in. Between them stood Matthias, his triumphant expression more arrogant than ever. A cluster of other hunters on either side of him trained their weapons on Nathan and Thane. One held a modernized crossbow. Two others wielded what looked like bazookas on their shoulders.

Fear inundated every cell in Nathan's body. Fear for Thane, and fear for Violet. He needed to get them to safety. *Come on, Delano. Think!*

He scrambled to his feet.

"Stay down, slith," ordered Matthias.

The hunter with the goatee yanked the wire, bringing

Nathan crashing to the ground. He bit back a grunt of pain. Thane moaned, clutching his leg.

"Stay with me," said Nathan in a low voice only Thane could hear. "We need to get through this, you understand? For Violet."

Thane caught his gaze. With his jaw set, he gave Nathan a curt nod. "For Violet."

"You take out the ginger." Nathan stared directly at Matthias and, in a louder voice, said, "I'm gonna start with the ugly one."

Matthias grinned, his eyes glittering with bloodlust. He raised a hand and curled his fingers at Nathan. "Come at me, slith."

Nathan focused his remaining energy and sprung. As before, his speed was shocking, but this time it wasn't enough. While he was still in the air, the two hunters with the bazookas took aim, one at him and the other at Thane. They fired.

Nathan flailed uselessly as the projectile expanded into a net, which wrapped around him on impact. Once again, Nathan slammed into the dirt.

His spikes would cut him free. Diamantium could slice through almost anything—

Nathan's body shuddered as a shock of electricity pulsed through the net, sending explosions of pain through his very core. The combination of his and Thane's roars and the high-pitched electric buzzing almost shredded his eardrums. Then, in an instant, the electrification stopped. Numbness tingled through his extremities—except for his barbed leg, where the pain had intensified.

He and Thane both groaned. Nathan tried to turn his head, but the net allowed only a few inches of movement before it hugged tighter to his face.

"So what now?" One of the hunters kicked Nathan's ribs. "We taking these back to be harvested?"

Matthias rubbed his jaw. "Nah, I think I got a better idea. It'd be a waste to harvest them so early." He pointed to Nathan. "I want to see this one in action."

The ginger shook his head. "But this slith is marked. The client said that *this* slith in particular—"

"I know what the client said." Matthias's eyes narrowed in warning, and the other man dropped his gaze, his lips pursed. Placing his hands on his hips, Matthias turned back to Nathan, his shark grin wide. "Besides, we can delay the transaction for a while and make a bit of extra money in the meantime."

"What about this one then?" asked another hunter as he kicked Thane.

Thane bared his teeth, but the net kept him pinned.

Matthias cackled. "Bring him along. He's got enough fight in him to be a good bait dog at least. Where's Axel?" he called over his shoulder.

"He's still out looking for Sagan" came the reply.

Matthias pinched the bridge of his nose. "Hopefully he returns soon. And hopefully with that boy skewered on his trident." He groaned in frustration. "In that case, one of you go and get the tranqs from the vehicle. The last thing I want is one of these sliths thinking they can escape. Again."

One of the hunters took off.

Nathan wrestled against the net. No, no, *no!* This couldn't be happening. He needed to get to Violet. She needed him.

"Hmm, while we're waiting for the tranqs . . ." Matthias's eyes glittered way too much for Nathan's liking as he gestured for the remaining hunters to huddle closer. He spoke in a voice too low for Nathan to decipher, but judging by the malicious grins on the hunters' faces, it didn't bode well. As one they swaggered away, leaving only Matthias and the two controlling the electrified nets.

Nathan's heart raced.

Matthias crouched down beside him, his hands resting on his knees. "I'll admit, you've been a bit more trouble than I expected."

A bright orange light lit up in Nathan's peripheral vision. He turned just as the aroma of petroleum and smoke seared his lungs. One of the hunters was dousing Nathan's porch with gasoline from a red plastic jerrican. Another lit a fuel-soaked rag and threw it onto the porch.

*No! No! No!*

But there was nothing Nathan could do. Flames blazed up instantly with an audible *whoomp*, engulfing his beautiful timber home. He strained against his bonds. He needed to stop the fire. He needed to save all of Violet's framed photos that lined his hallway. He needed to make sure the flames didn't reach her room—the safe place she could always come back to. He just had to—

"Time to go, boys," said Matthias.

Something sharp bit into Nathan's thigh. He growled, fighting harder to free himself. He ignored the throbbing ache in his calf, the intense heat of the flames, and the rancid smoke in his lungs. But a new numbing sensation took over his body, tingling from his fingers to his toes. If only he could—

A black shadow encroached on the edge of his vision. His legs and arms began to relax. His vision blurred and his mind grew groggy.

*No! Fight it! Stay awake! Stay awake! Stay . . . a . . .*

The blackness consumed him.

# DIAMOND SMEARED WITH BLOOD

Violet slammed on the breaks, and the jeep veered off the road and onto the shoulder, its tires crunching deep into the gravel. Her body whipped forward and back as the car jerked to a stop and the engine stalled to silence. For a moment, her racing pulse hammered in her ears.

*What the hell just happened?*

She checked the rearview and side mirrors, but the road behind her was empty.

*Please tell me I didn't hit them.*

She should get out and check if they're all right. But a small part of her remained cautious. She swiveled in her seat and looked out the back windows. Nothing. She couldn't see anything.

Except . . . Was that . . . ?

A figure was lying on the ground a few yards away on the other side of the road. They were still alive. Even from this distance, Violet could see the rise and fall of their chest.

Her switchblade was still in her hand. She gripped it tighter, then got out of the jeep. Her shoe scuffed a stone, and it clacked a few times along the road.

The person turned their head at the sound, and Violet's jaw dropped.

"Sagan!" The stark blond hair and sea-blue eyes were unmistakable. She sprinted over and collapsed at his side. "Are you okay? What were you doing in the middle of the road?"

Sagan's eyebrows shot up. "Violet—" He sucked in a few gulps of air. "Violet, you're here, and you're . . ." His features hardened into a frown. "You can't be here. You have to go."

She inspected his grazed skin and fresh bruises. His lower lip was split, and blood trailed down the side of his face from a cut at his hairline. Her hands flew to her mouth. "Oh no! I *did* hit you."

With a groan and a wince, Sagan propped himself up on his elbow, his other arm clutching his abdomen.

"Stop. Don't move," said Violet. "I'll call an ambulance. Oh, Sagan, I'm so sorry." She dug into her jeans pocket for her phone, then realized it was still in the car.

Sagan latched on to her wrist. "Go!" he yelled. "You have to get out of here!"

Violet froze at his sudden ferocity. "What? No. I can't leave you here. I just hit you with my car. Just let me—"

He shook his head, then grimaced. "No. It wasn't you. It was"—he dragged in a ragged breath—"Axel."

"What? What do you mean it wasn't me? I . . ." She ran her eyes once more over his injuries, this time noticing that the blood on his face was dark and caked, obviously not a fresh wound. "Sagan, what happened to you? Who's Axel?"

A twig snapped. They both looked up.

A towering man slunk out of the forest behind them. He looked directly at Violet, his face cracking into a menacing grin. A tingling sensation crawled over the back of her neck and skittered down her spine.

Sagan's grip on her wrist went from tight to bone breaking. "How the hell did that thing find us?" His voice was so quiet she almost didn't hear him. "No. You can't have her."

The man let out a high-pitched laugh, like a witch's cackle.

The handle of Violet's switchblade dug into her palm as her thumb found the button to release the blade. But she paused, eerily transfixed, as the man turned his face to the sky.

Before Violet's eyes, he began to transform.

The smooth texture of his flesh roughened into scales that shimmered in the sunlight, and sharp crystal spires burst through his clothes. A second set of lids flickered over the eyes he now fixed back on Violet. His malefic smirk deepened—right before a forked tongue whipped out from between three sets of fangs.

"Violet, *run!*" Sagan roared.

She heard his warning, but her body refused to move. This man—or rather, this creature—was horrifyingly similar to the monster that had killed Lyla. Her mind screamed in physical and emotional agony as the reinstated memory burned through her consciousness.

The thing sprang toward her and Sagan, its powerful legs propelling it high into the air.

Violet sucked in what she assumed would be her last breath and did the only thing that came to mind. She threw herself facedown on top of Sagan. Every muscle, fiber, and cell tensed as she anticipated the fatal impact.

Instead, a shriek pierced her ears, and the sensation of warm rain splattered her back. Something heavy thudded to the ground a few yards away and skidded over the asphalt. Violet dared to peek; the creature was writhing and wailing in the middle of the road. Blue liquid sprayed from one of its thrashing limbs.

Another man with a bushy gray beard emerged into

Violet's view and casually strode over to the creature, a glimmering trident in hand. A few other weapons, including one that looked like a crossbow, were strapped to his person.

The creature paused its thrashing as Gray Beard drew close, then it charged him. The two locked into a vicious battle—man and crystal trident versus vengeful beast.

Violet saw her opportunity. "Come on, Sagan. Get up." She ignored his protests and pulled him into a sitting position.

"Wait, I need my bag." Sagan snatched a black bag by his thigh, which Violet immediately yanked off him and slung over her shoulder. She grabbed hold of Sagan, wrapping one of his arms around her neck to help raise him from the ground. He groaned and winced but quickly gave up fighting her efforts to help him. She stumbled a bit under his weight, but they managed an awkward shuffle in the direction of her jeep.

"Sagan, I've seen one of those things before. It . . . it killed Lyla."

"I know."

"What? How—"

The pained wails of the creature grew more gargled and desperate. The battle was clearly going in favor of Gray Beard.

"I don't think that thing is going to last much longer," said Violet.

"Hmm," grunted Sagan. "We still got to get outta here."

They sped up toward the jeep. The ferocious roars and clangor behind them began to die down.

"Hurry," said Sagan.

Three more steps to go. Then two.

A final shriek tore from the beast, then silence.

Another surge of adrenaline rushed through Violet. She didn't risk looking back. Instead, she yanked open the passenger side door, threw the bag in, and helped Sagan climb into his seat. He closed the door behind him as she ran around the front of the vehicle and climbed into the driver's side. Her phone, now in the footwell, blared its shrill tune again, but she ignored it.

Thankfully she'd left the keys in the ignition. The engine started with a flick of her wrist. She glanced in all the side and rearview mirrors, and her heart skipped a beat.

The deceased creature was lying in the middle of the road, but the man who'd killed it was nowhere to be seen.

"Where is he?"

A quick two-tone whistle came from Sagan's window. They both turned to find Gray Beard grinning at them, the crossbow-like contraption in his hands.

"Now, where do you two think you're going?"

Violet's body went rigid and her eyes widened; the crossbow bolt was trained directly on her.

When neither Violet nor Sagan spoke, the man's grin fell, but the bloodlust glint in his eyes remained. He gestured with his weapon. "The way I see it, you've got two choices. You can both come with me alive or . . . not alive." He shrugged one shoulder. "Either way, you're coming with me."

Sagan's hand felt for the bag that was between him and Violet.

"Uh-uh," warned the man. "Don't even think about it, Sagan. Hands where I can see them. You too, missy."

Acid bit at Violet's throat as her stomach threatened to empty.

The glittering head of Gray Beard's crossbow bolt caught Violet's eye again. She needed to get out. Her mind screamed at her to get out. Run! But fear still paralyzed her. She could slam her foot on the accelerator, but at what cost? Would Gray Beard's crossbow hit her or Sagan before she could get the car moving?

Sagan raised his hands.

Gray Beard looked pointedly at her when she didn't move. Her breath quickened into shallow pants as she dropped her switchblade into her lap and also raised her hands.

The man smirked. "Glad to see you can both follow simple instructions. That'll make my job easier."

She jolted at the man's sudden husky laughter.

"You should see the looks on your faces. Especially yours." He pointed to Sagan. "How primitive do you think we are? Did you seriously think we would let you steal that slith and escape so easily? You *stupid* boy."

Violet's mind whirled. What was this guy talking about? What on earth was a slith? And why did Sagan steal it? What kind of trouble had Sagan got himself involved in? Sagan was . . . he was . . . Actually she hardly knew. Violet hadn't seen much of him after Lyla's death.

Sagan was still faced away from her. She had no way of guessing what he would do next.

"I'll come with you," said Sagan. "Just let her go."

Gray Beard met his request with an incredulous look. "How stupid do you think I am? You seriously think I don't recognize a bounty when I see one?" He rummaged in one of his jeans pockets and pulled out a crumpled piece of paper.

The paper had a photo of Violet on it. Her stomach dropped. He wasn't implying that . . . *she* . . . ?

Her fingers twitched, aching to grab the steering wheel.

The arrow flashed in the sunlight as the hunter bounced on his toes, chuckling. "Hell, it must be my lucky day. Not only did I stumble across *another* slith"—he inclined his head to the creature on the road—"but then you lead me straight to your little payday girlfriend here." He pointed his weapon at Violet.

Her heart pounded, threatening to break through her ribcage.

He crumpled up the paper, put it back in his pocket, then whistled. "This girl's bounty is worth a fortune. I'm gonna enjoy this month's bonus, that's for damn sure." Gray Beard's amused expression turned stony. "Now, turn the car off and get out."

Sagan didn't move, so Violet didn't either.

The man raised the crossbow, setting his sight on her. "I won't say it again," he said, each word slow and deliberate.

For a few heartbeats, no one even seemed to breathe. The hum of the engine filled the silence.

Then the shrill tune of Violet's ringtone cut through the tension like a chainsaw. She jumped in her seat. In the half second it took her to glance at her phone in the footwell, Sagan moved with lightning speed.

Gray Beard jolted back with a half spin as Sagan sliced a dagger across his shoulder. He growled and attempted to re-aim the crossbow at them.

"Drive! Drive! Drive!" Sagan yelled.

Violet shifted the car into gear and slammed her foot on the accelerator. Panic gripped her throat as the jeep didn't take off straightaway, instead skidding and fishtailing on the gravel.

Just as she felt the car's wheels finally grip solid road, Sagan screamed.

She looked over at him. A metal crossbow bolt had pierced straight through not only the car door but also Sagan's leg, just above the knee. The arrowhead glittered as if made from diamond—diamond smeared with blood.

"Oh, no! Sagan!"

"Don't slow down! Drive faster!" he yelled through gritted teeth.

The engine revved louder as she accelerated down the

road, but she kept glancing over at Sagan. His black jeans grew darker and glistened around the metal jutting out of his leg.

"Tell me what to do, Sagan. How can I help?"

"Just drive. Whatever you do, don't stop." He made a tourniquet with his belt around his upper thigh, then paused for a few moments, sucking in a few deep breaths.

"What are you doing?"

Sagan didn't answer. He took hold of the tail end of the bolt and began shoving it farther through his thigh, crying out in pain as the bolt inched forward.

"What are you doing?" Violet shrieked. "Stop it! I'll get you to a hospital as soon as I can."

"No hospitals. Just keep driving," he said, his words laced with torment.

"Sagan, stop! You're making it worse."

He continued, hissing in agony. "I have to pull it out."

"Please, just wait until I can find a hospital. A doctor will cut it out."

"I said no hospitals!"

"Fine! At least wait until I pull over so I can help you."

"No! Don't stop! They'll find us if you do. This thing has a tracking device inside one of its barbs."

"What?" Violet rubbed the heel of her hand against her forehead. "Are you saying that guy is tracking us?" She looked in the rearview mirror, expecting a vehicle to speed into view.

"Yes. That's why I need to get rid of it as soon as possible." He groaned, his hands dripping crimson as he shoved the barbed bolt farther.

Violet wished she could cover her ears and drown out Sagan's agonized cries. With one last wretched moan, he yanked the bolt free and held it up. Spindled barbs beneath the arrowhead still clung to red chunks of his flesh.

Violet's gag reflex kicked into action, and the acrid taste of bile hit her tongue. She covered her mouth with one hand.

Sagan flung the bolt out of the window and slumped back into his seat. Sluggishly, he rummaged once again into his bag and pulled out a glass vial containing a white pearlescent liquid.

"Whoa," said Violet. "What's that stuff?"

"It's best you don't know." Sagan pulled off the stopper. He poured some of the liquid onto his leg, then tilted his head back and took a sip. Gagging, he wiped his mouth with the shoulder part of his sleeve.

"Who was that guy?" Violet asked.

"Axel."

Violet took note of Sagan's other injuries. "Why is that Axel guy after you? What happened?"

The next few moments were quiet, apart from Sagan's ragged pants. "I did something that really pissed off my father. He sent Axel after me, who ambushed me at my house. I managed to escape out the back door, and I cut through the forest until I found the road out of town."

"And what about that other guy—that thing with the scales and spikes?"

"It was . . . umm . . ." He mumbled the next few words as his head began to droop.

Violet shook his shoulder. "Sagan? What was that thing?"

He raised his head with a heavy intake of air. "It was a Veniri."

"A what? What is a—"

Sagan kept talking. "But don't worry, Violet . . ."

She couldn't make out the rest of his words, other than something about a shield.

"Why was that guy after me?"

No answer.

"Sagan?"

She glanced over at him. His eyes were shut, and his head slumped to one side.

"Sagan?"

Still no answer. She tapped on his shoulder. "Sagan, I need you to tell me where to go."

Nothing.

She choked on a sob and gripped the steering wheel, trying to swallow her rising panic. What the hell did she know about escaping from psychopathic beard guys? What if he was still tracking them? What if he managed to get another device attached to the back of the car? She should stop the car and check.

No! Sagan had told her not to stop. That would give Axel the opportunity to catch up.

She pressed harder on the accelerator, and the engine roared. The trees on either side of the road whipped by faster. Faster. Faster.

A shrill tune blasted up from her footwell. She jumped and let out a startled shriek, causing the car to wobble and weave into the wrong lane. The ringing continued as she released some pressure on the accelerator and got the car back under control. She glanced at Sagan, but he hadn't even stirred.

Reaching into the footwell, she spotted Gus's name flashing on the phone's screen.

"Gus?"

"Violet! What the hell is going on? Are you okay?"

"Yes, I'm fine. At least . . . I'm . . ." Her words caught in her throat.

She could hear Autumn in the background. Then both their voices became loud and clear, talking over each other, as Gus—she assumed—put the phone on speaker.

Relief overwhelmed her panic, and she burst into tears.

"Oh my gosh, guys. You have no idea how happy I am to hear your voices."

"Violet, what's going on?" asked Gus.

Violet heaved a few teary sighs. "It's a long and crazy story."

"Tell us *everything*," demanded Autumn.

## SEH'VUTHI

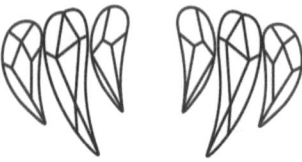

Foggy tendrils of awareness prodded the edges of Nathan's mind. How long had he been asleep, and how long did he have before he was dragged back into oblivion? Profound exhaustion tugged at his limbs, but something nagged at him—something he needed to do. What was it?

Tight mesh clung to his body, binding his legs together and his arms to his chest. He tried to wiggle his fingers, but he barely managed a weak twitch. A tingling sensation tickled his scales. He was in Veniri form? Why? When had he changed?

*Where am I?*

He was on his back, his body gently rocking as a growling hum sent vibrations through the hard surface he was lying on. He had to be in the back of some kind of vehicle. A van maybe? Something else lay on his left, bumping into his shoulder at regular intervals.

With a slight jolt, the swaying stopped. The vibration beneath him continued, though the growling hum had quieted to a soft purr.

With a faint *click* and *bang*, a car door opened and closed.

A few seconds later, the back door swung open, casting a bright light onto Nathan's closed eyelids. Even the minuscule action of raising his heavy lids was near impossible, but he managed to open his eyes long enough to drag his gaze over a familiar face.

*Thane.*

"It's about time you showed up, Axel," said a male voice from outside the vehicle. "Where's the Branstone boy?"

"Gone," said a lower, more gravelly voice.

A string of violent curses followed.

Nathan tried his best to keep the fog in his brain at bay as he listened to the rest of the conversation.

"Keep your knickers on," said the guy called Axel. "I managed to get a tracking barb in his car." He grunted as if lifting something heavy. A second later, something thudded next to Nathan on his right. "I found this one when I was chasing the boy."

The first voice huffed. "Did you have to stab it so many times? I'm going to have to hose all the blood out when we get back. Why couldn't you have used stun nets like we did with these two?"

Axel scoffed. "Where's the fun in that? So you got the runaway then? Where'd the other slith come from?"

"Dunno. Picked it up with the runaway."

"Seems like these things multiply quicker than we can kill them."

"Just as well. The more we kill the more we get paid."

Axel chuckled. "Speaking of getting paid, I found that girl too. She drove off with the boy."

"That Violet girl?"

Nathan's attention peaked. *Violet.*

"Yep" came the reply.

A tongue clicked. "I still don't understand that bounty. What's so special about her? She's just a human."

"As long as I get paid, I don't care," said Axel.

"Then let's go get 'em and get paid."

The door banged shut, and before long, the swaying recommenced.

Nathan's pulse began to race. Where were he and Thane being taken? He searched his mind, trying to peer past the blackness that shrouded his memories. Anything to give him a clue.

Those men had mentioned . . .

*Violet!*

Where was she? Where was Violet?

Her face materialized through the fog of his mind's eye with startling clarity, almost as if he could reach out and touch her. But greedy tentacles of dread latched on to her shoulders and arms and twisted around her neck, snatching her back. She screamed, reached out to him, begged him to save her, but the tentacles stifled her cries. They were dragging her toward a grassy field with three tombstones—the graves of Nathan's closest loved ones.

*No! Not Violet too!*

In his mind, he lunged and grabbed her extended hand, using every ounce of his depleted energy to pull her into a tight embrace. Instead of fighting him, the tentacles ensnared him too and dragged him along toward Violet's doom.

A yell cut through Nathan's nightmare. Fierce expletives came from the front of the car.

"That damn boy got rid of the tracker!"

"So which way do I go now?"

"I don't know!" roared the voice.

Nathan's black fog drowned out the developing argument. He couldn't fight it anymore. In his mind, he still clutched Violet tight as the tentacles released their hold, retreating back into the depths.

Then the fog swallowed him and Violet, sending them both into a deep abyss.

* * *

"Nathan?"

Nathan stirred at the soft sound of his name.

"Nathan? Are you awake?"

He tried to answer but only managed a groggy moan.

"Nathan, wake up."

He opened his eyes and blinked; darkness pressed against his vision. "Thane?"

"Yeah, it's me" came the reply from his left.

Nathan tried to turn his head, but the net over his face still hampered his movements. "Damn it," he said as a rush of memories flooded back, reminding him of the grim situation they were in. Thankfully, the fog in his mind had cleared somewhat. The tranquilizer was losing its effect. "Where are we?"

"I don't know," said Thane. "It feels like we've been driving for hours."

"How long have you been awake?"

"Um, not sure. Maybe an hour? I tried waking you up, but you were pretty out of it."

Nathan groaned. His stiff body desperately needed repositioning, but there was no chance the net encapsulating his body would allow it. "Any chance you've figured out where they're taking us?"

"None." A few seconds of silence passed before Thane continued, panic edging into his voice. "So what do we do now? How do we get to Violet? We need to get out of here and go find her. We need to—"

"I know, I know. Just try to stay calm." Nathan wasn't about to admit his own escalating panic. "At the moment there's nothing we can do, unless you've managed to get free of your net."

"Nope. Believe me, I've tried."

Nathan drew in a long breath through his nose. "Okay, so we'll just have to wait. Once we know what's going on, then maybe we can come up with a plan."

Nathan tried to keep his mind from spinning, from uselessly analyzing and reanalyzing all that had happened in the last few days. He needed to focus on something else—talk about something else.

"So, you've been spending all this time with Violet. How did you keep your tattoo hidden?"

"Scarves at first. Then I came across a concealer that did the trick."

"It must not have done the trick very well if she saw it."

Thane groaned. "I had a lapse in concentration, and I, um . . . forgot to put it on. And as you can imagine, all hell broke loose."

Nathan couldn't help a small scoff. "What did you expect? Her trauma was so extensive the shield couldn't hide every-thing. That detail became the padlock to her memories. Seeing your tattoo was the trigger to unlock it all." Nathan tried to shake his head, but the net held him firm. "She must have been in agony when it all came crashing back."

Thane groaned. "Yeah, that part was the *worst*."

"Yeah, I bet."

"Up until that moment, things were going great. Other than the incident with the girl at her college, Violet was . . . happy."

Nathan stared at the darkened ceiling of the trunk. "How you guys met—you know, the second time."

"Right, the second time," said Thane after a nervous laugh. He recounted the story of bumping into Violet at the coffee shop. "After that we just began hanging out, you know, just chatting over coffee and chai. And then I . . ." Thane cleared his throat. "I helped her out with one of her assignments, and then we . . . actually, there was this, um . . ."

"What?" Nathan asked when Thane didn't continue.

"There were these weird golden lights."

Nathan frowned.

"I have no idea what they were," continued Thane. "It was kinda freaky."

"You said they were golden?"

"Yeah."

"Did they radiate from your skin?"

"Yeah. How did you—"

Nathan cursed under his breath. Regardless of what he thought about Thane's relationship with Violet, this was more serious than he'd imagined. And clearly, it was out of his control. "What color were Violet's lights?"

"Violet's? What do you mean? She . . . there were only golden lights."

Nathan released a heavy breath.

"Nathan? Do you know what it is?"

"What you experienced was the beginning of Seh'Vuthi."

"No," said Thane after a pause. "It can't be. That's . . . that's forbidden."

Nathan let out a bitter laugh. "According to Queen Idalia, but it isn't within her power to control, despite how much she and her mother tried by outlawing all talk and teachings about it. It just became exceptionally rare, especially when the breeding program was introduced. But when it happens, it's a power to be reckoned with."

"Wha . . .? How do you know all this?"

"I've seen it twice. Once when I was a child, around the time it was outlawed. An uprising began, led by two Veniri who were bestowed with Seh'Vuthi. The reign of Queen Imoranda almost came to an end. Unfortunately, the

Seh'Vuthi couple was captured and executed, and Queen Imoranda brought down her wrath on the Veniri people and rebels alike."

"That's not the version I heard," said Thane.

Nathan chuckled. "Yeah, well, the royals would prefer the truth be lost, but there are still too many of us who remember what really happened."

"Hmm. So, what is Seh'Vuthi? What does it do?"

"It's when . . . Let's see . . . How can I explain this?" Nathan's eyes searched the darkness. Why did he have to be the one to give this explanation? He'd rather reveal that Santa Claus isn't real, or that crab salad actually doesn't have any crab in it—not this "birds and the bees" stuff. "Uh . . . what you experienced is the beginnings of a, for lack of a better word, 'soul-bind.' It's when you, your soul, has found someone it wants to bind to. Your golden lights were a proposal."

"What . . . ? Proposal? As in . . . marriage?"

Nathan cringed. "Essentially, yes. But instead of white dresses and tuxedos, like Erathi weddings, the Seh'Vuthi is more profound. It's more metaphysical. Your soul starts to take on broad elements of the other person—what they see, what they feel, and how they perceive things. Anything that helps you understand them on a deeper level. However, the process of Seh'Vuthi is only completed if the other person's soul accepts your proposal."

"Oh . . . so, how do you know if the other person has accepted?"

"Their lights appear as well, and eventually your souls intertwine. I don't know if it's the same for every Seh'Vuthi couple, but things like mental communication abilities are established—maybe special abilities that only one member had is now shared with the other. What used to benefit one now benefits both. That's the main reason why the Seh'Vuthi

Veniri rebels were able to nearly overthrow Queen Imoranda, and why she decided to outlaw it."

"Wait a minute," said Thane, "you said you'd seen this twice. Who was the other couple?"

Nathan opened his mouth but couldn't produce an answer.

"It was you, wasn't it?" said Thane after a few moments. Nathan couldn't see Thane's face, but the shock in his voice was obvious. "But . . . with who?"

"I'd rather not talk about it." Nathan closed his eyes, allowing the lull in the conversation to drag out. A face from long ago pushed to the forefront of his mind. Her smile and glow were as radiant as ever, only darkened by the shadow of his own grief.

"Suit yourself."

Thane shifted in the darkness next to him. "I'm not sure I like the idea of any of my abilities transferring to Violet," he eventually said. "The last thing she needs is to become a filthy killing machine. I think I would prefer to avoid Seh'Vuthi and just stick with the Divine Oath."

"What?" Nathan exclaimed. "Tell me you didn't. Tell me you didn't pledge the Divine Oath to Violet."

Thane didn't answer.

"But she's not royalty. She's not even Veniri."

"I don't care," said Thane, his voice edged with steel. "I won't waste my oath on any Veniri, especially not that foul beast Idalia, who thinks she can—"

"Bite. Your. Tongue," wheezed a new voice.

Nathan froze.

Between raspy breaths and audible gulps, the voice in the darkness continued, "Renounce your words, and I will be merciful on Her Divine Majesty Queen Idalia's behalf and spare your life."

Deep resentment leached through Nathan's body as he

recognized the voice. "Kronan," he said through gritted teeth. He flicked out his tongue through the mesh and, sure enough, caught the putrid stench of Kronan's soul-scent.

Kronan gave a wheezy cackle. "You have no idea how long I've waited for this day, Nathan—the day I finally end your life."

Something heavy shifted on Nathan's right. A surge of both fear and fury pumped adrenaline into his veins, and with a surge of desperation, he fought to free himself from the net.

Then all became quiet as the vehicle turned off.

Without warning, the back door opened, and a bright white light streamed in. Through his squinted eyelids, Nathan registered three hunters looming over them.

Kronan leaped past Nathan with a gurgled screech and latched on to one of the hunters.

"Geez, Axel." A hunter whistled. "I thought you said you killed this one."

"Huh." A fourth hunter with a gray beard stepped into view. "Looks like I was mistaken."

As the three hunters wrangled Kronan, Axel leaned in, grabbed Nathan's netting, and yanked him out of the vehicle. Nathan *ooph*ed as Axel dropped him unceremoniously onto the ground. A few seconds later, Thane thudded next to him.

Kronan's screeches eventually died down to panting wheezes.

Nathan tried to take in as much of his surroundings as he could. He was lying on timber. The lapping melody of water drifted up from beneath the planks, and the strong smell of salt filled his lungs with each intake of air. Gulls screeched above him. Nathan turned his head as much as the net would allow and spotted several boats gently rocking at the edge of the boardwalk.

Axel once again gripped Nathan's netting and dragged

him over a gangplank, then down some stairs into a boat's cargo hold. Finally, he shoved him into a crate made of familiar green-tinged metal. The door of the crate slammed and locked shut, and soon after, another hunter threw Thane into the crate next to him.

A face with a familiar shark grin appeared between the crate's slats. Nathan gritted his teeth, fighting hard against his bonds.

Matthias leaned in. "Save your strength for the fight pits, slith. And make sure you do me proud."

With a wink, Matthias turned, and the other hunters followed him up the stairs. The last closed the door behind him, plunging Nathan's world once again into darkness.

## 27

## SPICED RICE

VIOLET CLOSED HER EYES AND TILTED HER HEAD BACK, enjoying the sun's warmth. Beside her, Autumn collapsed back on the picnic blanket and leaned against her shoulder.

"How are you feeling?" Violet asked, resting her cheek on top of Autumn's head.

Autumn sighed. "Actually, I'm feeling like a really crappy friend. I should be there. But I . . . I just can't." She turned her face into Violet's arm, a sob shuddering through her.

"It's okay." Gus sat on Autumn's other side, and both he and Violet wrapped an arm around her back. "We can have our own memorial for her. One where we binge her favorite movies in Hello Kitty shirts while eating an assortment of her favorite Japanese snacks."

Autumn sniffled out a small laugh. "Actually, that sounds awesome. The other service is likely to be way more formal and somber, not like Bessie at all."

"Yeah," agreed Violet, although she too felt a pang of guilt for not being at Bessie's memorial service. When the three of them received an email stating the details, they'd seriously discussed going—even bought plane tickets—but when the day came closer, Autumn's grief spiked. Violet understood what Autumn was going through—what it was like to not be ready to say goodbye.

"All right, done," said Gus. "When we get back to the house, I'll make an online order for an obscene amount of Japanese junk food."

"Awesome." Autumn wiped away her tears.

"What about you, Sagan?" said Gus. "Are you in?"

Sagan stood at the rocky edge of the creek a few feet away. "I don't think so," he said with a slight shake of his head. "I didn't know her."

"Bessie won't mind," said Autumn. "If anything, she'll be pissed to be missing out."

"Still, I wouldn't want to intrude," said Sagan.

He bent down, picked up a pebble, and tossed it into the water. His face crinkled into a slight wince as he massaged his thigh. He'd been walking more and more since he and Violet had arrived at Gus and Autumn's compound just over a week ago, but he still hadn't fully recovered.

"Come and sit down, Sagan." Violet patted the rug beside her. "Give your leg a break."

"Yeah, come on," said Gus. "No one's going to think you're any less macho if you just relax for a while."

"No, I'm fine." He crossed his arms and readjusted his stance.

Gus leaned back on his elbows. "Suit yourself."

The conversation lapsed into silence, allowing the sounds of nature to meld into the forefront. Gushing creek water bubbled and churned in an undulating tune, with the low roar of a nearby waterfall adding its own bass notes. Birds flitted and chirped, and the wind rustled the long grass and reeds by the water's edge.

Violet's eyes followed a radiant blue-and-green kingfisher hovering over the water. Its wings flapped at an incredible speed. Then, with stunning grace, it dove into the water, only to resurface a second later with prey secured in its sharp beak. It flew to a low-hanging branch over the water, smacked the fish's head on the branch, then gobbled it down.

She chewed her lip, mulling over the events of the past few weeks. Some of it still didn't feel real.

It had taken her several days to drive to Gus and Autumn's little hippie community, with only a few fitful naps in between—fitful due to her new nightmares of crystal tridents, barbed arrows, and creatures with forked tongues. The faceless man was no longer the center of her dreams, but his presence still constantly haunted the shadows of her mind. Every now and then, his face configured itself into Thane's.

Sagan was barely conscious for the whole drive. When he did wake, it was only ever long enough to take another swig from the bottle of white pearl liquid. He'd question their whereabouts, but she would hardly get an answer out before he was unconscious again.

Several times she'd had the urge to pull over at a police station, but for what? What police officer would believe she'd seen a man with a crystal trident kill a reptilian humanoid, and now the man was after her? Plus, Nathan was a cop. She'd trusted him. How could she possibly trust a cop that she didn't even know?

When she'd finally reached Gus and Autumn's property near the ocean, she'd nearly collapsed from exhaustion and relief.

Gus's mom, Dawn, was a doctor for the compound and was swift to take care of Sagan, who was even swifter in his recovery, much to everyone's shock. After only a week, his wound already looked like an old scar. Violet had a strong suspicion the mystery liquid in his black bag had something to do with it.

On the drive over, she'd told Gus and Autumn everything over the phone. She couldn't answer a lot of their questions, such as what the creature on the road was or why Axel was after her. When Sagan was finally conscious enough to hold a lengthy conversation, Gus and Autumn had bombarded him with questions too. He kept tight-lipped at first, but it didn't take long for him to crack, especially after Violet insisted she at least had a right to know why a bounty order had her photo on it.

Every answer Sagan gave brought up at least ten more questions. Violet's mind boggled with Sagan's compendium of new words. *Veniri, Diamantium, Erathi.*

The word *Erathi* amused her. It was what the shifters called humans; it was what *she* was. And as for the shifters themselves, if she hadn't seen for herself the creature with the forked tongue, she would've guessed Sagan's little bottle of pearly white liquid was actually a hallucinogenic of some sort.

But despite all the new information he provided, Sagan couldn't shed light on why the guy with the gray beard was after her. Couldn't or wouldn't, Violet wasn't quite sure which. But the term he'd used was "being hunted."

A shiver ran through her at the memory of his words.

The faint ringing of a bell caught everyone's attention.

"Lunchtime." Gus jumped to his feet and held out his hands to help both the girls up. He and Autumn folded up the picnic blanket, then led the way along the walking path toward the ringing lunch bell.

Violet waited for Sagan, who carefully made his way up the slight incline where the rocky creek's edge met the grassy field. His bad leg wobbled on a rock, and he stumbled forward.

Violet rushed down to meet him. "Here, let me help you."

"Thanks, but I can manage."

Violet ignored him and took hold of his arm, draping it over her neck.

"I said I can manage." Regardless of his hard tone, he didn't push her away. His limp was slight, but Violet could tell he was still in pain despite his poker face.

"You should take some painkillers when we get back."

He scoffed. "I can handle it. I've been through worse."

"Really? How much worse? Did you lose the whole leg last time?"

He huffed, but a corner of his mouth twitched up. He looked down at her and held her gaze. The cobalt edges of his irises faded to almost white around his pupils, and a few flecks of pastel blue speckled the white rings.

Violet broke eye contact and stared at the ground. To her slight relief, Sagan dropped his arm from her shoulders, and she let her own arms fall to her sides. They continued to walk a few inches apart as the walking path moved into an orchard. Bees hummed and weaved around them to find the flowering trees and vines.

"So, how long do you plan on sticking around here?" Sagan asked.

She'd been asking herself the same question over the last few days, especially whenever Gus and Autumn talked about going back to college. She wasn't sure she could go back and live a normal college life after everything that had happened.

"I'm not sure. Is there a chance that guy with the trident is still after us?"

The house came into view on the other side of the trees.

"It's likely," said Sagan after a pause.

"Do you think we're safe here?"

"If they haven't found us by now, then yes. I think, for the moment, you're safe."

"Good, 'cause I'm running out of places I can go." She huffed out a long breath. Her chest felt tight at the memory of finding out Nathan had been friends with Thane all along. Some days she hated Nathan; others she sat with her thumb hovering over his speed dial number, trying to gather enough courage to talk to him. Her mind whirled with so many questions, and yet, they all boiled down to just one. *Why?*

She couldn't stay in the guest room of Autumn's house forever, but she also couldn't fathom returning home—back to Nathan's place. Not right now, but then again, maybe never. His betrayal had cut her deep.

"At least you've got a home to go back to," she said, hugging her arms around her torso.

"No, I can't go back."

"But surely your father—"

"No!"

She jumped at his outburst.

He stopped walking and looked at her. "I won't go back. Especially not to *him.*"

His expression stirred a long dormant memory of a sleepover at Lyla's house. Violet had woken in the middle of the night needing a glass of water, and she'd accidentally eavesdropped on a vicious conversation Sagan and his father were having in the study. Matthias had Sagan pinned against the heavy wooden desk, one hand latched on to his son's throat.

"You don't talk about her. Ever," Matthias had growled, an inch from Sagan's face.

Sagan's eyes narrowed at his father, defiance and rage evident even from where Violet stood peering into the study.

"But she's *my* mother," countered Sagan.

Matthias had reacted with a cracking backhand, then left Sagan to cradle his cheek.

Sagan's severe expression now was the same as it had been that night.

"Okay," said Violet. She had no idea what else to say.

Sagan didn't respond. Instead, he broke eye contact and continued the rest of the way a few steps in front of her.

Over the next few weeks, Violet fell into a relaxed routine. She volunteered to help out wherever possible, trying to keep her mind busy with chores rather than worries and fears. Even doing the laundry for everyone was welcome—until she came across the clothes she'd been wearing when she found Sagan on the road. Patches of dried iridescent blue were splattered across her pants and all over the back of her jacket. In the end, she didn't bother washing the blood-splattered clothes. Instead she bundled them up and threw them straight into the trash.

Where Gus's mom was a brilliant doctor, Autumn's mom, Skye, was a brilliant cook. Gus's family, along with Sagan—who'd taken up residence in their spare room—joined in for most evening meals. The delectable feasts comprised nearly all homegrown produce. Violet had developed a particular fondness for homemade yogurt and freshly baked bread.

Gus wasn't joking when he'd told her he knew macramé. He was an enthusiastic tutor, guiding Violet's hands to form the knots and weaves.

"That's it, now you're getting the hang of it," he commented one night on one of her knots. "A few more days of this and you'll have your own macramé hammock."

"What? Days?" Violet winced. At least two of her fingers had the beginnings of new blisters, and the skin of several others was already starting to peel from the previous day's attempt.

"Here." Gus grabbed a few strands of rope. "I'll work on this side."

A few feet away, Autumn sat with her laptop at the kitchen bench, a regular sight when they weren't out in the yard. Her headphones were on, and the staccato clacking of her keys melded with the rhythm of her mother's cooking. Pots bubbled and sizzled on the stove, creating mouthwatering promises for their upcoming dinner. Skye was the mirror image of her daughter, from the decorated dreadlocks right down to the toe rings.

Sagan sat at the end of the kitchen counter, away from the group. His elbows rested on the countertop as his eyes focused on some faraway thought. He played with a section of the black chain poking up from his shirt collar, rolling it between his fingers.

Since that day at the creek, he'd clammed up. He still tagged along on some of their chores and activities but only observed from the side. Other times he would disappear for hours, showing up again at dinnertime.

Violet's apprehension that he would leave altogether grew each day. She hadn't had the courage to talk to him since that day at the creek, but she didn't necessarily feel awkward around him. His presence, as well as Gus's and Autumn's, soothed the unease that grew inside her every time she was by herself or trying to fall asleep at night.

Every now and then, her anxiety became so strong she thought she would either faint or throw up. Whenever that happened, she'd force herself to focus harder on her task or get the cousins to tell another story of their mischief from when they were kids. Anything to help push the feeling away.

"I'm going to my room," announced Autumn. "Let me know when dinner's ready."

"Sure thing," said Violet, not looking up from her macramé.

"So"—Gus lowered his voice so only she could hear —"how are you holding up? You know, after the whole 'Thane thing'?"

Violet's chest pinched. "I'm fine." She looped a strand of rope into another knot, a little tighter than necessary.

"Okay, good. I just wanted to make sure, because I know you really liked him, and—"

"I don't want to talk about it, Gus." She looped another knot, yanking it even tighter than the last.

"Okay," said Gus in almost a whisper. "I'm sorry for bringing it up. It's just . . . I'm a little concerned about you. That's all."

Violet dropped the ropes and rubbed her eyes with the heels of her hands. "I know, I'm sorry." She gave him a small apologetic smile. "I just can't deal with it all right now. I just . . ." She sat up straighter to take a huge breath into her lungs, then slumped with the heavy exhale. "You're right, I really did like him. There are some days that I really miss him. I miss being with him, and the person I was with him. With him I felt . . . free. Uplifted. But then I think about his tattoo and what that means, and I just . . . I just *hate* him." She winced and played with a rope's fraying end. "You probably think I'm stupid."

"No, not stupid," said Gus. "I think being confused is totally understandable. He took advantage of you and your trust."

"Yeah. So did Nathan." She held back a sob. His betrayal hurt the most.

Gus's brow creased and he shook his head. "I still don't get it. What was his deal? Why would he be friends with the guy that kidnapped you? It doesn't make any sense."

"I know. I've been going insane trying to figure it all out."

"Yeah, I bet. Well"—he patted his shoulder—"anytime you need a shoulder to cry on, just let me know."

Violet chuckled. "Thanks, Gus."

"Dinner's just about ready," called Skye, wiping her hands on a tea towel. "Sagan, do you mind starting to serve while I set the table?"

"No problem."

266

Gus hopped up and headed for the back door. "I'll go get Mom, Dad, and Uncle Cruz."

"And I'll go get Autumn," said Violet, dropping her macramé thread.

She went and knocked on Autumn's closed door, but there was no answer.

"Autumn, dinner's ready."

Silence. Violet waited a few seconds, then turned the door handle and peeked inside.

Autumn was sitting on her bed with her legs outstretched. Her laptop rested on her thighs, and she had on her Bluetooth over-ear headphones.

"Autumn, dinner's—"

Violet's eyes widened when she realized what her friend was focusing so intently on. Autumn held her gold metallic clutch a few inches from her face—the same one from the black light party—and whatever was inside cast a bright orange light onto Autumn's face.

"Autumn? What—"

Autumn looked up, slammed the clutch shut, and stuffed it under her pillow. "Violet! What are you doing? Heard of knocking?"

"I did knock."

"Oh. Maybe knock a little louder next time." Autumn forced a grin.

After a few awkward moments, Violet finally said, "Um, dinner's ready."

"Okay, cool," said Autumn, making no sign of leaving. "I'll be out in a few seconds. I just got, um . . ." She stabbed a finger at her laptop. "I just got to finish up something here."

Violet slowly nodded but couldn't quite stop herself from glancing at Autumn's pillow, where she'd hidden the gold clutch. "Okay. I'll, uh, see you out there."

"Cool." Autumn bobbed her head enthusiastically.

Violet closed the door behind her and frowned. What was Autumn up to? Making her way back to the kitchen, she realized she was too hungry to focus on unraveling the enigma that was her friend. She might fish for answers later.

She joined Sagan behind the kitchen counter, her shoulder bumping into his as she reached for a plate.

"Sorry," she said.

"It's fine," he replied, cutting into a loaf of warm bread. Tendrils of steam escaped with each new slice.

Violet reached for Skye's signature dish of spiced rice— one of her favorites. Star anise and bay leaves, along with a spiraled cinnamon stick, could be seen through the condensation on the underside of the glass cover. A cloud of aromatic steam billowed upward when Violet raised the lid, her mouth watering.

But when the scent of cinnamon hit her nose, her stomach lurched, and she couldn't stop herself from gagging. She covered her mouth with both hands, the lid slipping from her fingers and falling to the ground. She barely registered the crash and spray of shattered glass.

Her world spun. Distorted echoes hammered her eardrums. Sagan's face blurred before her, his eyes wide and his mouth forming incoherent words.

And then blackness flooded her vision.

* * *

A steady beeping dragged Violet from sleep. She was nowhere near ready to be awake. She reached an arm out in a groggy attempt to switch off the alarm, but something caught her hand.

Opening her bleary eyes, she saw an IV tube running from the top of her hand to a machine, which was the source of the beeping. She sat up and blinked, and the infirmary room of the community compound came into focus, the place where Gus's mom worked and where Sagan had spent most of his time when they first arrived.

"It's about time you woke up." Gus sat in a chair nearby.

"What happened?"

He came over and perched on the edge of the bed. "Well, long story short, we were about to sit down for dinner when you decided to pass out."

"What?" She rubbed her forehead, trying to remember, then moaned. "Oh, no. I broke Skye's glass lid."

"Don't worry about it." Gus waved a hand. "She's more worried about your feet."

"My feet?" She winced, now aware of a slight ache in her soles and a tightness that went from her toes to her ankles. She threw off the blanket, the sudden movement making her head spin.

"Easy," said Gus. "You better take it slow."

She waited a second or two for the world to become still again, then drew her legs up and inspected the neat bandages wrapped around both feet.

"You stepped on the glass before you totally blacked out. You're lucky Sagan caught you before you hit your head on anything. He was the one who carried you here."

"How long have I been out?"

"Well, a while. It's been two nights."

"Two nights?"

"Yeah, it was a bit of a worry. Mom's been running some tests to find out what happened. She said she should have some news today."

The door flew open and Autumn burst in. "Finally! You're awake!" She ran over and wrapped Violet in a hug. "You had me worried, you jerk."

Violet chuckled and hugged her back. "It's good to see you too," she said through Autumn's dreadlocks.

Behind Autumn, at the foot of the bed, stood Sagan.

"Hey," said Violet, "I hear you're the reason I don't have a cracked skull."

He put his hands in his pockets and shrugged. "Your feet are cut up pretty bad."

Autumn rolled her eyes. "She's trying to thank you, doofus."

Gus laughed, and Sagan shot them both a look. His mouth twitched, then his eyes found Violet's again. "You're welcome. How are you feeling?" The corners of his eyes creased with concern.

"I'm fine." Violet nodded, but the movement started the world spinning again. "I think," she added, grimacing, and slumped back on the plump pillows.

"What's wrong?" Gus asked.

"I, um . . . I'm feeling dizzy."

Gus grabbed the chart at the end of the bed. "Do you feel sick, like you're about to throw up?"

"No. At least, I don't think so."

He read the beeping machine and jotted down some notes on the clipboard, then proceeded to check her blood pressure, temperature, and heart rate.

"Since when did you become Doctor Gus?" Violet asked.

"It's his hidden talent," said Autumn, beaming with pride.

"What? I thought macramé was his hidden talent."

Gus smirked. "I, ah, started helping my mom out when I was a kid. It began with simple things, like handing her a bandage, but I kind of developed a knack. When I got older, she'd let me do simple stuff if she was busy with another patient, and then she'd check over what I'd done when she got back."

He was pulling out a new IV bag from a nearby supply trolley when Dawn and Skye came in.

"Hey, you're awake," said Skye.

"Glad to see you're up," said Dawn, her relief evident in her smile. She and Gus started conversing in a medical jargon Violet hadn't even realized Gus was fluent in. He offered the IV bag to his mother, but she gestured for him to continue hooking it up himself.

"There, that should do it," he said after he was done. He turned to Violet. "As far as I can tell, everything should be okay. You were a little dehydrated and hypotensive due to not drinking enough fluids over the last few days, so I've started another IV fluid to correct this." He gave her a reassuring smile. "You should feel better soon."

Violet's eyes bugged.

"You poor thing." Skye pressed a hand to Violet's forehead. "You're probably hungry too. I'll go and whip you up something to eat." She planted a kiss on the top of Violet's head before leaving the room.

"Thanks, Gus," said Violet, still a little amazed to see him in such a different role. She turned to Dawn. "So, do you know why I passed out?"

Dawn's mouth pinched into a thin line. "Gus, Autumn, Sagan, will you give us a few minutes?"

She received immediate protests from Gus and Autumn, and Sagan looked as if he would rather eat hot coals.

"It's fine," said Violet, raising her voice over the arguments. "I don't have a problem with them being here."

Dawn placed her hands on her hips, giving the cousins a pointed look. Violet had a feeling they were going to receive a lecture later.

"I did receive some test results today," said Dawn, turning her attention back to Violet. "Some were a little perplexing, but others make sense due to your symptoms." She clasped her hands together, and her lips pinched again, this time into a tight smile.

"Violet, you're pregnant."

# EPILOGUE

MATTHIAS CHECKED THE TIME AGAIN, RELEASING A LOW GROWL at the glowing numbers on the watch face. How much longer did they have to wait for these damned things? He peered impatiently into the surrounding trees, beyond the bright beams and deep shadows cast by the floodlights from the vehicles behind him.

A soft whimpering issued from a square crate on the ground, about two-thirds of Matthias's height and made of green-tinged Metallikite. Gradually, the noise grew into a shrill, animalistic squabbling.

"Shut up!" barked Axel. He kicked the crate again and again, but the sound only grew louder.

Matthias squeezed his eyes shut and pinched the bridge of his nose. "Axel, would you please—"

A high-pitched shriek quaked though Matthias's eardrums. His eyes flew open just as Axel yanked his trident out from one of the gaps in the crate.

"I said *shut up!*" Axel roared.

The shriek fell to a quiet sniffling that stopped a few

moments later. A small trail of pearlescent liquid trickled out from the crate, pooling among the leaf litter.

Matthias sighed. "Axel, would you please stop damaging the product. There isn't going to be much of it left if you keep spilling it."

Axel grunted. "Damn noise was grating on my nerves."

"And the kicking made everything so much better," said one of the hunters behind them.

Axel spun as someone else snickered. He pointed his trident in the direction of the hecklers. "Another word out of either of you and I'll use you as bait for the next hunt."

The snickering stopped, but Matthias didn't have to turn around to imagine the scornful looks Axel was probably receiving. Axel was a fierce and impetuous hunter, but his brutish personality didn't earn him much respect from the others.

Twigs and leaves snapped and crackled under Axel's heavy boots. "How much longer are we going to stand here? We've been waiting for hours. Bet those blasted things have gotten themselves lost."

Matthias inhaled sharply through his nose and spoke through gritted teeth. "What are the chances of them being lost when the whole damn forest knows exactly where we are from all your racket?" He gave Axel a pointed stare, and the man was at least smart enough to don a sheepish expression and cease fidgeting.

"I'm just saying," said Axel in a more hushed tone, "I think we should pack up and leave, take the product to one of our established clients. You know, stick with our own. Since when do we make deals with our prey anyway? First the human girl, now this." He kicked the crate again but with less force than before. "Do we even know what they're going to do with it?"

Matthias raised his shoulder in a half shrug. "As long as they've brought our payment, I don't care what they do."

Axel grunted. "Even if they plan to use it against us?"

"How could they possibly use it against us?" Matthias didn't care for Axel's conspiracy theories, but even pointless conversation was better than this damned monotony.

Axel scrutinized the crate. "Well, you know what they say about the Yranum and immortality. We can't have our prey figuring out how to become immortal, now, can we?"

Matthias scoffed. "*We* haven't figured it out yet. What makes you think they will?"

"But—"

"I see something. Over there," said one of the hunters behind them.

Matthias flicked his attention to the trees ahead.

"I see it too," said another hunter.

"There's another over there."

The murmurs and chatter picked up as movement in the shadows advanced toward the clearing. Matthias became hyperaware of the crystal machete strapped to his back and the collection of other weapons secured to his body.

After several seconds, the shadows solidified into a number of humanoid silhouettes that stepped into the floodlights.

Axel gave a low whistle. "Look at all that glitter." He leaned in closer to Matthias and whispered, "I say we take 'em. That's more than enough Diamantium for my retirement fund right there."

Matthias ignored him, examining the Veniri. Maybe twenty stood before them, with likely double that number hidden out of sight. All the ones in plain view were in full shifted form. He had to give them credit; it was much harder to track a slith without knowing their "human" identity.

*Not impossible though.*

None of the Veniri wore any clothing; their iridescent scales and Diamantium shards were on display, from head to toe. Tiny rainbows glinted across the ground, tree trunks, and foliage from the plethora of large spikes extending from the creatures' knees, elbows, and collarbones.

The dazzling glimmers pulled an image to the forefront of Matthias's mind: a young girl's face, her expression anguished yet hopeful. She reached out to him, but before she could touch him, the sentinels of his ambitions and deepest desires locked the memory away. Only her shrieking scream lingered in his mind.

*Daddy, please!*

Matthias's hands clenched into tight fists at his sides. He forced his attention back to the scaled demons before him. Hate churned with ferocious potency in his chest, and his fingers itched to take hold of his own Diamantium spike holstered by his hip.

After he got what he wanted, he would slaughter every last one of these abominable creatures on this goddamned earth.

Several Veniri flicked their tongues out of their triple-fanged mouths. Others hissed, their otherworldly eyes locked on Matthias. He frowned, scanning the scaled creatures a few times. Something wasn't right.

All of them were male.

He folded his arms. "Where is she? I made it very clear she was to be here this time. No queen, no deal."

Two of the Veniri broke rank and walked forward on their three-toed feet, their movements lithe and slick. A few hunters had described them as raptor feet, like in dinosaur movies, but to Matthias they were just oversized chicken feet waiting to be lopped off at the knee and served up as entrees in Yum Cha restaurants.

They halted about a foot away from Matthias, close

enough for him to make out the complex patterns of teal, white, and black scales on their hides. The bright illumination at the base of each Diamantium spike almost made him squint.

Matthias shifted his hands to his hips. With three swift moves, he could have these things gutted and twitching out their last moments of mortality on the ground.

The one that stood eye to eye with Matthias glanced at the crate. "Is that all of what you promised?"

Matthias raised his chin and looked at the thing through hooded eyes. "Like I said before, 'No queen, no deal.'" He enunciated each word as if speaking to an infant.

The slith's features crinkled into a scowl. Then it flicked out its tongue.

With lightning speed, Matthias whipped out his hand and caught the slimy muscle. It wrapped around his wrist with a squelch, and he yanked hard until the creature's face was an inch from his. "Don't you poke this disgusting thing at me," Matthias hissed through his teeth.

The slith let out a guttural growl and tried to thrash out of his grip. Matthias saw the rage burning in the pathetic being's eyes. He tugged once more, then released the tongue and shoved the creature back. It stumbled and fell to the ground. A few hunters laughed; Axel guffawed the loudest.

A deep rumble reverberated in the chest of the second slith. The thundering sound grew louder as others around the clearing took it up, joining in the war cry.

Matthias smirked. Despite their warning of an attack, not one slith moved an inch. *Interesting.*

Turning to the others, the slith on the ground hissed out something unintelligible. The rumbling stopped. The creature stood up and gestured to the side of the clearing.

Two sliths stepped out from the shadows, dragging a

third between them. Its head was hunched forward, and blue liquid trailed in its wake.

The one whose tongue was yanked stepped behind the newcomers and, with one hand, clasped the forehead of the slumped slith and tilted its head up. A laborious wheeze escaped its lips.

Matthias knew a broken creature when he saw one.

Its eyes flew open and its mouth gaped as an elbow blade burst through the side of its neck. The creature released a throaty gargle, and every breath was a laborious wheeze. Streams of blue coursed down its chest, weaving rivulets through scales and crystal spikes.

"Are they trying to do our job for us?" Axel mumbled.

Matthias cocked his head to the side and narrowed his eyes. What on earth was this ridiculous display about? "Wow," he said, his voice monotone, "I'm so impressed. I could—"

He cut himself off as blue smoke effervesced from the slith's shimmering trails of teal blood.

Matthias snatched his dagger from his belt and took a step back. "What the hell's going on?"

Axel's trident appeared in the corner of his eye, and the rest of the hunters flanked him and Axel, their weapons held out. The blue smoke danced in the air before Matthias, growing thicker until it coalesced into the apparition of what looked like a human woman.

The hunters' shouted threats turned to stunned silence.

She was the most beautiful woman Matthias had ever laid eyes on. Her hair, crown, and outfit were outrageous and downright seductive. A hand rested on her cheek, and her pinky finger stroked the bottom lip of her smug smile.

Axel's trident inched forward and stabbed at the apparition. The blue wisps undulated around the crystalline prongs.

"What kind of trickery is this?" growled Axel.

No one bothered to answer him. The spectacular woman didn't even break eye contact with Matthias as Axel continued to stab at her.

Matthias shoved the trident away. "I thought I said 'face-to-face.'"

The wraith's delicious smile deepened. She dropped her hand and glided forward until her nose was an inch from his. "What do you call this?"

Her tender voice sent shivers down Matthias's spine. A corner of his mouth tilted up into a half smirk. "Cheating."

She placed a hand on her chest and laughed; the sound was like a glass wind chime. "Did you really think I wouldn't take precautions?" She clicked her tongue and shook her head. "Not so clever then, are you, hunter?"

Matthias's smirk faded, and a muscle twitched in his jaw. "Well, then, by all means, educate me." He gestured to the blue smoke. "Why don't you start by explaining how you're doing this?"

"Hmm . . ." She placed her smoky hand on his chest. Her fingertips trailed across him as she circled to his back. "That, my sweet, is such a dull topic."

Matthias's skin tingled under his clothes. Could he really feel her touch, or was he imagining it? His finger twitched toward his Diamantium blade, but as Axel had already demonstrated, his weapon would be ineffective against this wraith. "Why don't we discuss the deal at hand?" he said. "Did you bring what I asked?"

She returned to her position in front of him and steepled her fingers under her chin. "That depends. Have you brought what I asked?"

For a few moments, Matthias didn't move. The nerve of this creature, this so-called *queen*. She was beneath him in every sense of the word. If only she'd shown up in the flesh and not as a coward in the form of this . . . this . . . *smoke*, he'd have taught her how to show him respect.

Her steepled fingers began drumming a slow beat, and her pleasant smile began to harden.

How he wanted to wipe that impatient smile off her face. A few scenarios ran through his mind, but logic reminded him that none of his savage imaginings would help him in this current situation. He'd hang on to those ideas for after he achieved what he wanted.

For now, let her think she had the upper hand.

"Axel, move out of the way."

The big man hesitated, then let out a few indecipherable mumbles as he shuffled to the side. The smoky wraith's smiled broadened as she dropped her gaze to the crate. She glided over to inspect the box, trails of blue vapor twisting and curling behind her.

After circling the crate a few times, she paused on the other side and turned her attention back to Matthias. "How many are in there?"

"Three."

The queen raised a delicate eyebrow. "I thought you said the Yranum were rare?"

"They are," said Matthias, unable to resist a smug grin.

"Hmm . . ." The queen dipped her head slightly. "I must confess, dear hunter, I had my doubts about reaching out to you, but you have succeeded where many of my servants have failed."

Matthias smiled. "Like I said to you at the start, this is what I do best."

She returned his knowing smile. "If that's true, then please enlighten me as to why there's been a delay on the bounty of the male Veniri?"

Matthias's jaw clenched as the slith in question flashed through his mind's eye. Nathan Delano, the one who used to be a detective in his hometown. That slith had been living in plain sight for years. Hell, that thing had even investigated his own daughter's murder. How had he never picked up on the fact that it wasn't human? He'd never imagined one was capable of slipping past his radar. Never again would he allow that to happen.

"Rest assured I have my best men on the case. You will be notified as soon as he's in my possession."

She narrowed her eyes. The expression was probably meant to intimidate him, but it just made him more resolute. He wasn't ready to give up that slith. Not yet.

"Forget him for now." She waved one hand. "There is another I seek more urgently."

This was starting to become a trend. What was the story behind all of these bounties?

A Veniri stepped forward and held out a folder. It was a missing persons case file. With exaggerated indifference, Matthias perused the contents. On top was a grainy surveillance photo taken almost twenty years ago of a woman in a hospital gown. Beneath it was a second much clearer, much more recent photo, likely of the same woman in her mid to late forties. She wore a dark coat and scarf, and her loose brown hair hung past her shoulders. The photographer had captured the woman glancing backward as she walked down a busy city street.

There didn't seem to be anything special about her—until he came across the name. Gloria Chambers.

*Chambers? Does that mean—*

"I want this woman acquired swiftly," said the queen, "either alive or dead."

Matthias slowly nodded, still scanning the document.

*—disappeared from hospital—last seen wearing—baby girl abandoned—father unknown—*

He slammed the file shut, passed it to Axel, and raised his chin. "Consider it done. My price will be another—"

"Yes, yes," said the queen, dismissing him with a flutter of her fingers. "Once I have her, you'll be duly compensated."

Matthias bared his teeth in a wide grin.

"Where's the girl?"

"Ah-ah-ah." Matthias waved a finger. "I want to see what's owed to me first."

He didn't miss the subtle twitch of her mouth, the only sign of her irritation.

She raised an arm. Two more Veniri entered the clearing, carrying a large wooden chest between them. They placed it on the ground in front of Matthias and opened the lid. Shards upon shards of Diamantium glittered within, and from what Matthias could see, they were elbow shards, knee shards, and large collar-bone and spinal shards—everything Matthias's clients demanded the most. To get a stash this large of these specific spikes, his men would have to harvest at least fifty Veniri.

Axel whistled his appreciation.

Matthias put his hand on his hips and raised his gaze back to the wraith. "I want to see the tomes."

She twitched an amused eyebrow and, after a heartbeat, gestured again. Another two Veniri emerged from the shadows. Matthias's eyes widened and his pulse raced when he saw the heavy burdens they were carrying. Each Veniri held an ancient tome. Even without a close inspection, Matthias knew both tomes were made from solid gold and inlaid with gems and precious stones.

This. *This* was what he'd dreamed of since he was a child. At least, this was the beginning of bringing his dream to fruition. His siblings, father, and grandfather had all merci-lessly ridiculed him for years, but they wouldn't be laughing anymore. How the Veniri had managed to get their filthy hands on these precious Erathi artifacts he didn't know. But that was a mystery to solve at a later date.

The two Veniri stood side by side near the queen. Matthias took a step closer, but he stopped when several Veniri hissed and moved in front of the tome bearers.

He glared at the queen. "I need to confirm their authenticity."

She smiled, clearly enjoying this hold over him. "Where's the girl?" was all she said.

It was Matthias's turn to rein in his irritation. He raised a hand and gestured to the hunters behind him. Within a few moments, four hunters brought out a long blue polyethylene icebox and placed it between Matthias and the queen.

A hungry look entered her eyes. "Open it," she ordered.

All the hunters turned to Matthias. He let the moment drag a little longer than necessary, then nodded. One of his men leaned down, flicked up the four latches, and opened the lid. Axel began shuffling again, and Matthias shot him a glare.

A white fog drifted out of the icebox as the queen swept over to it, blue tendrils swirling in her wake. After a few seconds, the fog dissipated, revealing the body of a young girl lying on a bed of ice cubes. Her long brown hair fanned out over the ice, and blue veins spiderwebbed across her pallid, almost transparent flesh. Across her neck was a gruesome gash.

Matthias had been furious when he'd discovered the useless hunter he'd sent after Violet had killed the wrong girl. After about a week of being unable to locate their true target, they'd decided to reclaim the wrong girl's body from the morgue. Fortunately, the girl who was mistakenly killed looked a lot like Violet, and as long as Matthias got what he wanted, he didn't care what happened after the queen figured out she'd been deceived.

The blue wisp tilted her head to peer down at the girl. Without looking up, she raised one hand, and one of the Veniri approached the blue icebox. It leaned down to take hold of the girl's shoulders.

"What are you doing?" Matthias demanded.

"I need to confirm her authenticity," said the queen.

Matthias narrowed his eyes. He didn't appreciate her tone, or the reuse of his own words, or the chance his deception was about to be revealed.

Axel began shuffling again.

Ice cubes chinked as the Veniri rolled the girl onto her front.

Matthias frowned. What was this slith looking for? He shared a loaded glance with Axel.

"No scars," the Veniri said with a hiss.

*Scars?* No one had mentioned anything about scars.

The Veniri stood and shot Matthias an accusatory look. "This is not Violet Chambers."

Within a split second, the queen wraith was an inch from Matthias's nose.

"You dared to deceive *me!*" Her voice no longer tinkled; instead, it was like a nail being dragged across a pane of glass.

Matthias's whole body shuddered with adrenaline. He flicked a glance down at his extended arm; the tip of his dagger pierced right where the wraith's heart would be. Turquoise wisps snaked and undulated around his hand and the Diamantium dagger.

In Matthias's periphery, Veniri and hunters alike closed their ranks around himself and the queen, both sides ready to spring into attack at their leader's command.

"Careful, *slith*," Matthias warned in a low voice. "Just one word from me and none of your kind will be returning home tonight."

The queen bared her teeth, not a hint of her former pleasantries left. Even in her fury, she was still a goddess of beauty. "You are failing to comprehend that if I don't get what I want, then you also don't get what you want."

Matthias's face twisted into a scowl. The command to attack was on the tip of his tongue, but a glance at the tomes stopped him. Of course he and his men could take the tomes by force and obliterate every last slith in this clearing, but there were more tomes than these two. And as of yet, no hunter had been successful in finding where the Veniri were hiding, let alone where the tomes were stashed.

His chronic frustration rose. Satellites could track phones and devices all over the earth—they could even provide a close-up image of a car parked in one's own driveway—and yet, the technology still wasn't efficient enough to find where this queen and her Veniri scourge were lurking.

Matthias swallowed bile as panic churned in his gut. He still needed to maintain this temporary alliance. There was no guarantee he would find the Veniri city in the near future.

Time for plan B.

"Curtis!" he shouted. Everyone grew still. "Where's Curtis?"

"Here, boss." One of the hunters walked up to him.

"You were the one who brought in this bounty. Now, tell me, who is this?" Matthias latched on to the back of Curtis's neck and dragged him over to the ice chest. Curtis grunted as his face was shoved an inch from the dead girl.

"*Who is it?*" Matthias roared when Curtis didn't answer.

"It's . . . it's that girl, Violet."

"No," said Matthias through gritted teeth. He took out his phone with his free hand, pulled up a picture of Violet, and held it under the hunter's nose. "This is Violet."

Curtis's eyes grew wide. "But . . . but, boss, you said—"

Matthias raised his voice over Curtis's stammering. "I will not tolerate being lied to by my own men." He released

Curtis's neck and turned to address the other hunters. "Let this be a warning for anyone who thinks they can deceive me." He reached back for his Diamantium machete, swiveled, and with a wide arc of his blade, severed Curtis's head off at the shoulders. The head thunked to the ground, and the rest of the body collapsed forward in a heap.

Not bothering to clean off the blood, Matthias holstered his machete and turned back to the queen. "Forgive me, Majesty. My men have failed both of us." He laid a hand on his heart. "I will ensure this never happens again."

The queen's eyes burned with a wild intensity, and a corner of her mouth rose in amusement. Matthias knew that expression all too well—he himself often made it directly after a kill. Bloodlust, the desire for more.

She glanced at the Veniri who had inspected the girl's body, and it lashed out its tongue.

A muscle twitched in Matthias's jaw. He swore the next tongue he saw was going to join Curtis's head on the ground.

The Veniri turned to the queen and said, "Almonds."

Matthias frowned. What could that possibly mean?

The queen regarded Matthias with a lazy blink. "You say this will never happen again?"

"You have my word and my sincerest apologies."

"Good."

Triumph replaced his gnawing panic.

Her wispy apparition glided over to him, bloodlust still lingering in her placid expression. "Fair warning, hunter, I will not be so merciful next time." Despite the threat in her words, her tone was low and husky, as if speaking to a lover. "For now, I will uphold the rest of our agreement, the Diamantium for the Yranum. However, I now expect to receive *all three* of my bounties without any further delay, and this time, I want them all *alive*."

Several Veniri moved forward to take the Metallikite

crate away, renewing the cries and whimpers from within. The tome bearers began to follow, moving toward the edge of the clearing.

"Wait! The tomes!" Matthias called out, taking a rushed step forward, painfully aware that his tone and expression were a little too eager.

The wraith regarded him with narrowed eyes. "You will get your tomes when I get my *authentic* bounties."

"Then I've changed my mind about the payment for the Yranum. I want the tomes instead of the shards."

A mix of emotions flashed across the wraith's face before her features smoothed into neutrality. She folded her arms. "That was not what we agreed."

"No, but you're forgetting that I managed to acquire *more* than what was agreed. So I'm changing the agreement."

The queen narrowed her eyes. Her gaze cut into his very core, and for the first time in a long time, Matthias found it hard not to look away from someone's challenging glare.

*She's not human.* He reminded himself. She was filth. She was an abomination, an unnatural atrocity.

"The tomes for the Yranum, or no deal."

The queen sneered. "I will not—"

"Boys, stop the crate," demanded Matthias.

He forced himself to maintain eye contact with the queen, but in his periphery, he could see his men block the path of the Veniri with the crate. Despite the Diamantium weapons trained on them, the Veniri showed no sign of giving it up.

Matthias gave the queen a smug grin. "There are plenty of other buyers who would be willing to pay a substantial amount for this small Yranum family."

A tinkering laugh escaped her. "I'm curious to know which one of your buyers will pay you what you want most."

"And what about you?" Matthias retorted. "Which of your

sliths will be able to acquire more Yranum for you? You said yourself that none are capable."

Triumph bubbled in Matthias's chest as the queen's expression turned stony. He had her. There was no way she was going to leave without the Yranum in her possession.

At last, she waved a casual hand. "Fine, I will allow the payment to change. But only for *one* tome." The queen closed the gap between them until her face was a few inches from his. "This is the last time the deal changes. And from now on, I expect you to address me as Your Highness."

As the queen waited for his answer, she scrutinized him with a slow blink. He couldn't read her expression. If he was honest with himself, there were elements about her that intrigued him.

"Done," said Matthias, then after a few moments, he added, " . . . Your Highness." He didn't bother hiding his derision.

An unmistakable edge of darkness pervaded her broad smile.

Ignoring the glares of protest from his men, Matthias gestured for them to move away from the crate. "It's fortunate you came to your senses," he said.

Steel glinted in her eyes, but she didn't drop her triumphant demeanor as the crate disappeared into the night. Once it was out of sight, she flicked her hand, and a slith with the tome appeared at her side.

Profound excitement shuddered through Matthias, from the center of his chest to the tips of his fingers. With some effort, he schooled his features into nonchalance. This was the closest he had ever come to one of these artifacts. Hell, he was probably the first Erathi to lay eyes on one in a millennium. His eyes danced over the inscriptions and colored inlays on the tome's golden cover. He hated the idea of the other tome remaining with the sliths, but it was only a matter of time before it, too, would be in his possession.

The slith started to pass the tome to Axel.

"No!" exclaimed Matthias. He darted forward and shoved Axel out of the way. When he latched on to the tome, the weight of it made his knees buckle. He adjusted his grip and managed to struggle upright, but not before the wraith arched an eyebrow and curled her mouth into a smirk. Even the slith who had held the tome looked at Matthias with condescending amusement.

Heat rushed up his face and neck, but with his tome in hand, he didn't care.

"As for the rest of our transaction," rang the queen's chiming voice, "don't take too long, my sweet. I, too, have others who are interested in what I have."

Her teeth glinted with her final smile, and the wispy blue image dispersed into nothing.

Matthias clenched his jaw, but the flare of rage was short lived. He had the book. That was all that mattered,

Without delay, the sliths all melted back into the shadows; the last of them carried away the chest of Diamantium.

And once again, the hunters were alone in the clearing.

"Axel, take off your jacket," said Matthias.

"What? Why?"

"Just do it," he ordered, carrying his treasure to the back of one of the pickup trucks. He gestured for one of the hunters to drop the tailgate and told Axel to lay his jacket on it.

As gently as he could, he placed the tome on top of Axel's jacket. The spotlights from the truck cast every glorious detail of the ancient artifact into sharp relief.

"That's it?" Axel grumbled, coming up beside him. "After all that, this is all we get? Gold?"

"This isn't just gold, Axel," said Matthias. He ran his

fingers over the ridges and grooves of the embossed cover. The design was more glorious than he'd ever imagined. Inlaid gems and precious stones adorned ancient Egyptian figures, hieroglyphs, and symbols.

"Okay, so we got some gold and some pretty rocks," Axel scoffed. "Diamantium is worth a hundred times more than any of that."

A few of the other hunters chimed in their agreement.

"It's not the gold that's of value," said Matthias. "It's what's inside." He opened the tome to its first page, revealing another magnificent image of Egyptian figures in their iconic profile design. His greedy eyes scanned the hieroglyphic text, and his heart thumped faster as he recognized some of the phrases. He turned to the next page, then the next. Each gem-studded image was more detailed than the last.

He stopped at the final two pages—a double-spread depicting a woman with outstretched arms. She wore a stunning crown and beautiful multicolored gown. From her shoulders fanned glorious wings of malachite and lapis lazuli, each feather tipped with gold.

"This is it, boys," said Matthias. He glided his fingers over the rippled surface of the blue, green, and gold feathers. "We're going to get our wings back."

# ACKNOWLEDGMENTS

Wow! Where to start?

Writing this book has been a really fun and exciting but also a stressful, intimidating and epic journey. And of course, there are a number of people who without them, there would be no such thing as "Shards of Venus".

First off, I owe a phenomenal thank you to my Lord and Saviour, Jesus Christ. Without His amazing sacrifice, I would have ended it all long ago. I give all credit to You, my Father in Heaven and the Holy Spirit for my life and all that is good in it. Thank You!

To my wonderful husband, your support and encouragement has been stellar! A huge thanks for your feedback and involvement in this journey so far. Words cannot express how grateful I am, nor how much I love you.

Annabelle, you are such a delight and you bring me so much joy. You are so creative and imaginative, I'm always eager to see what you create next. I love you so much!

A big thank you to Mum for raising me, for being there whenever I need, for feeding my Enid Blyton addiction and for introducing me to authors such as Frank E. Peretti, C.S. Lewis, and J.R.R. Tolkien. I think I can safely blame you for sparking my wild imagination, haha!

A big thank you to the rest of my family! I'm so blessed to be a part of such a wonderful clan. It means a lot to have your love and support in all the good times and even the bad.

The Writer's Unite Group; Carleton Chinner, Julie Dickson, Tim Edwards, Suzie Eisfelder, Tarryn Mallick, and Katarina Smythe. You guys are AWESOME! I'm so glad I found you guys and eventually plucked up the courage to share my budding little story. Thanks for all the feedback, the support, the great laughs and the motivation to keep writing.

Adele Ritchie, Treece and Dan Stubbs, Lisa Meehan, thanks so much for being available to hear all my crazy ideas and helping me to brainstorm and fix several of my plot holes. You guys rock!

A big shout out to all my beta readers, Beryl Peachey, Beth Joyce, Donna Thornton, Gail Donges, Kylee Beauclerc, Karen Drescher, Kat Eveans, Kerrianne Draper, Kristy Phebey, Monica Murray, Rebecca Hampson, Rosie Barlow, Aunty Sandra Coleman and Tessa Wakefield who volunteered their precious time to read through my manuscript and to provide me with honest feedback. Taking on a beta reader role is an epic job and I'm truly grateful.

Kirstin Andrews, thank you so much for all the work you put into editing my story. It's been such an honour to have you as my editor. Words cannot describe how grateful I am. Thank you!

For the amazing cover, thanks so much to the amazing team at Deranged Doctor Design for your fantastic work in bringing my world visually to life. Wow! I can't stop looking at it.

I hope I haven't forgotten anyone. If I have, I'm so sorry! xoxo

# ABOUT THE AUTHOR

Tjalara Draper began her writing career at the start of 2016 when the stories in her crazy imagination kept growing. After a short online course in Creative Writing, she was thoroughly convinced she needed to pursue her all-time dream of becoming an author. "Shards of Venus," a paranormal/urban fantasy about shifters was the first pick of all her story ideas.

She's wife to an amazing man who is currently training to become a doctor, and mother to a spitfire of a daughter, who becomes more creative and outgoing with each day that goes by.

When Tjalara isn't writing her next book or tackling laundry monsters and wrestling dishwashing shenanigans, she's bound to be somewhere flying on wishing chairs, swimming with the mermaids, marking her skin with shadow hunter runes, raising dragons, or being a poison taster for the commander.

GET IN TOUCH:
    Website: www.tjalaradraper.com
    Facebook: Tjalara Draper Author
    Facebook Group: Tjalara Draper's Reader Lounge
    Instagram: tjalaradraper_author
    Amazon: Tjalara Draper, Shards of Venus